HE HAD ASSUMED THAT DIVORCE WOULD BRING RELIEF AND RELEASE . . .

Once he had had a marriage. Now he had a post-card from Port-au-Prince with a beach scene. It wasn't signed; it just said, in Jessica's carefully manicured script, "You're free now."
Free.

The word sank into him like a stone. Instead of relief, he felt a kind of interior pain that varied from dental-drill intensity to a secondhand ache. He was free. He was . . .

STARTING OVER

"A modern *Pilgrim's Progress,* a journey through America . . . with all of our contemporary hang-ups, frustrations and temptations."
—*Chicago Tribune*

"A rare pleasure." —*The Kirkus Reviews*

D1384878

STARTING OVER

Dan Wakefield

A DELL BOOK

To my following brothers and sisters,
nephews and niece: Wayne, Margaret, Wayne Jr.,
and Daniel Kelley Shaun, Dorothy, Michael,
Liam, and Kate O'Connell with love

Published by
DELL PUBLISHING CO., INC.
1 Dag Hammarskjold Plaza
New York, New York 10017

ISBN: 0-440-18301-4

Reprinted by arrangement with
Delacorte Press/Seymour Lawrence, New York, New York
Printed in the United States of America
One previous Dell printing
New Dell printing—October 1979

The author wishes to express special thanks to Robert Manning and the entire staff of the ATLANTIC MONTHLY *for providing the felicitous facilities and fellowship which enabled him to finish the novel during the long Boston summer of '72.*

The past is a dream and the future is
a mist. The great moments pass away.
What amuses man is to be puzzled,
not to know the outcome of a
boxing match or a baseball game.
A man is never satisfied.

—MUHAMMAD ALI
in *Sports Illustrated*

There were only three things I was
afraid of—God, sex, and being alone.

—MERCEDES McCAMBRIDGE
on The Steve Allen Show

PART ONE

1

Potter was lucky; everyone told him so.

"You're lucky," they said, "that you didn't have any children."

Divorce wasn't any bowl of cherries, of course, but as long as there weren't any children involved it wasn't an irreparable damage, like the sundering of a full-blown family. Just the busted dream of a couple of consenting adults. When Potter met new people and the subject of his recent divorce came up, he was congratulated so often for not having any children, he was tempted to start passing out cigars of celebration, saying heartily, "It wasn't a boy—*or* a girl!" But instead he did the appropriate thing, which was to shake his head in a kind of thoughtful wonderment and breathe a relieved *whew*. Nobody loves an ingrate.

Potter indeed was glad that he hadn't brought any innocent parties into the mess, but the fact that things could be worse is little comfort when they're bad enough. The truth was, divorce had disappointed him. Maybe, like marriage, he had expected too much of it.

He naturally assumed that when he got the divorce he would feel a sense of relief and release.
He had spent five tumultuous years with Jessica,
the last four of them in a state of holy matri-
mony, the last one of those in a state of desperation that he felt sure could only be alleviated by
divorce. It took that year to persuade his wife it
was best for both of them, and she finally agreed
to go down to Haiti for one of the quickie splits
offered there. It was one of the popular spots for
such transactions since Mexico had, in effect, gone
out of the business.

A lawyer told Potter the Dominican Republic
would be better, legally, but Jessica said since
the whole thing was his idea anyway, and as she
was only doing it as a favor she ought to get to
go where she wanted and stay on afterward for a
vacation. Potter had offered to give her the
household goods and three thousand dollars from
his savings account of $4,172.37 so that she
would have time to re-settle if she wanted, and
take a break from work for a while. They both
agreed it was fair for their own circumstances,
though sometimes Jessica mumbled the word
"alimony," which made Potter very nervous and
anxious to accede to her wishes. As to the divorce site, she explained that the Dominican Republic sounded drab and official, while Haiti had
"color." Potter privately imagined that she wanted to go to Haiti in order to offer herself as White
Queen in some voodoo ritual gang-bang, just to
spite him, but he couldn't raise that as an argu-

ment and so gave in. He got a postcard from
Port au Prince, with a beach scene. It wasn't
signed, it just said, in Jessica's carefully manicured script: "You're free now."

Free.

The word sunk into him like a stone.

Instead of relief, he felt a kind of interior pain
that varied from dental-drill intensity to a secondhand ache.

"What you're feeling," said Arnie, "is only
natural."

Arnie was a hip psychologist who lived on some
sort of commune around Nyack, and came in
three days a week to the Hotel Royalton in mid-
town Manhattan, where he held office hours,
counselling the numerous theatre and music
people who liked his informal, wide-ranging approach to their hangups. The public relations
firm that Potter worked for handled a lot of
show business clients, and through them he had
heard considerable praise for Arnie Freiheiter,
and had met him informally at parties, so that
making an appointment with him didn't seem
like such a big deal as going to a regular shrink
in an Upper East Side office. It just seemed like
dropping around for an hour or so to chat with
Arnie. Still, Potter was somehow annoyed by the
fact that Arnie sat cross-legged on the couch,
without any shoes or socks on. Potter felt that
if a guy was going to deal with your problems
he might at least put his shoes on.

"What the hell is natural about it?" Potter asked. "What I'm feeling?"

Arnie shrugged. "Like," he said, "any kind of split. Like you leave home when you're a kid, you feel homesick."

"But I *wanted* to leave," Potter said. "My wife, I mean."

"Right. Just like the kid may have wanted to split from the scene at home and go away to camp, but then when he gets there he's homesick."

"You mean to say I'm homesick for my wife?"

"Look. When you split from someone, no matter how bad it was, you feel a loss. You were used to your marriage. It was comfortable."

"Fuck it was comfortable."

"I don't mean like that. I mean in the sense that it was familiar."

Potter felt like thanking Arnie for his time, but he knew the hour wasn't nearly up and it would have seemed rude to leave. He would have given his left nut for a stiff belt of Scotch, but he knew that Arnie didn't drink. In fact, Arnie was in the process of rolling a joint.

Potter shared it with him, as he always did when offered grass, because he had learned it was more of a hassle to refuse and have to hear lectures about the glories of the weed and how you just weren't getting it down in your diaphragm if you weren't getting high. Potter was a drinking man and grass only made him sleepy, but he smoked it to be sociable and forestall people from preaching at him.

Potter took a deep drag, coughed, and passed the damn thing back to Arnie. He concentrated on holding it in, tried to think it into working, and began to *think* of all the other times he'd been through this—picturing people, places, rooms —when he realized Arnie was asking him something.

"What?"

"I asked," Arnie repeated, "if you'd ever read Doris Lessing."

Potter admitted he had not, and Arnie explained that more and more of his women patients had been laying her books on him, and he'd really begun to get into her stuff. He advised Potter that if he wanted to be able to have a meaningful relationship with a new woman, he would do well to get into Lessing himself. Potter nodded, squelching a yawn.

"Lessing," he said, as if making a mental note.

Cabs were battling below, on Forty-fourth Street. The Algonquin, with its marvelous cocktail lounge, was only a stone's throw away. Potter figured he might just stop off there for a quick one on his way back to the office. Arnie had uncrossed his legs, stood up, stretched, and reached into his shirt to scratch at his belly. He said he'd be happy to see Potter again next week, his fee was forty dollars. Potter wondered if that included the joint. For the same amount, he could buy five fifths of good Scotch. Which is what he would do from now on.

Olney and Sheperdson, the PR firm Potter

worked for, was holding a cocktail party at Sardi's to introduce the press to the cast of *Serenity!*, a new improvisational musical based on the Bhagavad-Gita. Heskel, the man from *Billboard*, was nudging Potter and pointing at one of the girl *Serenity!* singers, all of whom were dressed in minisaris. "I could meditate on that little ass of hers for quite a spell."

"Nice," Potter commented, "very nice."

Bud Olney, the firm's senior partner, was passing out paperbound copies of the Bhagavad-Gita. "Here you go, Heskel," he said, winking, "this'll elevate that mind of yours."

"My mind is elevated just to the level of all these twitchy little asses."

"Seriously," Olney said, his voice lowering a register, "you ought to talk to some of these kids. This isn't just a hype, you know—every member of the cast has studied meditation in India for at least three months as a prerequisite for joining the production. Tell him about it, Potter."

"That's right," Potter said. "Three months."

Olney moved on, and the *Billboard* man shook his head at Potter with an envious grin. "You lucky bastard."

"Huh?"

"Heard you got divorced. Got nothin' to tie ya down."

"Oh—yeah."

"Me with a family at the wrong fuckin' time in history. Hey—look at *that* one."

"Nice," Potter nodded.

He didn't want to disillusion anyone by men-

tioning that even though divorced he felt generally miserable, and the prospect of screwing a
Serenity! singer didn't do much to dispel the
gloom. No matter what went on in his head,
though, Potter looked the part of a guy for whom
things came easily, and that aura was good for
his business. He moved with a casual grace and
style, and his curly black hair invited the fingers
of girls who liked to tousle it. He had a charm
that was partly Irish, from his father's side, and
a tinge of southern from his mother and from
growing up in Washington, D.C., and going to
college at Vanderbilt. His father was a career
man in the State Department, and it might be
said that Potter inherited or assimilated traits
of "diplomacy," though he never thought of his
old man's stern demeanor as being "diplomatic"
in the ameliorative sense of the word. Unlike his
father, Potter talked glibly, and had a knack for
tuning into other people's feelings and outlooks.
Businessmen trusted him instinctively, and the
far-out clients he handled from the world of
Rock soon came to accept him in spite of his
consistent Brooks Brothers dress. Everyone thought
him pretty dashing.

It occurred to Potter—as a man who dealt in
images—that perhaps he'd feel better if he tried
a little harder right now to behave according to
his own image, and so he stoked up his charm,
and asked a *Serenity!* singer to lunch.

Her name was Cressy, and she had big, dewy

eyes. "Are you sure you're not married?" she
asked.

He assured her he in fact was officially divorced (he had the postcard to prove it), and she
seemed to relax.

"It's not a moral thing with me," she explained. "It's just bad karma to make it with a
married man."

Potter assured her he understood, and things
went pleasantly enough for a while. Then Cressy began picking at her chicken salad in a la-
conic manner. Something else was on her mind.

"Why do people get divorced?" she asked, her
eyes large and vacant.

"Why—uh—it's different," Potter said sweetly. "Every case is different. You know—like Tol-
stoy's 'unhappy families.'"

The literary allusion was lost on Cressy; Potter stared intently at a tiny dab of mayonnaise
on her lower lip, which was pouting slightly out-
ward. He imagined leaning over to lick it off,
but only smiled, patiently.

"Why did *you* though? Do it?"

"Simple," Potter said, lifting his palms upward. "My wife and I couldn't live together."

"Didn't you love each other?"

"Madly and passionately."

"Well—what was the problem, then?"

"I just told you."

"*Loving* each other?"

"It's a hard thing to live with, day in and day
out."

"I guess I don't understand," she said.

"Maybe you will. Sometime."

Cressy grew despondent and grumpy, refusing dessert and monkeying with the strap on her watch. Potter called for the check.

The next morning he woke around ten with a specially bad hangover. He was not in the small, cluttered apartment on Christopher Street he had sublet from a girl at his office who had moved in with an electric guitarist on the Lower East Side. But he knew from the noise he was still in Manhattan. The garbage trucks were gorging themselves in the street below, making that high metallic groan as they swallowed the muck that the city had prepared for their morning feast. Potter thought of them as a herd of mechanical dinosaurs that would someday take over and rule the whole island. And, just down the block, came the headsplitting rapidfire bursts of a pneumatic drill that was ripping up the street again. Potter turned and looked beside him in bed, groggily expecting he might see his wife—now former wife—but saw instead a stranger he had picked up the night before at Julius's. She was a secretary somewhere or other. She was not especially pretty, and had vomited on the stairs. The girl moved toward him under the sheet, yawning. He put his hand gently on her shoulder.

"I'm going," he said.

"Hmmm? For breakfast?"

"No, for good."

She jerked up, as if slapped, blinked her eyes, and pulled the sheet around her shoulders, protectively. "Well thanks one hell of a lot."

"I'm sorry. It's not you. I mean I've got to get out of this whole damn thing."

He flung himself out of the bed and started pulling his clothes on, frantically, as if he were leaving a burning building.

"*What* whole damn thing?" the girl demanded.

Potter waved his arms, wildly, trying to encompass what he meant. All he could say in explanation was: "New York."

2

Instead of going to work that day, Potter went to Boston. He often fled there when things seemed to be closing in on him, took a train or a shuttle flight and holed up at Max and Marva Bertelsen's fine old brownstone in Louisburg Square, the ritziest part of Beacon Hill. It was a haven, a place to unwind and calm down from the jangle and rush of New York.

He caught a one o'clock train from Penn. Station. It was New York spring and the day was warm and drizzly, the tops of the taller buildings shrouded in smog. Potter didn't like to fly in that weather—but even more important, he wanted the luxury of slow, suspended time that the train would afford. He went to the snack car —a compromise combination of diner and club car, and ordered a club sandwich and a beer. He finished quickly, then settled back to enjoy a series of slowly-sipped Scotch and sodas. He was calmed by the rocking motion of the train, the rain slurring the windows, and the wet towns and cities he could watch from the safety and warmth of the car, isolated. He had bought no papers or magazines, but chain-smoked and sipped his drinks, not exactly trying to "think things out," but hoping something would come to him, some new idea or answer.

Around New London, Connecticut, he recalled a magazine article he had read a month or so before in his dentist's waiting room. At the time it meant little to him, but now seemed extremely significant. It told how different guys in middle age had completely changed their lives, had left lucrative but unsatisfying jobs and careers and even professions and set out to find true fulfillment, even though it meant less money and prestige and more hardships. A veterinarian who had built up a terrific practice in Beverly Hills had thrown it all up, including his house with kidney-shaped swimming pool and Jaguar XKE, and gone to Oregon to work in a lumber camp. An auto executive who was rising up the corporate ladder and leading the good life in fashionable Grosse Point, Michigan, had chucked everything to become a male nurse. The owner of a textile mill in West Virginia had sold out to some conglomerate and taken his wife and children to live on a commune outside Puerto Vallarta, Mexico, where they learned to make pottery and tie-dyed bedspreads.

All over the country, it seemed, growing numbers of people were giving up the grind, getting out of the rut they were in, and doing what the hell they pleased. It wasn't just the kids anymore. It was solid, respectable people like auto executives and veterinarians. Not many perhaps, but a growing trickle, a discernible stream. Potter himself knew a couple who had left the publishing business and bought a working farm in New Hampshire. They had sent out a mimeographed newsletter to their old friends in New York, reporting how happy they were and explaining they were "into crop rotation."

When Potter graduated from college in '58, nobody did that stuff; at least nobody you knew, nobody who had a good education and a chance of making it in business or the arts or professions. Only the weirdos, the copouts and dropouts who couldn't cut it anyway left the mainstream of American opportunity, spurned the golden current of success, and really meant it. But now, if you left a good job in a leading law firm and went to northern Vermont to tap maple sugar, you were sort of envied. At least you weren't scorned. The truth was, as far as Potter could figure it, nobody gave a shit anymore. There was something nice about that. But it was also a little bit scary, as if in the middle of a game you were playing the rules had been changed, or just forgotten about, and you had to pretty much make things up as you went along and pretend you knew what the hell you were doing. On top of that, Potter was uncomfortably aware that for him a good part of the game was already over. He had just turned thirty-four. That was pretty near the halfway mark, or maybe even way past it, the way he was boozing. Time to shit or get off the pot if you were going to make a new move, really start over. And what better time than now, the first year of a new decade? The Seventies. Stretching ahead, as yet only four months soiled.

"You don't have any children," Marva Bertelsen said. "You're free to do anything you want."

Potter took a swallow of Drambuie. It was sticky, like his mind felt. "The hitch is," he said, "I have to want to do something."

He looked to Max, hoping for an answer, a direction, hoping he might say "Go west, young man," or "Take up the plough," and Potter would do it. But Max only sipped at his espresso, looking knowledgeable but inscrutable.

Potter met Max in the Service, when they both were stationed at the Navy Department in Washington. Potter as a yeoman typist, Max in the psychiatric division. Max was a shrink, and though Potter never saw him on a professional basis, he kind of adopted him as a father. Max was only three years older than Potter but seemed a lot more than that, maybe because he was so goddamn calm and in control all the time. When Potter met him, Max had recently finished his training analysis, and he seemed to be one of the few people Potter knew for whom that process had "worked." There was something comforting about the result, but also something Potter found a little bit scary. It was something in Max's calm, unruffleable demeanor; as if some wire had been unhooked, the one that connected you with anger and frivolity and unpredictable thought and action. Max smiled a lot, but seldom if ever laughed. When something struck him especially funny he would smile and say, "That's very funny."

"Those guys in the magazine article," Potter said, "the article I was telling you about—they all seemed to have some burning desire to do some particular thing they'd never been able to do—but I can't think of anything like that. Becoming a lobster fisherman or something. You know."

"What about—your acting?" Marva asked brightly.

"Come on, Marva, that's over," Potter said forcefully. "Done. Dead. Buried. Gone."

"OK, I just thought."

"What about teaching?" Max asked.

"Teaching *what?*"

"What you know about—the theatre. Even public relations."

"Who the hell wants to know about *that?*"

"You might be surprised," Max said with a smile.

"Don't worry, Phil," Marva said, "Max knows *everyone.*"

Potter didn't doubt that.

When Max and Marva went to bed, Potter stayed up, keeping the fire in the library going, drinking giant Scotch and sodas, pondering his possible futures. He wished, in a way, he could just move in with the Bertelsens—like a black-sheep son, unfit for employment—and hide in the warm safety of their house, their friendly protection, their ordered lives.

The thought of the old dream of acting reminded him of the dangers of the world outside,
the dangers of caring and desiring, of wanting
something so bad you can taste it, but having it
always recede before you until in order to live
at all you had to turn your back on it—swear
off it as surely as an alcoholic swears off the
sauce—and for something less, something else.

The dream had become a memory, still vivid
and painful. When Potter finished college and
the Navy and came to New York, he came with
the casual assumption that—with time and the
breaks and professional training—he would
emerge as a new Marlon Brando or Jason Ro-
bards, and after a successful run on Broadway
in a new Tennessee Williams hit, he would hop
off to Hollywood, swatting producers away like
gnats, and do the star bit, but not let himself be
taken in. He played in his mind many times the
scene in which he politely told the roomful of
Hollywood moguls that he couldn't accept their
fantastic offer for the lead in the screen version
of a new Harold Robbins novel, but had chosen
instead to return to New York and do Shakespeare in the Park for scale.

After four years of making the rounds, with
his smile and his folder of glossy profile photos,
he landed one part in a TV drama series in
which he dashed into a room and said, "Telegram
for Mr. Bostwick."

It did not lead on to bigger things.

One afternoon at a casting call for parts in a
new TV crime series Potter was sitting on the
usual bench, crowded with other palmsweating
aspirants, his head aching and his feet sore,
wanting to take a piss but afraid to be gone in
case his name was called, when a door was flung
open from the inner sanctum, the warm secret
source of carpeted power, and out came a girl
he saw around a lot at parties, who was bright
and on her way up and treated him with a flirta-
tious sort of friendliness. Her name was Made-
line and she never wore makeup except on her
eyelids. They were purple. Potter moved slightly forward, simply to greet her, but before he
could open his mouth she flashed by him, and,
though her eyes never fell upon him, never
made the slightest flicker in his direction, her
long delicate arm, as if guided by radar, reached
out at the moment she was precisely perpendicu-
lar to him, and her longnailed fingers made a
quick, fleeting ruffle through his hair, while, at
the same split-second she said, "Hi, Love," and
then she was gone, with her papers and her power and her purple eyelids.

Potter sat for a moment not moving; his scalp,
where her fingers had flicked across it, felt on
fire. He did not see the room, or the people in it,
but he stood up and moved, in a trance, to the
elevator. It came, and he pressed the lobby button and stood facing front. He turned right, out
the glass revolving doors, and with his mind as
blank as a newly washed blackboard, he walked
to the nearest city trash basket and stuffed in the

folder containing his résumé and his glossy photos and walked on, as if guided by an electronic beam, to the nearest sign that said LIQUOR, walked in and asked in a pleasant monotone for a quart of Cutty Sark, hailed a taxi, went back to the apartment he shared with a girl named Tandy who had graduated magna cum laude from Bryn Mawr and was working her way up in publishing and said she would help pay the rent and do the dishes and whatever the fuck needed to be done to help Potter make it in the theatre because she believed both in Potter and the theatre.

When she came home she found him in his underwear guzzling from the bottle, glassy-eyed, and when she asked what had happened he explained, "I quit."

For a while she tried to reason with him, told him how that sort of thing happened all the time to everyone, tried to taunt him, appeal to his machismo, but finally she understood that something had clicked off, that indeed the big theatre dream was as busted inside him as a pricked balloon, and that nothing could patch it together and blow it up again; and when she was sure of that she set down her cup of Medaglia d'Oro and lit a Pall Mall, and after exhaling a long, thin stream of smoke, like a line drawn across the empty air, she said in a calm, thoughtful voice: "You'll be drunk tonight. And puking in the morning. When you're through, get your shit together and clear the fuck out."

Potter said nothing.

Thinking back, he wished he'd had some kind of line of farewell. He at least could have done a quick buck-and-wing and said "Remember me to Herald Square."

The old saw that "those who can, do; those who can't, teach" was part of the vague prejudice Potter had carried with him against the academic life, but that seemed no more applicable now than many of the other set assumptions he had grown up with in the Fifties. Teaching had the potential for the sort of personal satisfaction that people seemed to value more now than old-fashioned success, and Potter was willing to give it a fling if any institution was bold enough to grant him the chance. Knowing the market was already glutted with Ph.D.s, he couldn't imagine that his own academic background, which sported nothing gaudier than the now perfunctory B.A., would qualify him for anything. But Max Bertelsen, who knew what was happening, said that Potter's practical experience might just be of interest to certain institutions whose programs were now in flux.

Gilpen Junior College was in flux.

It was one of the many brownstone schools of higher education on Beacon Street, former family houses converted into factories of learning, ranging from certified distinction of a minor sort to high-priced havens for middle-class kids who had nowhere else to go, were not yet ready or willing to marry or work, and whose parents could afford the luxury of a largish tuition in

exchange for the solace of saying "My son/
daughter is at Gilpen Junior—you know, in
Boston." This college, as well as many others
scattered through the metropolitan area, had
flourished for a while with fairly staple servings
of a liberal arts stew, and a boast of being small,
selective, and "giving special attention to the
individual student." But along with many other
private colleges, Gilpen had felt the pinch caused
by the end of the postwar baby boom, rising costs,
the growth of state institutions with vastly lower tuitions, and had brought in a new dean who
was a real live wire to revolutionize its program
to meet current needs and trends.

As Dean Guy M. Hardy, Jr., explained it, "The
day of the Ivory Tower is past. In fact, 'the past'
is past. What's happening is Now, in education
as in other fields."

Dean Hardy tamped his meerschaum and his
brow furrowed in studied seriousness. His greying hair was styled in a brush-cut, and with his
snapping little eyes and pudgy, lineless pale
moon face, he reminded Potter of an apprentice
FBI agent. Actually, he had "been in government" before going into higher education. From
the way Hardy spoke of "being in government"
it sounded as if he had probably held some sensitive post pretty high up in State, but Potter knew
from Max Bertelsen that Guy Hardy had served
in the nether regions of the USIA, editing
a quarterly designed to capture the minds of the
intellectuals in Central America and producing

a series of Brief Lives of American Presidents
for Radio Free Europe. He had also seen overseas
duty, holding down the post of librarian at the
American consulate in San Salvador for eighteen months.

"The world is changing, and with it, education," Hardy continued.

Potter tried to concentrate.

He gathered that Dean Hardy had been sucking around the Harvard Crowd, and had through
some such connection gained entrée to the
Bertelsen salon. That was big potatoes in the
Boston-Cambridge intellectual circuit, and Potter understood clearly the reason he had been
granted the interview was because of high rec-
ommendations from Max.

"So we stress," said Hardy, "Communications.
We do not have 'Freshman English' as such, but
a wide-ranging course of study designed to meet
the needs of students growing up into one of the
most media-oriented societies known to man."
He paused, proudly, and said, "We call this core,
required line of study 'Contemporary Communications in a Media-Oriented Society.' "

"Very apt," said Potter.

"Or," Hardy chuckled, "as the students call
it, 'Con Com.' "

Potter smiled.

"Max tells me you've done quite well in public relations. What brings you to consider leaving the field?"

Potter got out a cigarette, paused, and sizing

up his audience in the way that he would a prospective client, proceeded artfully to feed the
Dean every cliché he figured he would gobble
up, all covered with a thick sauce of sincerity.
When he finished, Hardy was clearly impressed,
and said he liked the idea of having some faculty who had come by their experience "in the
real world of push and shove."

"I can honestly say," Potter said with a grin
of camaraderie, as if sharing a personal insight
with a man of the world who would understand,
"I've done my share of pushing and shoving."

Hardy winked, and nodded. He offered Potter a position as instructor, teaching two sections of Con Com—and a prize!—a seminar in
public relations.

For that one, Potter mused, he could take the
class to lunch, have each student drink four martinis and abstain from any food; the ones who
could return and work until five would pass
the course. After the interview, Potter walked
down Beacon Street and into the Public Gardens, where he sat on a bench, feeling expansive
and excited, looking around at this curious old-
new city, seeing it now not just with the appreciative eyes of the tourist but the proprietary
feeling of a soon-to-be citizen of the place. It
was the way he once felt when he was new to
New York, sitting on a bench in Washington
Square.

3

Trees and grass.

Grass and trees.

Potter rented a ground-floor apartment in an old frame house on a quiet street in Cambridge where traffic jams of contentious taxis and demolition crews from Con Edison seemed as unlikely as cattle stampedes. He figured as long as he was fleeing New York he might as well get as far away from its spirit as possible, and so chose to live across the river from Boston in the more pastoral, less-citified world of Cambridge. It was only a ten minute commute by subway, and the subway itself was a joyride compared to the roaring, rocking, hellbent human cattlecars that blasted back and forth beneath the boroughs of New York in their underground chambers filled with pestilent air and ages of grime. The subways Potter took to Boston from Harvard Square were brightly-painted trolley-type cars that reminded him of childhood and a less frantic era. And, in what Potter considered an extra dividend of the trip, the trains clanged up from un-

derground to cross the Charles River on a bridge
that provided the passengers a sudden, sun-glint-
ed view of water and sailboats, skyline and sky.

Potter sat at his bowed-out living room window with a glass of instant iced tea, just looking
at the green, luxuriating in the sight, devouring it, letting it feed him. It was one of the important factors in making his move, and it
helped him to view it as rational and right. He
felt the presence of grass and trees might even
make him drink less. Bring order. In New York
you had to drink just to clear the soot from your
throat. Burn off the grime. In New York you
had to drink for your goddamn health. Or your
job. Just by leaving his PR job, Potter had elim-
inated all the expense account luncheons with
three martinis and a brandy for dessert, and all
the freebie cocktail parties after work. He vowed
not to drink in the daytime anymore, and figured that ought to be easy since there wasn't any
reason for it now. That was certainly a plus for
his change; in fact, almost everything he could
think of about his new move was a plus except
for a considerable cut in salary, but in its own
way he looked on that, too, as a healthy change.
It would be good to live frugally for a while,
help in his desire to simplify and purify his manner of existence.

Those were the pleasant kinds of thoughts that
came to him while looking out the front window, but when he had to turn back into the
apartment itself he felt less assured and confident

of things. Not that there was anything wrong
with the apartment; it was the sort of place that
prompted everyone to say, "You could really
do a lot with it." The problem was, Potter did
not know how. What furniture he and Jessica
had accumulated during their marriage he had
left for her own use. He hated the painful process of "dividing up," and anyway he didn't
want to bring the furniture of his old life into
his new one. He only brought books and records. Marva Bertelsen had been kind enough to
take him to Jordan Marsh to pick out a rug for
the living room, and help him get the necessary
linen and towelling. She also showed him a sec-
ond-hand furniture store in Cambridge where
he bought a couch for the living room, a mattress and springs for the bedroom, and a beat-
up desk and chair. He picked up a couple of
canvas sling chairs for the living room, and im-
provised a coffee table by setting a varnished
door on some cement blocks. He had meant to
use the blocks for putting a bookcase together,
but he thought the coffee table more important,
so that left the bookcase still to be done, and
in the meantime he kept the books in the old
liquor boxes he had packed them in, and shoved
them against the wall in the living room where
the actual bookcase would be when he got
around to setting it up. The walls were white
and nude, except for a travel poster of Rio de
Janeiro that Potter hung with thumbtacks.

Supplying the kitchen turned out to be the

hardest part of all. It was hardest because when
Potter went to buy the minimal stuff he needed,
it reminded him of all the times before he was
married when he had moved from one place to
another, finding it easier to leave junk behind
and pick up a new set of pots and pans and
dimestore dishes and silverware to start with
again. He bought four of everything, anticipat-
ing a girl for himself and a nice other couple
they would entertain with quiet gourmet dinners at home. Selecting the cheapest stuff he
could, he rushed through the ordeal as quickly as
possible, throwing in dishtowels and potholders
and paring knives at random, performing the
task with a feeling very much like swimming
underwater. When he finished, he took his rattling packages and ducked into the nearest bar
for a double Scotch on the rocks.

Once he recovered from the essential furnish-
ing, Potter bought a marked-down portable stereo, a model that probably was mostly sold to
Puerto Ricans new to the mainland. He was being frugal. He even figured he could do without
a television.

In a few weeks, he changed his mind about
that.

Potter had stayed on at Olney and Sheperdson
through most of the summer, working hard,
padding his expense account more than usual,
and saving as much as he could for the coming
time of his new, more stringent circumstances.

He moved into his place in Cambridge in early September, in time for the hot gold burst of Indian summer that fired the whole city with a heightened glow. Scores of schools and colleges and universities began preparation for a new semester, and the atmosphere was charged with a pleasant sense of anticipation.

Except for quiet dinners at the Bertelsens', Potter didn't do much in the way of social life, nor did he desire to yet. It was an intermediate time for him, a pause between his old life and new one about to begin. There were times like that when he found it was best to hold back, to wait, to be alone as much as you could stand it, to try not to press things. Potter had a roommate in college who referred to such times as periods in which he "devoted himself to science" —read a great deal, tried to get some exercise, refrained from alcoholic or sexual or emotional binges, in general rallied his forces, got into shape for the good times to come.

You had to believe, of course, that the good times indeed were coming, and that wasn't always easy. Sometimes Potter was stricken with doubts and regrets, wondering if what he was doing made sense. Sometimes the thought of Jessica opened in his mind like a sudden wound, and he would wonder where she was, what she was doing—who she was doing it with. The line of the old song, slightly revised, would ring through his head in a cruel taunt: "I wonder who's fucking her now?" He heard she was back in New

York, and was thankful he wasn't there himself
where he might run into her, walking hand in
hand with some new lover, looking cool and
glamorous.

He walked a lot. Every morning he walked
the eight blocks into Harvard Square, where he
bought the Boston *Globe* and *The New York
Times* and went to breakfast at a cafeteria on
Brattle Street where you could sit and pore over
the papers, refill your coffee, and not be rushed
into eating up and moving on. After breakfast
he walked down to the Charles and strolled along
the banks. Occasionally he found a game of
touch football he could get into. That was one
of the best things. The running and jumping
and throwing and blocking that brought sweat
to the body also washed the mind clean. He
would walk home pleasantly aching and exhausted, take long showers, get into his bathrobe, and
settle down to read. He hadn't read so much in
years—not only books for his courses, but novels
in paperback whose titles he had bandied about
at cocktail parties with the bluff assurance he
got from culling descriptions in reviews. Around
midnight he would flick on the tube and burrow
into bed for the talk shows and late movies that,
with enough Scotch, usually got him to sleep.

He thought of it not as a bad time, but a
"thin" one. He had found that time itself
changes in different periods of one's life—sometimes it seems fat with events and decisions, vic-
tories and defeats, each moment full—and in

other periods time seems thin, one-dimensional,
the hours long and slender, stretched like a wire.
It was that kind of time now and he accepted it,
moved with it. Patiently. Restrained. Carefully
hopeful.

The week before the fall semester began at
Gilpen Junior College, Potter was invited to a
cocktail party at the home of Dean Hardy. The
Dean lived in Cambridge in an old but socially
suitable two-story frame house convenient to the
shrines of Harvard, whose mere physical presence gave him comfort, and, as he admitted with
what seemed to Potter a lascivious smile, "stimulation."

The Dean had rented a Harvard student,
handsomely blond and red-jacketed, to serve as
bartender, and also had on hand a glum professor of history from Harvard, who sighed and jin-
gled the change in his right-hand pocket a lot,
and whose conversation mainly consisted of gruff-
sounding grunts. Potter wondered if he, too, had
been rented for the occasion.

The Dean's wife, Lucy, was a birdlike woman
with tightly curled hair and a manner of fluttering sincerity that led her to grasp the hand of
each guest in both of hers with a tight little
squeeze of welcome. She was everywhere at once,
moving at what seemed to be the speed of people in silent movies.

Dean Hardy made a special point of introduc-
ing Potter to Professor Don R. Sample, who was

Chairman of the Communications Department.
Sample had earned his Ph.D. at the University of
Illinois College of Communications, and had
taught journalism all his life. He had written his
thesis on automotive trade publications, and was
regarded as one of the leading authorities in that
field, having served as special consultant for what
he referred to as "the Honda people," in the area
of publications.

"I understand that you—uh—have had a good
deal of experience on the practical—umm—
side," Sample said.

"I was in public relations," Potter answered.

Sample, an extremely tall, gaunt fellow,
leaned slightly downward to address Potter, rocking slightly as he spoke. "The Dean," he said,
"values the practical side very highly."

"Fortunately for me," Potter smiled.

"Indeed."

The edges of Sample's mouth twitched in a
movement that indicated something between a
smile and a sneer. His long face looked remark-
ably grey. Potter had the feeling that if Sample
coughed, dust would come out.

The Gilpen faculty members at the party
seemed a pretty motley crew, ranging from academic types like Sample to a longhaired young
man whose background and expertise seemed
even more "practical" than that of Potter. Buford explained that he was, by profession, a television repairman, as well as a Gilpen instructor.

"What do you teach?" Potter asked.

"Television repair."

"Where?"

"At Gilpen. It's a required course for all Communications majors."

Potter smiled, not knowing if Buford was putting him on, but the young man seemed completely sincere.

"Dean Hardy feels," he explained, "that if 'The Medium is the Message,' as McLuhan says, it's important to know how our most significant medium of communications really works, from the inside out."

"Ingenious," Potter said.

Buford shrugged. "It follows."

"I suppose it does."

Potter went to get another drink.

An amiable man with red hair and a bright pink face introduced himself as Gafferty, a fellow instructor in Communications. Perhaps because of his open smile, or because he asked the Harvard bartender if he'd mind just fixing him a glass full up with whiskey and a little ice, Potter took an instinctive liking to the guy, and asked him if faculty members as well as students were required to be experts in Television Repair.

Gafferty laughed, his cheeks growing pinker. "Ah, would ya believe it now? The scholar of the future will carry a monkey wrench instead of a book."

"I take it McLuhan is pretty big around here."

"Rather a patron saint, I'd say."

A tall, graceful young woman drifted by and Gafferty hailed her, throwing an arm around her bony shoulders in a friendly, fatherly way, presenting her to Potter. "Would you believe this beautiful girl is a *Scientist?* A doctor of chemistry, that most occult study."

She gave Gafferty a peck on the cheek, and held a thin long hand toward Potter. "I'm Alison Farr," she said.

Gafferty went to get her the drink she had been on the way for, and Potter gave her a rudimentary résumé of himself. As he spoke, he felt almost hypnotized by her eyes. He usually didn't notice women's eyes. It was not that Alison Farr's eyes were large and brown that engrossed him, it was the expression in them—a hurt look, as if someone had cruelly and unexpectedly rapped a ruler hard across her knuckles. Otherwise she seemed terribly calm and self-possessed.

"I lived in New York a while myself," she said. "When I was married."

"Oh?"

"I'm not. Married anymore."

"Oh. Me, too—either."

It was a bond, like people who have just met discovering that they both were expelled from the same university, or both recently had their appendix removed.

Two drinks later, when the party around them had reached a decibel of clinking and clattering sound that had them squinting in order to hear each other, Potter suggested they go out to dinner. Alison said if he didn't mind potluck she'd like to just go back to her place and eat, she wanted to relax.

Potluck turned out to be a wonderful *coq au vin* that Alison said was no trouble at all. She explained that she loved any excuse to cook well, it was kind of a hobby with her, took her mind off things, but she found it hard to do by herself.

Potter nodded. "It's like touch football," he said.

"Football?"

"I mean, it turns your mind off. But you can't do it alone."

"Oh. Yes."

Alison put on a record of Leontyne Price singing famous arias. It was lovely, but almost painfully intense. Like Alison. Potter found he was afraid of that right now. The intensity. He liked Alison Farr and he would like to go to bed with her, but he knew it would not be casual and amiable and safe. He did not want to have to look into those huge hurt eyes of hers afterward, did not want to be involved in their depths.

It was the time when he would make his move with her now or not, and she knew that, and evidently knew his thoughts and doubts, and said, "I guess I'm very serious, right now. About things. And people."

"I know. And I guess I'm not. Not now, anyway. Or can't be yet, or something."

"Good night," she said.

Potter stood up. "Thank you," he said. "For the dinner. And everything."

She nodded, her eyes closed.

"Good night," Potter said.

Potter had no special assignment for registration day at Gilpen, but he thought he ought to show up. He scotchtaped a schedule of classes and office hours to his door, and then went down to the first floor where students were signing up for classes. It was crowded and a little confusing, and Potter just milled around aimlessly for a while, till he ran into Gafferty and asked if he'd like to go out for a beer.

"Splendid suggestion," Gafferty said.

They walked down Beacon and across the Commons over to Jake Wirth's, which Gafferty swore would be worth the walk. It was an old German place, one of the oldest restaurants in Boston, Gafferty said, and one of the few of any age where a man could still get an honest sandwich and a good draft beer. The place was large and plain, with bare wood tables, and Potter liked it. They each had a stein of dark.

"You seemed to be hittin' it off nice with lovely Alison," Gafferty said. "At the party."

"Oh—sure. I mean, she's a very nice person."

"Lovely girl. Been through a rough time, with divorce and all."

"I know."

"I was sort of hopin', you and she—"

"I don't think so. I think we're both too much in the same—uh—sort of condition. It's hard to explain. I just got divorced myself recently."

"Oh, I'm sorry. It must be a hard thing on a person."

"Yes. No matter how you cut it. You can't make it light and easy. I take it you're married?"

"Married? Ah, that hardly covers it, man. Been married ten years, and I've got myself nine children. And the wife, of course."

"*Nine?*"

"I can field my own baseball team."

"Jesus. Nine."

Potter felt a sense of awe at the enormity of it, and in one way an overwhelming relief that he had no such burden himself. But in another way it made him feel empty, one-dimensional, a dropout from the population explosion, an outsider from the great Dickensian family tradition. He had a fleeting sense of being in a contest with a man who was about his own age and in general his own profession, and the score was a lopsided 9-0 against him.

"In a way," he said, "I envy you—that big family."

"Ah, but don't we all envy the next man? Me of course envying your carefree life, with lots of girls and no house deeds and diapers."

"Sure," Potter grinned. "And I hope you know, of course, I'm sure, that my life is about as glamorous as yours. Falls as much short of the image, anyway."

The two men felt at ease with one another, and they drank and talked themselves into a state of camaraderie and boozy philosophizing that led Potter to ask his new friend what he "wanted out of life."

"Ah, I've been asked that a number of times. All I can answer is—and I really mean it—I'd just like to feel up to snuff."

They both broke out laughing, and Potter said, "If you can do that—feel up to snuff all the time, or most of the time, you've really accomplished something."

"Surely I believe that," Gafferty said. "It's more than I've ever got for very long. But Jesus, man—I don't mean to complain. I love to teach, when I teach what I love, and I manage to do that most of the time. In spite of the requirements. I mainly teach the Irish poets. If that doesn't count as the grandest 'communications' man has come up with, I'll eat my hat. I teach that McLuhan fellow for a week or so, and then I get to the real Communications—Yeats, Joyce, Synge, O'Casey . . ."

As Gafferty spoke enthusiastically of his teaching, Potter began to feel an excitement and apprehension about his own, about his upcoming classes, thinking if he was going to do it he damn well might as well do it right. He would read some more, prepare some more; he would give it his best, whatever that now was worth.

4

Potter felt he had prepared himself well for the
first meeting of his seminar in Public Relations.
He had thoroughly read and underlined *Theory
and Practice of Public Relations* by Castorp and
Billingsgate, which after considerable delibera-
tion he had chosen as the principal text for the
course. Furthermore, he had scoured the recent
issues of the *Public Relations Journal,* a periodi-
cal of the PR trade, or, as the editors would probably prefer it, the profession. While actually
working in the field his attention to that publi-
cation had been small, limited usually to occasions when he had nothing else to take with him
to the bathroom for scanning while sitting on
the pot. But now he felt it was part of his responsibility as a teacher to keep up with what was going on in his subject, have all the up-to-the-min-
ute stuff at his command.

He read with careful interest an article on
"Public Relations in the Classroom," which said
that in most courses theory was being stressed
over practice, and quoted Hunter P. McCarthy,

head of the Public Relations "sequence" at West
Virginia University, who felt that PR courses
were being "absorbed into a more psychological-
communicological approach." Hunter P. Mc-
Carthy said further that "As man's senses extend,
the chief business of our society will be catering
to those extended senses, and public relations
practitioners should be in the vanguard of service
to man's extension." After reading that declaration several times Potter was still not sure what
exactly it meant, but it certainly gave him a
heady feeling, knowing he was in the vanguard
of something, however elusive. He was amused
and reassured by an article on "PR People in
Retirement," which reported that "In-depth
study finds them happy, involved, useful, and
well-adjusted to a new way of life." As one now
allied with the business, if only as a teacher, Potter could surely look ahead to a contented time
of pasturing in his declining years.

Potter alluded to the article in his introduc-
tory remarks to the seminar, one of several notes
of wry humor that he struck, hoping to set the
tone in a breezy, informal way; and hoping also to win the hearts of each and every student.
He was surprised at how important it seemed to
him to be loved by his classes; his performance,
casual as he hoped it appeared, was as studied
and consciously timed as if he were on the stage,
facing a first-night audience in the starring role
of his career.

Potter ended his spiel, lit a cigarette, and

looked around the table for questions, confident
he was prepared to field any and all. But the first
one asked was the one he had not expected, was
not in his notes or research or calculations, and
he had not prepared any smooth way to handle
it. It came zinging in from left field, though Potter was sure it had not been intended that way
by the questioner, a clean-cut studious young
man. Mr. Stevenson. Foster B. Stevenson.

"Sir," Mr. Stevenson asked, "you mentioned
something of your own experience in the public
relations field in New York City. Could you tell
us, please, how it happened you decided to enter the field?"

Potter could feel his cheeks growing warm.
The faces of the fifteen students seated around
the long mahogany table turned toward him, interested, attentive, expectant. Potter coughed.
It sounded like a sudden explosion in the silence
of the room. He began to speak, knowing he had
to, groping awkwardly, hearing disjointed phrases
come out, like "Well—you see—at that time—uh,
I was—but first I should explain—"

His groping for the manner in which to most
suitably answer the question did not mean at all
that he had forgotten it, or that it was the slightest bit unclear in his own mind, for as soon as
the question was asked he saw with perfect clarity the actual time and place when he decided
to go into public relations; it was one of those
scenes that were indelibly retained in his memory because it marked so definite an end to one

part of his life and the beginning of another, a
demarcation as definitive as a wedding or fu-
neral, a divorce or a graduation.

Potter was standing in the middle of a room
that tinkled with cocktail glasses and conversation. It was after he'd been kicked out by Tandy
and had been living on a fold-out bed at the
apartment of a guy from his old acting class,
and waiting tables at Allen's on the Upper East
Side. Several friends stood amiably about, none
of them noticing that the usually gregarious
Potter had fallen silent for an untypical period
of time, and that when he finally spoke, his comment did not seem related to the chit-chat
around him.

"I'm hungry," he said.

The three or four people standing by him
stopped their own conversation and looked at
Potter with curiosity.

"Why, Phil," one girl said helpfully, "there's a
whole ham and turkey right over there on the
table. Would you like me to fix up a plate or
a sandwich for you?"

He shook his head, his expression fixed in a sort
of trance. "That isn't what I mean," he said.

"Well—uh—what is it—you're hungry for?"
the girl asked, warily now. "Steak or something?"

"No," he said, still evidently staring at something beyond or above the people who were now
so attentively watching him; whatever he saw
was beyond the party, the room, the evening.

"We could fall over to Thompson Street and

get some Italian food, if that's what you want," his roomie Al Solonkis said.

"That isn't what I want."

"Well for the love of Jesus, will you tell us what in the name of God you want?" Al burst out.

Potter suddenly smiled, as if the trance was broken, and looked at his friends as if they should have understood all along what he meant that he was hungry for now, what he really wanted for the first time in his life.

"Money," he said.

Once it happened it seemed only natural—all too natural, Potter thought—that he was just right for public relations. Going with Olney and Sheperdson, who handled a lot of theatrical clients, made it seem even more natural, an extension of his former interest. Shouldn't he have known it all along?

He had feared it all along.

But that was not the sort of thing to tell the young people gathered in his brand new seminar; it did not convey the sort of image he wished to create for either himself or the subject. Whatever hostility or disrespect or condescension he felt about the field, he figured in part, at least, was due to the fact that it was not what he started out wanting to do at all, but a very distant second choice, not even in a sense a choice at all, but a seemingly inevitable solution, a half-baked bargain with a charming sort of devil. But if students were attracted to the sort of work and life that public relations offered, he saw nothing shameful about it, did not wish to discourage them, and hoped in fact to give them as much advice and good counsel, intellectual stimulation and accompanying entertainment as he possibly could.

After his initial fumbling with the question, he spoke of the "challenge" of the field, tried honestly to take into account the financial attraction it had for him after years of playing the starving artist, how it was in fact related to his old love, the theatre, not merely, in the case of his own firm, in gross press-agentry for stars, but in the planning of long campaigns for top-notch serious Broadway productions, promotion of meaningful cultural events, fund-raising for a topflight symphony—oh, a rich variety of noble works and deeds. But as he spoke of these things his mind was far away, thinking of how he was able to continue the job as long as he did, after the novelty of new work and a good income had worn off, how he was able to not only keep plugging away but to strive for even greater rewards —and the explanation of that was even more inappropriate for the young ears of the students in his opening seminar, for the answer was inextricably tied to his affair and eventual marriage with Jessica.

She was a model. Tall, of course, and tawny, sharp bones and big eyes; small chest, long slim legs that he recognized from his fantasies, from TV bath oil commercials, from *New York Times*

Sunday Magazine hosiery ads. She seemed very bright and very vulnerable, unsure beneath the cool gloss of her beauty. He met her at a cocktail party and after two drinks, he mentioned, off-hand, as if it were something quite natural and matter-of-course, that he intended to marry her.

"Oh?" she asked; lashes lifted in an interested, inquisitive way.

They went to bed together later that evening, and didn't really get up again for three days, except to make forays into Jessica's kitchen for booze or yogurt or frozen steaks. The attraction was of a kind that is sometimes described as electric.

"Something must be wrong," she kept saying.

"Why?" he asked.

"It always is."

"But this," he assured her, "is different."

She cried a great deal, especially when, a year after meeting, they were married. Because, she said, of being so happy. He asked, with increasing irritation, why being happy made her cry, and she said because it couldn't last.

Time proved her right: a little over four years, in which they moved here and there around Manhattan and Brooklyn Heights, tried her working and her staying home, tried shrinks and booze and pot and pets, second and third and forty-second honeymoons, summer houses and winter vacations, infidelity and urban renewal; tried everything but Children. And both of them, despite

benevolent advice from friends, balked at that—
until they had worked things out for themselves
they vowed not to bring any innocent parties into
the act.

On their fourth Christmas Potter insisted that
they refuse the invitations of family and friends
and just be together, the two of them; he had
some Dickensian fantasy of the holiday bringing
them together. Tight-lipped, she agreed, after
making it clear how nice it would be to see her
sister in Moline and her sister's children and her
alcoholic brother-in-law who sold for John Deere
in the Quad Cities area. Potter mused on the
warmth and comfort to be found in a big old-
fashioned Christmas dinner at home, with the
phone off the hook and carols on the hi-fi.

Jessica was busy in the kitchen most of that
Christmas morning; busy but silent. When she
served the dinner, Potter thought it would never end; she bore in the bird, then the trimmings
—cranberries and sweet potatoes and creamed
onions and succotash and homemade bread and
buttered carrots and hominy grits—each dish
laid down like an indictment against him. When
the table was laid, laden, loaded down, she sat,
primly, her face drained of color, her eyes
alarmingly wide and calm, and said smoothly,
"You wanted a Christmas dinner—here it is."

Potter had several creamed onions and then
ran to the bathroom and vomited.

"No appetite?" she asked, solicitously.

They made up, then and many more times,

but it was then, over the groaning holiday table, that he knew, for certain, it was over.

But whatever criticism he could make of the time with Jessica, he could never complain that it was dull, and during it he worked with her in mind, with the two of them in mind, with the prospect of all that they might do and have, to urge him on, and he knew if it had not been for her his career in public relations would not have been as long or as productive or as lucrative.

But that would have been—to say the least— as difficult to explain to a college seminar as it would have been inappropriate. So Potter kept his private life to himself and managed to get through the hour tossing out generalizations that he hoped were not too namby-pamby and anecdotes he hoped were not too irrelevant. When the time was up, though the day was unseasonably cool for September in Boston, Potter's shirt was soaking wet.

Potter discovered that teaching a class was in a way like making love. Sometimes he did it with great enthusiasm, artfully building up interest and getting a rising response of excitement that peaked with a mutual rapport between himself and the students. Sometimes he did it because it was expected of him, and he forced himself to go through the motions, mechanically, ending sooner than he should have, leaving both himself and the class feeling grouchy, disgruntled, unsatisfied.

He felt pretty sure of himself in the PR seminar, and after his beers with Gafferty, he devised
his own way of teaching the Communications
sections. It was required that the classes read
and study current periodicals—newspapers, magazines, the underground press, trade publications
—and Potter picked a selection he felt comfortable with and interested in. It was also required
that McLuhan's book *Understanding Media* be
read, and after that the individual instructor was
allowed to "build up and out." Gafferty did it
with the Irish poets, and Potter struck on the
notion of doing it with Shakespeare. He even
got the idea from McLuhan, who wrote in *Understanding Media* that one could create "a fairly complete handbook for studying the exten-
sions of man" by reading Shakespeare; he
pointed out that in *Othello* Shakespeare was
concerned with "the transforming powers of new
media," and that *Troilus and Cressida* is "almost completely devoted to both a psychic and
social study of communication."

Eureka! Under the approving mantle of Mc-
Luhan himself, Potter devised a Communications course that included *Othello, Troilus and
Cressida, King Henry V.* A production of *Lear*
that he saw as a kid at the Booth in Washington
had originally turned him on to the theatre, and
after the performance, thrilled, he went to his
father's library and one by one took down the
little blue volumes of the complete set of Shakespeare, devouring each with wonder and excite-

ment. Reading the plays again, discussing them, reciting in class those lines, those rolling cadences, inspired his teaching and gave him new energy. He wanted to convey this richness to his students, to make them see, hear, and feel what was there; he wanted, indeed, to communicate.

He liked the students. None were especially brilliant, or militant, and that was fine with Potter. For the most part they seemed pleasant, and bright enough. He enjoyed the realization that he was being paid to help them, to tell them what he knew and what understanding he had of the books and subjects they discussed; and, in such discussions, he found that he made new discoveries himself, that sometimes a student's question or comment would open up an unexpected angle of viewing a thought or situation, and he found that such occasions brought him a quiet kind of pleasure.

He soon learned that his office hours, his consultations with students, were not strictly limited to matters academic. Halligan, a tall, serious Vietnam veteran, invited Potter to have a beer with him, and with the second glass, confided that his girl was pressing pretty hard to get married.

"She's bought these dishes," Halligan said.

"Dishes?"

"A whole set of this very expensive kind. More than regular people would ever use. You know, the kind that break easy."

"I think I know the kind."

"So before, we'd just been talking about get-

ting married, but now that she's got these dishes,
she says we have to really get going on it, that's
what they're for. To start your marriage."

"I take it you're not so anxious to get married."

"Well, I think I love her, you know, and I
know that we should probably—well, we'll eventually have to get married, I guess, but—Jesus.
I don't know. The idea of having to cart all
those dishes around, it makes me feel sort of
closed in. Like you start accumulating all that
stuff, and you can't just take off or anything."

"Not easily," Potter agreed.

"I guess I hadn't really thought about marriage. What it would really feel like."

"Well, I'm afraid I'm not a very good person
to tell about marriage," Potter said.

"You're divorced, you mean."

"How did you know?"

Halligan shrugged. "Things get around. About
faculty."

"Oh. Well, anyway, my own marriage just
didn't work, but it doesn't mean it's not right for
other people."

"I guess you can't tell until you do it."

"I'm afraid not."

They didn't resolve anything, nor did Potter
wish to influence Halligan's decision on matri-
mony, but it made him feel good, that the guy
would want his advice, would regard him as
someone to talk things over with.

Potter felt he was getting along pretty well

with the students, felt that in general they liked
him, and he was surprised when Lester Harnack
said he'd like to give him some advice about "student relations." Harnack was a part-time instructor in Communications who had published a
couple of poems during the Beat era, and was
said to have once hitchhiked from New York
City to Wilkes-Barre, Pennsylvania with Greg-
ory Corso. Harnack had kept pace with the
changing styles of the counter culture, and now
lived in a communal house in Boston's South
End, a "transitional" neighborhood.

"At least let your hair grow," Harnack coun-
selled Potter. "The way you dress—it creates a
kind of barrier between you and the kids. I'm
not just speaking of academic bullshit—I mean
the girls. A lot of these girls really swing, and
they're looking for father figures. If you know
what I mean."

Potter knew. He thanked Harnack, but said
he thought he'd stick to his old-fashioned style,
he was pretty much set in his ways. He was well
aware that his Brooks Brothers garb was a kind
of uniform—just as Harnack's Wrangler pants
and boots and buckskin shirts with fringe was
another kind—but it was a matter of pride with
Potter to stick to the style he'd grown up with
even though it was no longer in fashion, in the
spirit in which one might continue to wear the
colors of some once-illustrious regiment that had
since gone from glory.

Besides that, Potter wasn't interested in student seduction. Aside from disliking the cliché nature of it, the prospect of such involvements seemed messy and complicated, and Potter was trying to avoid that. He was waiting for some kind of clear-cut, mutually satisfying relationship.

But he was getting tired of waiting.

PART TWO

1

A woman friend of Potter in New York called
to tell him she heard he had got a divorce and
moved to Boston, and she wondered if he'd like
to meet a nice available lady who was also recently divorced.

"I assume," Potter said, "that this lady is not
only divorced, but that she has two children."

"How did you know that?" his friend asked.

"A feeling," Potter said. "Probably telepathic."

Potter knew because he had begun to suspect
that in the great IBM machine of life, his mat-
ing card had been programmed in such a way
that he was only allowed to meet a woman if she
was divorced and had two children. He had nothing against divorced women with two children
—some of them he had met were admirable human beings, attractive and intelligent, yet the
fact that since he had started going out in his
new life in Boston, except for the fragile Alison
Farr, he had not met women of any other cate-
gory, had begun to spook him a little.

Sometimes things go that way. There was another time in Potter's life, back in his early New York days, when every girl he met was in her third year of analysis. Not her first year or her fourth year, but her third year. During that phase, when he met a new girl and they had had enough drinks to get into the personal shit, he would look at her appraisingly and say, "I bet you're in your third year of alalysis," and the girl would be amazed by his insight, wonder how she had given herself away, what unconscious clues he had picked up, but Potter would only smile, mysteriously.

When you got into one of those trends there was no use going against it. Potter assured Marva he would call her friend.

He nosed his newly bought secondhand Mustang convertible down the dark, winding streets of Cambridge reeking of High Karate cologne and cursing the goddamn thoughtless residents who didn't have numbers on their houses. It was hard enough to find the right street, there were so many little odd ones that curled around—it was almost as bad as Greenwich Village, but with fewer lights and more trees. Then when you finally got the right street you'd be lucky to find a single visible number on a house, and Potter had to get out and go up to someone's porch, straining his eyes to make out a faded gold-chipped combination of numbers; and all the time worried that someone would think he was a prowler or student revolutionary or Peeping Tom and either call the police or simply shoot him down on the front lawn. Just getting out of New York City wasn't any guarantee of safety, not anymore. You could just as well be clobbered in a riot in Harvard Square as mugged in Central Park.

He was supposed to be looking for a green, two-story house, but it was hard to make out even the colors; in the moonless night, most everything looked grey. In the next block he found something faintly greenish, with a bright bulb lit on the porch, and figured that must be it. He cut off the motor and drew in a long, deep breath, bracing himself. He had broken another personal promise, another one of those "last things in the world he would ever do," and that was go on a blind date. A blind date with a divorcée who had two children.

But it was better than sitting at home watching television, drinking a continuous series of Scotch and sodas, and, with an incredible exertion of will, making himself put a frozen TV Mexican dinner in the oven, repeating the incantation that If You Drink You Have To Eat. It was one of the thin threads that he felt separated him from being a real alcoholic, and he strove mightily to cling to it. But there were times when, alone with a bottle and a TV movie he had seen six times before and never liked in the first place, it seemed it might be altogether easier and less painful to stick his own head in the oven rather than a frozen TV dinner.

He got out of the car and looked up at the

house. The woman and her children lived on the top of the two stories—they had the upper half of the box to themselves. He wondered what manner of lady he would find inside when he opened the door of this particular box—you could never tell from the advance descriptions. And he knew she was in the same suspension wondering no doubt what sort of character would be emerging from his own little box of a car, into her box of a house, hoping no doubt, against all the odds, he would be just the understanding fellow to want to share a box together with her, even with the two children thrown in. Or maybe she was sour on it all and wanted nothing more than a temporary diversion that would keep her own head out of the oven.

Potter sighed and shrugged: Well, he told himself, there's nothing like romance. He had promised himself he would not be disappointed; that he would expect nothing out of the ordinary in the way of looks. She had not after all been touted as Miss Massachusetts, or even a runner-up in the Cambridge preliminaries. And yet, though he had tried to fight down his particular fantasies, her name had conjured up, in spite of his rational protestations, something exotic.

"Hello," she said. "I'm Renée Gillespie."

She was in fact, rather pretty; "striking" even would be an appropriate term. Good bone structure, large green eyes, a pretty mouth. Her fine black hair was pulled discreetly, stylishly back at the back of her head, with a gold clip. She wore a dark, handsomely embroidered blouse, and a long skirt. She was poised, but somewhat withdrawn, not out of coldness, Potter felt, but a sense of vulnerability. She was, in looks and manner, altogether admirable.

And Potter was so stricken with disappointment he could barely speak.

In spite of all his intellectual preparedness, the fantasy that had sprouted out of the name "Renée Gillespie" had flowered in his imagination, blooming into some Alexandrian temptress, a French courtesan who had married an aged wealthy Jewish merchant who was killed in some international arms deal, but who in his will had provided her with the means to achieve her doctorate in Biology at Harvard.

Though he had known, in fact, that her husband was a professor of mathematics who had left her for a graduate student and taken a position with a Washington think-tank.

He was disappointed not only in her, the real Renée Gillespie, but even more in himself, for his stupid and adolescent fantasy that came easily from her name. If only her name had been Harriet Smith, or Mary Ellen Klein.

"Won't you come in?" she asked.

"Oh—yes."

He smiled, trying to compose himself.

The baby sitter hadn't arrived yet, so Potter had to take off his coat and sit down. Renée offered him a glass of Dubonnet, apologizing that she had nothing else in the way of alcohol. Potter accepted; he hated the syrupy sweetish taste of Dubonnet, but he would have taken anything with alcohol in it.

The children appeared in the hallway, staring at him.

"Hi," Potter said. He forced a grin.

"Say hello to Mr. Potter," Renée said brightly. "That's Scott, and Teresa."

Scott, a skulking lad of around ten, glared hatefully at Potter. Teresa, a golden-haired little doll in bunny-print pajamas with feet, sucked avidly on her thumb.

"C'n I have a Coke?" Scott asked his mother.

"You've already had one today."

"C'n I have a half a one?"

"One's the limit. You know that, dear. Let's not argue."

"Aw, Christ."

"Behave now, Scott. There's company."

Scott turned his back toward Potter, and asked in a semi-whine, "Who's gonna sit for us?"

"DeeDee."

"She's stupid."

"Scott, you'd better snap out of this mood and act like a grown-up boy or you're not going to watch any television."

Renée said this quickly, in a level, heartfelt monotone, and came from the kitchenette with a glass of Dubonnet and a determined smile. She sat down in a large armchair that was beside the sofa, and brushed back a wisp of hair. Most of it was black, but there were these wispy little ringlets of grey right around her ears that wouldn't stay put.

Potter said "Thanks," and took a quick sip of the Dubonnet.

"Say hello to Mr. Potter, Teresa," Renée asked hopefully.

Teresa was still rooted to the spot where she first emerged from the hallway, staring unblinkingly at Potter and working the hell out of her thumb.

"Hi, Teresa," Potter said in what he hoped was a jovial, winning manner, "how are you tonight?"

Teresa bit down harder on her thumb, and slowly, relentlessly, tears started streaming down her cheeks. She suddenly bolted and ran for her mother, burying her curly little head in Mrs. Gillespie's long skirt.

"Teresa, hon, there's nothing to cry about!" Renée said.

"She's a-scared of that man," Scott volunteered.

"I'm really harmless," Potter said feebly. His neck itched.

"Mr. Potter's a *nice* man," Renée said.

"How do you know?" Scott asked. "You never even met him till just now."

Potter felt a deep, pure urge to smack the kid, just once, as hard as he could. Instead he took a belt of the Dubonnet, narrowed his eyes, and said, "You're right, Scott. For all you know, I might be The Boston Strangler, recently escaped from prison."

Renée's face gave way to a sudden twitch, but she quickly resettled it into a smile and said, "Scott, dear, why don't you see what's on television?"

Teresa was bawling harder now, despite her mother's reassuring strokes and pats.

"Is he really The Boston Strangler?" Scott asked.

"Don't be silly. Now go and see what's on."

"I was just kidding," Potter said.

There was a knock at the door, and Renée jumped up, leaving Teresa to bawl by herself, and let in the baby sitter. Potter thanked God she was fat. There was no worse torture than having to drive home one of those exotic, long-haired twitchy-assed baby sitters after a lackluster night on the town with a harried divorced lady. Potter prayed for ungainly baby sitters.

When they finally got to Chez Dreyfus, and were seated, Potter ordered a double Scotch on the rocks.

"I don't usually do this," Renée said, "but I think I'll have a martini. A Very Dry Martini."

"You deserve it," said Potter.

"I'm sorry it was so—hectic. They're really nice kids, but—"

"I understand. It must be hard."

"Their father lives in Washington, now, and he only gets up about once a month."

"It must be tough on the boy. Especially."

"On me, too. When Daddy comes now it's a big occasion, like a holiday. He's Santa Claus, and

I'm the wicked witch who makes them do all the things they don't want to do."

"Yeah. It's really tough, I guess. I guess I'm lucky, in a way. I'm divorced, but we didn't have any children."

"Yes," Renée said, "that's probably fortunate. If the marriage didn't work."

Potter agreed. They drank to his good fortune.

By the end of the meal, Potter had a sharp headache over his left eye. He had asked for a booth when he called for reservations, but they got there late and had to either stand and wait for another twenty minutes or be seated at a table in the midst of the room. It was too bright, and the talk and clatter all around them made conversation more difficult. You had to really concentrate.

Renée ordered coffee and flan for dessert, and Potter had a brandy.

"This is a real treat," she said.

"I'm glad."

Potter liked her. She was gentle, kind, intelligent, sometimes funny; but over it all was a fringe of sorrow that clung to whatever she said and did; outlined her, defined her. It was not self-pity. Potter thought it was justified, and yet it unnerved him. Sadness is not an aphrodisiac. He wished that he wanted to fuck her, and hoped that perhaps he still could work himself into such a desire.

When he asked her to come by his place for a drink she studied her watch, longer than it took to figure out what time it was, and said, "Well, just for one."

"Sure," he said. "A nightcap."

He put on a cheerful-sweet Joni Mitchell album, popped a couple of Excedrin, and fixed them each a drink; his strong, hers weak. An act of chivalry.

"Is that Judy Collins?" she asked.

"Joni Mitchell."

"I get them confused. All those pretty young girls singing their love songs."

"Yeah. I know what you mean."

He knew that she meant she hated their guts. He put on a classical guitar record, and Renée smiled, and leaned her head back on the couch. Potter put down his drink and kissed her, gently, tentatively. At first she hardly moved and then she leaned into him with full force, her mouth wide and hard on his with a sudden, fierce hunger. He pressed her against him and then she suddenly pulled away and averted her eyes. "I'd better go."

"Can't you stay—a while?"

She sat for a moment, drawing her lips in. Then, without looking at him she clutched his hand in hers, pressing it tightly. "If you don't mind running DeeDee home, and you still feel like it, you could come have a drink at my house."

It would happen, then.

He took a half a fifth of Scotch with him, and had a stiff one when he got back from driving the mute, gumchewing baby sitter home. Renée had changed into a blue nightgown, a quilted house-coat, and big, floppy comfortable slippers whose fur was soiled grey. The radio was tuned to a symphony.

Potter took off his jacket, loosened his tie, and sat down beside Renée on the couch. Her hand squeezed his and she leaned against him. He closed his eyes and took a burning swig of his drink, then turned to match his mouth with hers. She came alive all over, digging her nails in his back, squirming and sobbing and gasping. Pot-ter struggled out of his clothes, still keeping his mouth on hers, yanking and jerking his way out of shirt, belt, slacks, and Renée wrenched free of her robe. Potter, now only in socks and shorts, fell upon her.

She whispered "Wait," and swiftly pulled her nightgown over her head; it floated to the floor, making a blue puddle. Potter pressed down on her, feeling himself grow, and she started tug-ging down his shorts, when she suddenly froze.

"What—"

"Shh."

There was a creak in the hallway.

Potter didn't move or turn to look.

"What are you doing?" the boy's voice asked in a sleepy grouch.

Potter closed his eyes as tight as he could.

"You get right back to bed this minute imme-diately," Renée said in a quaking sort of hiss, "you get right back to bed and go to sleep."

After a silent infinity, she let out a sigh, and Potter raised his head. Renée was sitting up, but huddled over, her hands pressed against her temples. She looked cold and bony and frail, like a refugee or a prisoner who had just been stripped of his only clothing.

"Jesus," Potter said softly. "I'm sorry."

"Don't be."

Potter sat up on the couch. His head was throbbing, and his prick had shrunk to what felt like the size of a cigarette. Renée picked up her nightgown and draped it around her shoulders, shivering. Potter looked down at the heap of his clothes, inside out and messily tangled. It looked to him like a snapshot of his life.

When he left he kissed her lightly on the forehead and said he would call her.

She thanked him for the lovely dinner.

The day after his date with Renée, Potter had to teach. He had an Alka-Seltzer, three aspirin, and a glass of orange juice for breakfast, but still he felt nauseous and aching. The minutes ticked off like separate eternities. He repeated himself, coughed a lot, and could hear the restless motions of legs crossing, pages riffling, throats clearing, and yawns. Between classes he went to his office, closed the door, and sat with his head on his desk. For lunch, he had one of the secretaries in the English office bring him back a grilled cheese sandwich and a chocolate malt. By the time he got through his PR semi-

nar in the afternoon he was beginning to revive,
but he still felt shaky. He figured fresh air would
do him good.

He strolled down Beacon Street toward Arlington, and took one of the paths that curled
into the Public Gardens. The air was cool and
brisk, and so were the people. No one was idling,
as they did in the Indian summer time, but all
seemed to walk with purpose, toward some appointed destination. The sky was cold, lavender
and pink. Austere. Potter stopped by his favorite statue, the one commemorating the discovery and first medical use of ether. The statue
was of a woman holding a child. On one side
of the base was inscribed a line from Revelation:
"Neither shall there be any more pain—"

Potter wondered if he reported to the emergency ward of the world famous Mass General
Hospital, whether they would give him a dose of
ether. If he were ever a president or dictator, he
would see that such a service was available to
the public, an emergency facility that would
dispense some sort of pill or gas or potion for
people who felt the kind of pain that came from
having nothing to do and nowhere to go and
feeling nothing inside.

In the absence of such a service, he walked.
He walked to the glorious statue of George
Washington on horseback, and then up the wide
center mall of Commonwealth Avenue, with its
grey and weather-greened statues of assorted
great men of the past. He stopped briefly at each

one, as he often did, reading the inscriptions
again, making a kind of silent visitation to their
memory. There was Alexander Hamilton, and
John Glover, a revolutionary soldier from Mar-
blehead. There was Patrick Collins, a turn-of-
the-century mayor of Boston, whose qualities
engraved in stone proclaimed not only that he
was honest and talented, but also that he was
"serviceable." Potter liked that. The notion of
being a "serviceable" man. But most of all he
liked the staunch figure of William Lloyd Garri-
son, at ease in a chair that seemed like a throne,
whose base bore the words of the great man himself declaring that "I am in earnest—I will not
equivocate—I will not excuse—I will not retreat
a single inch—and I will be heard." Actually
Potter didn't know a damn thing about Garri-
son except that he had been a leading abolition-
ist, but nevertheless the confident, uncompro-
mising words, the grand aristocratic sweep of
the sentiment, speaking from an age that seemed
more courageous and clearly defined in its purpose and conflict than his own amorphous time,
gave Potter a quick, adrenaline thrill. The whole
Avenue, with its solid statues, its great trees, its
fine old houses lining either side, had a stateli-
ness that Potter enjoyed.

He was finding in general that he liked Boston better than Cambridge. He liked the "old"
feeling of the brick sidewalks and yellow-
tongued gaslamps on Beacon Hill, liked the
open, majestic feeling of the Commons and the

Public Gardens, which were laid out on a more intimate, human scale than Central Park, and were less threatening; walking those paths, you expected to be panhandled, yes, but not mugged or raped or murdered.

Boston was grace and tradition to Potter. Cambridge was Harvard. Cambridge was students. Walking through Harvard Square, if you were not a student or someone who might be a student, you felt like an alien, felt as if you stuck out from the crowd, like a German tourist in the South of Spain. Every time Potter went through the Square, the Yeats line flashed automatically through his mind: "That is no country for old men." Old, in Harvard Square, seeming anything over thirty. At most. The atmosphere was youthfully oppressive.

When he got to Mass Avenue, Potter walked up to the Hotel Elliot at the corner of Boylston and had a couple of drinks in its pitch-dark cocktail lounge. Then he decided to blow a few bucks on taking a cab home, which would spare him a trek through Harvard Square.

Back at his apartment he prepared himself a large tumbler of Scotch and soda and ice, and turned on the seven o'clock news.

The war in Vietnam was still "winding down," like a busted alarm clock.

Martha Mitchell had made another of her famous late-night phone calls, bawling out someone who had criticized the Nixon administration.

Tension was high on the Israel-Arab borders.

Suburban mothers in Michigan were picketing against school-busing.

The Orioles had taken a lead on the Reds in the World Series.

The Celtics had a three-game win-streak going.

Derek Sanderson vowed that the Bruins would go all the way.

Tomorrow would be cloudy and cool, with scattered showers.

Potter found himself suddenly laughing.

They called that *news?*

He went to the kitchen to make a new drink, but first made a pledge to himself that he would eat.

The most simple substance available seemed to be a can of Hormel chili. Potter took it off the shelf, set a pan on a front burner of the electric stove, and got out the can opener. A do-it-yourself home dinner kit. He would do it a little later. First, he made the new drink.

It was situation comedy time on TV, and he pushed the button in, rejecting. Canned chili was bad enough without having to add canned laughter. He put a Judy Collins on the stereo.

When you're down in Juarez in the rain and it's Eastertime too—

Potter closed his eyes.

He woke, hungry and dizzy, the TV blank, the stereo scratching.

It seemed he had slept for days, but it was only a little past ten. He went to the kitchen, ground the can of chili open with a vengeance, scooped it out into the pan, where it made a soggy *plunk,* and turned the burner to Hi. Reaching for the Cutty Sark he stopped, took a deep breath, and instead pulled from the refrigerator a bottle of Gallo Rhinegarten white wine, filling one of the fluted glasses he had been given in the division of old wedding present spoils.

Wine with dinner. You had to make the effort. Stay civilized. He scratched his head, then took a bottle of Worcestershire Sauce from the cupboard and dashed a generous amount on the chili. Real gourmet action.

The chili hunk was beginning to sizzle, and he took a spoon and mashed it around in the pan. It looked like dogfood.

After dinner he poured himself a brandy, and lit up a mentholated Tiparillo.

He burped, and thought of Jessica's beef bourguignon. It was her specialty. It took all day, and was usually served with tears, but it was damn good.

Jessica.

After another Scotch he dialed information in New York, and got her number. J. L. Potter. What the hell, no reason they shouldn't talk. Be friends.

Lovers, even? Still? Again?

After one ring he hung up. It would only open an emotional spider's nest. When he talked to her again, even saw her again he wanted it to be out of some motivation more noble than loneliness, more gracious than despair.

2

Potter didn't much want to call Renée Gilles-pie but he didn't know anyone else to call. And besides, he thought she was nice; in fact he was convinced of that. He even thought maybe she was more attractive than he had felt she was on his first impression, distorted as that was by his fantasy of someone as exotic as he had con-jured up from her French-Jewish name. Of that, he was not convinced, but he wanted to believe it. One thing was sure: Saturday night was ap-proaching, a grim specter.

Saturday Night!

It was hallowed and feared and anticipated, lyricized in story and immortalized in song.

The loneliest night of the week.

The night when my sweetie and I used to dance cheek to cheek.

After Potter was graduated from Vanderbilt and went into the Navy he dated a Tri Delt from U. of Maryland, during the Holidays, and, on New Year's Eve, after a gallon or so of cham-pagne at a swell party in Arlington, Virginia, he had asked her to marry him. They became engaged. It was in The Papers. When he returned to his base in Mississippi, she wrote him a long, curlicued letter with circles dotting the i's, saying how glad she was to be engaged, and how she looked forward to the state of married bliss: "Just think," she observed, in a practical aside, "I'll have a Permanent Saturday Night Date for the rest of my life!"

Potter for some time had mulled over the notion of marriage bringing about a Permanent Saturday Night Date for the rest of his life, and his enthusiasm began to flag; the Engagement simmered down, then died, via letters and the lack of them.

But he understood what she meant, and how she felt about the Guarantee of having her Saturday night date card filled up for eternity. Beginning at puberty, all good American girls and boys were trained and drilled and instilled with the understanding that not having anything to do on Saturday night was a stigma so great that it marked the week as a failure, meant that you were Undesired or Undesirable or Undesiring, marked you as a malcontent or malcontented, a malignant and/or malingering member of society.

So you either went out, accompanied, or you hid. Pretended to be Busy, pulling the curtains of your room about you, the covers over your head, the lamps dimmed, the music stopped.

Ho ho ho. High school stuff.

College stuff.

Life stuff.

Potter felt sure that Senior Citizens were still plagued by it. It was worked inside your head so deep, you could never really get it out, never just sit around quietly somewhere in America on Saturday night, reading a good book, without feeling guilty or cheated.

But there was also a protocol that dictated that a girl, a woman, had to pretend to be busy by Thursday, or Friday, if she were asked out for Saturday Night, that a boy/man should not ask out a woman for that evening if it were too late, lest he insult her or shame himself. It was altogether tricky, even when one was an alleged Adult.

When Potter called Renée on Thursday afternoon and asked if she could have dinner with him Saturday, she said, "You mean Saturday *night?*"

He inhaled, squinting his eyes as he held the phone, and said, "Yes. *Saturday night.*"

There was a pause of age-old legendary painful feigning, as Renée, no doubt caught in her own images of social nicety, said hesitantly that if she could get a Sitter, yes, it would be OK. Which left open the possibility that only the problem of the Sitter was what might hang her up and might have prevented her thus far from accepting sundry other such invitations. Potter understood. He would check back with her to make sure she had got the Sitter, knowing already she would succeed in doing so, knowing with relief that he had filled up the hole of this soonest Saturday, for him and for her, before it swallowed them up, each vulnerable and singular.

Potter, relieved, whistled a tune.

The night when my sweetie and I used to dance cheek to cheek.

Very soon after Potter had made his Saturday Night Date with Renée, the phone rang. It was Marva Bertelsen. She wondered if Potter could come to a small dinner party on Saturday night. He explained he had already made a date. Marva explained that was too bad, because she had just the right girl for Potter.

"How do you mean," he asked, "just the right girl?"

There was a tantalizing pause.

"I mean, just the right girl for *you*," Marva said brightly.

"How do you know?"

"Well. She's *very* attractive."

"Mmmm."

"And *very* intelligent."

"Mmmm."

"Well, I guess you're not interested."

"I didn't say that."

"You just keep saying 'Mmmm.' "

"Mmmm."

"Well, it doesn't matter. She's in my pottery class. I like her, and I invited her over for Saturday, but you might not like her at all, come to think of it."

"Come to think of *what?*"

"Ohhhh. I don't know. When I think of it. She's really a glorified secretary. Works in personnel for United Insurance."

"So?"

"So, you probably want someone with a much more glamorous job."

"I didn't say that."

"I think she's very glamorous, as a person—herself—but right now she doesn't have what anyone would consider a glamorous job. Of course, she just got divorced not long ago, and she had to take what she could get. A B.A. in Psychology doesn't mean anything. Job-wise."

"Divorced?" Potter asked.

"Yes," Marva said with what sounded like a yawn. "You probably wouldn't be interested at all."

"I bet she has two children," Potter said.

"Oh, no. No children. She lives by herself in this really nice apartment on Beacon Hill. Wow. The biggest bed I've ever seen. Lots of incense and all. That sort of thing. Probably bore you to death."

"Not necessarily," Potter said.

"Weeeel. Maybe you could come by for dessert. Just to meet her. You probably won't see anything in her at all."

"Well, you never can tell."

Potter took Renée to have dinner Saturday night at a Greek place in Boston that Max Bertelsen had recommended, The Ommonia. It was a little bit overdone, with fake statues and a purple kind of lighting and a Greek combo, but it was rather festive, and Potter was in the mood for it. Renée seemed more relaxed than she had before, and quite animated; her fingers, long and white, made lacy patterns as she talked and laughed. She was wearing a white silk blouse with frilly cuffs, a maroon velvet midi, and black boots. Potter usually loved seeing women in boots, but somehow, Renée's were a little wrong. Instead of seeming sexy, they looked sort of orthopedic.

Potter wondered what the girl at the Bertelsen's would be like, the one who was divorced but had no children.

Renée finished off the last of her lamb and pilaf, and leaned back, smiling, in her chair. "Mmmm. I feel so indulgent."

"Good," Potter said. "I'm glad."

"I even think I might go overboard and have a Baklava."

Potter cleared his throat. He hadn't yet got around to mentioning that they were going to the Bertelsen's for dessert.

"Well," he said, "uh, we sort of were invited to these friends, of mine, after dinner. For dessert and coffee."

"Oh?"

Renée looked at him in a way that was interested, but slightly apprehensive.

"You'll like them," Potter said quickly. "But listen, you can have the Baklava too, if you want." He smiled. "Be *really* indulgent."

Renée straightened up in her chair and dabbed the napkin at her lips. "Oh, no. I'm actually stuffed, as it is."

Potter glanced at his watch. "Well," he said, "maybe we should go on over there."

He divided up the last of the Retsina, gulping his own down thirstily. It tingled pleasantly, like a mouthwash. They had knocked off a full bottle of the stuff.

The Bertelsens and their guests were still around the dinner table when Potter and Renée arrived, just a few bites into dessert. It was Indian Pudding. Marva was in her New Englandy mood. There was also Paul Tuckerman and his wife, Lynn. Paul was a bright young Urban man at Harvard whom Potter had met briefly at a Bertelsen cocktail party. Tuckerman was said to have done some very important work in Redevelopment, and was often called to Washington. When he referred in conversation to "John," he meant Mayor Lindsay. His wife Lynn had perfect teeth and displayed them often, in a stern, intimidating look that had the shape but not the spirit of a smile. She was working toward her doctorate in Education, and had a special interest in Criminal Rehabilitation. Potter believed her smile alone could significantly lower the rate of recidivism in any given Correctional Institution.

As Potter might have guessed, Hartley Stanhope was there. Stanhope, a lean man with distinguished grey hair, was a widower who had been the Bertelsens' ace Eligible Bachelor, at least until Potter arrived on the scene. Now Potter and Stanhope vied for the top spot, alternating in favor as their stock rose and fell with Marva. Potter wasn't really sure whether he disliked the man because of this rivalry, or because Stanhope occupied a secretive but influential position as a biological consultant to a government-backed Research Foundation. Potter imagined that Stanhope, the sort of scientific guy who smoked a pipe and sang in a Madrigal Group, probably thought up ways of poisoning the rice of the entire Asian land mass in the cleverest and most convenient manner.

Tonight, though, was one of the times that Potter felt less hostile toward Stanhope, perhaps because he knew that on this occasion Stanhope had been tapped as the Eligible Bachelor for dinner only after Potter had been unable to accept. Knowing that Stanhope was unaware of this made Potter feel even more benevolent toward him. And yet, there was an edge of jealousy, for Stanhope, even if second choice, had wound up as Dinner Partner for the Bertelsens' new female discovery, a divorcée without any children.

Potter took one look at Marilyn Crashaw and quickly looked away, fearing his immediate attraction to her would be embarrassingly obvious. He grasped Renée's hand under the table, and smiled at her. She looked at him suspiciously. He had never held her hand before.

After the Indian Pudding and espresso, the
party moved to the Library for cognac and conversation. As was customary on these occasions,
topics were discussed. Topics of Significance.
But Potter was only vaguely aware of them, as
they blurred across his mind, chalked words on
a classroom blackboard.

Inflation. Indochina. Administration efforts to
muzzle the press. Liz Drew's insightful piece on
"The White House Hard Hats" in the October
Atlantic. The "no-knock" law and its implications for the future of privacy. An Agnew joke.
Speculation on whether Pat Moynihan would
last it out serving the Nixon administration, or
return to Harvard. Where, it was generally
agreed, he belonged.

Potter tried to keep his eyes off Marilyn Crashaw's knees.

Marilyn wasn't really "pretty"; her nose was
too long, and had a slight bump on the bridge.
Her teeth protruded just a little, just enough to
be noticeable. Her figure was average, not fat
or thin, neither voluptuous nor twiggy. Her
hair was streaked blonde, and fell to her shoulders. Probably dyed or tinted. Maybe a wig or a
fall. You never could tell anymore. So what
was so terrific about her? Partly, perhaps, Potter was turned on by the way she dressed. It
certainly wasn't flashy by New York standards,
but it was not the conservative attire of the
thirty-and-over women in polite Boston-Cambridge society. The more style-conscious of

those ladies had gone for the Midi in a big way
this season, and the more traditional had stuck
to what looked to Potter like the old cocktail
dresses of the Fifties, but raised a little above
the knee instead of a little above the ankle. And
long hair was a no-no, except for their teen-age
daughters. Marilyn, who was certainly no teen-
ager, but probably around Potter's own age,
wore a plain white blouse with a gold-chain sort
of necklace, a miniskirt, and boots. The boots
were not extreme or kinky, but neither did they
look primarily practical, as if designed for spending a year at Ice Station Zebra. The outfit looked
good and Marilyn wore it with confidence, her
whole manner seeming assured and at ease, as
if to say Here I am, if you don't like it, too bad.
And Potter liked it, the overall impression. And
her eyes really topped it off. From the first glance,
her eyes seemed not only to look at him but to
look into him, saying a secret and intimate *hello.*

When enough time and conversation had
passed to be able to make a proper exit, Potter
took Renée's hand again, squeezed it, and said
to the others they had better be off, said good
night to each one in turn, and when he nodded,
stiffly, self-consciously, to Marilyn, she smiled,
and her eyes said *see you later.*

In the car going home Potter talked a lot,
faster than usual. He talked of the Bertelsens,
of the Boston scene, of the Harvard crowd, of
the evening. But he never mentioned Marilyn.
When they got to his place he made drinks and

put the classical guitar record on. He did not
really want to go to bed with Renée, but he
knew it would be taken as an insult if he did
not, if he did not at least try, and so he got pretty sloshed, and managed to do what he con-
ceived to be his duty. Through it all, he kept
seeing Marilyn's eyes. Afterward he drove Renée home, talking more, concentrating on not
mentioning the one thought that really occupied his mind: Marilyn. Renée was especially
silent, curled in her seat, huddled deep in her
coat. The only thing she said, just before the
car pulled up in front of her door, was a question asked in a tone of cool, pretended casual-
ness: "Who was that bitch?"

3

It was Sunday, the worst of days, the hardest one to get through alone. It yawned open, a pit of silence. There was little traffic, most of the shops and stores were closed, and the sidewalks were almost deserted. Potter once was able to fill up a large hunk of the day in football season by watching The Pros, but this year, on the second autumn Sunday, watching the Houston Oilers combat the Oakland Raiders, Potter was swept with a wave of depression; as the two teams blammed into one another, as a quarterback was thrown for a loss or sent a long bomb soaring into the waiting grasp of a fleet-footed receiver, as a fullback hurled himself into the enemy Front Four or a kicking specialist connected for a field goal, Potter had a deep and despairing feeling that he was watching the same game he had watched ten years before, that it was all the same, the plays and uniforms and the announcer's analysis, that nothing was different except Potter, who was ten years older, with little to show for it; that in another ten

years he would still be sitting of a Sunday afternoon and watching the same game, just that
many more relentless seasons closer to The
End. With a feeling almost of revulsion, he violently switched off the set, and had not turned
to Football since then. Which opened up a bigger hole in his Sunday—big enough for a mon-
ster fullback to plunge through without being
touched.

Potter woke groggily, his mind sodden, trying
to assemble the needed information. Cambridge.
Sunday. He looked at the clock. Shit. It was only a little after nine. He usually tried to sleep
till noon on Sundays; it gave him a running
leap forward in making it to the end of the day.
He turned over, squeezing his eyes shut, trying
to blank out his mind, but then he remembered
Marilyn Crashaw.

He would get her number from Marva and
call her today. He wasn't going to wait and
play coy. He wasn't going to play any games at
all with Marilyn. He had this instinctive sense
that he didn't need to, that she was going to understand him, that he would look openly into
those large eyes of hers and all sham would fall
away, all pretense become unnecessary. He
would take it slow, he would get to know her.
He didn't just want to get laid and go on to
something else, in the dulling old routine. She
was the first woman he had met since getting divorced whom he felt he might want to have a
relationship with, whom he felt it might be possible with. All that hope projected out of such

slim evidence, and yet that was all he needed;
he always knew, in the first hour or so, whether
anything really good could happen with a woman, anything beyond a lay. It might not work
out that way, but at least he knew if the chance
was there, the possibility.

He rousted himself out of bed and into the
shower, soaped himself up a terrific lather, and
actually sang, just like men used to do in the
movies to show high spirits—bellowing off key,
not caring, gurgling, enjoying.

> Pack up all my care and woe,
> Here I go, singing low,
> Byyyyye, Byyyyyye Blackbird . . .

Instead of going to one of the cafeterias in
Harvard Square that served sorry little eggs and
mushily congealed potatoes and soggy toast, Potter decided to treat himself, go into Boston, and
have a big hotel breakfast at the Statler. Afterward, he would go to the Commons and relax
with the Sunday *Globe*. He would not be
drowned by this Sunday, for he had something to
hang on to, something to buoy him up, over
the emptiness—a hope, a promise, a possibility of
fulfillment.

He nurtured the anticipation in himself
throughout the day, carefully, gently, protectively, and he felt it grow, a warm secret. In
the Commons, an unusual number of passers-by
seemed to smile at him, and he smiled back.
After a cursory glance at the Sports, he even

put aside the paper. He didn't feel the need as
he usually did in a kind of panic, like a starving
man gorging on stale bread. Today he wasn't
so empty.

Potter went back home around three, made
himself a Scotch and soda, and called Marva
Bertelsen.

"Thanks for last night," he said.

"Glad you could make it. And your friend.
What's her name?"

"Renée."

"Renée—Gleason?"

"Gillespie."

"She seemed very sweet."

"Yes, she is. She's a very nice person."

Potter could tell that Marva was going to get
her money's worth out of this call; she knew
damn well what Potter wanted.

"Yes, very nice, but frankly—"

"Yeah?"

"Well, she didn't really seem to be your type."

Potter took the phone off the table and lay
down on the floor with it. "How so? What's my
type?"

"Weeeel. A little more—flamboyant."

"That's very interesting."

"Don't you agree?"

"Well, maybe so. I never thought about it that
way."

"Oh, definitely. From what I've seen, you like
them a lot more flamboyant than—what's her
name?"

Potter closed his eyes. "Renée Gillespie."

"I mean, I liked her, myself. I was just thinking about her in relation to *you*."

"That's very thoughtful of you, Marva."

"Don't you think Paul Tuckerman's terrific? Someday he's going to be a sort of Kissinger, on the Domestic Scene, I'll bet anything."

Potter took a deep breath. "Goddamn it, Marva, will you tell me her phone number?"

"What? *Who?* You want the Tuckermans' phone number?"

"No, Love. I want your friend Marilyn's phone number, as I'm sure you well understand."

"Oh, *Marilyn!* Did you like her?"

"Yes, Marva. I liked her."

"Isn't that wonderful? So did Hartley. He called up this morning to thank me and—"

"Marva, I don't want to know about Hartley. I don't want to know anything about who he likes, or how much he likes Marilyn, or how much she likes him, or what they did, or what they're going to do. I just want her telephone number."

"I *thought* you two would hit it off," Marva said. "Let me see—I'm flipping through my book —I'm sorry you weren't free to come for dinner, I mean just with Marilyn, as her date, but oh—here it is. No, that's her office phone. Oh— OK. 266-1590."

"Marva, I want to thank you, from the bottom of my heart."

"Listen, keep me posted, will you? I'm dy-

ing to know what—well, I just have this feeling."

"Don't worry about a thing, Marva. 'Bye now."

" 'Bye, dear."

Potter freshened his drink, put on a Judy Collins, and, with the last warm light of afternoon
spilling through the front windows, he called
Marilyn.

Her voice was kind of husky, in the Lauren
Bacall style, and Potter was terribly excited by
it. Besides the sexy vocal quality, she sounded
very warm, and friendly. Just as Potter had anticipated. But when he asked her out for dinner
Wednesday night she seemed to get a little rattled. She explained she was taking a night course
in Existentialism, and it met on Wednesday from
7:30 to 9 P.M. He asked if Tuesday or Thursday
would be better and she sounded even more
nervous and slightly confused, then said that
actually Wednesday would be best, if he didn't
mind having a late dinner, and if he was able
to pick her up after her class. He said that was
perfectly fine, he would be there at nine o'clock.

When he hung up, he couldn't help wondering
if she was all dated up—if that fucking Hartley
had already horned in on her, or if she had another guy, or was having a secret mad affair with
her boss, who was married, or—

Potter stopped himself. He was going to take
it one step at a time. He was going to enjoy the
glow of anticipation that had warmed his whole
day. He wasn't going to spoil it. He put on more

records, which he hadn't done for some time when he was by himself. If he was alone, and lonely, romantic or pretty or soothing music only made him feel worse. But now, with a possibility of soon having someone to share that music with, someone he really wanted with him, it was all right. It was marvelous. He let Joni Mitchell serenade him with her pretty songs of love.

Potter whistled all the way to school the morning of his date with Marilyn, and breezed through his Communications classes with a verve and energy that surprised even himself. Unlike those days when he had said all he had to say, and saying it seemed to take sodden hours but the clock showed that only eighteen minutes had passed, this was a day when Potter was shocked when the class bell rang, for he felt he had only begun, that he needed much more time to explore all the possibilities he saw in the subject, which flowered beautifully before him. The ham in him was coming to the fore almost shamefully, as he recited passages, strode back and forth in front of his class, a captive audience if there ever was one, performing as if the area he paced between the front row of chairs and the blackboard was a legitimate stage. But what the hell, the students seemed to like it; they were being entertained. And Potter felt like entertaining.

When his second class had its all too brief hour ended at 12:20, Potter went humming out into the halls, ran into Gafferty, and proposed they really live it up and go have lunch at Bachelors Three. Drinks and all. When he saw Gafferty's hesitant smile, and watched the regular red flush of his face grow even deeper, Potter suddenly realized to his own embarrassment that it was all well and good for an irresponsible bachelor to go around having restaurant lunches with drinks as if still on a fucking expense account, but it was totally out of the question for a guy supporting a wife and kids. And if the number of kids were nine, such a lunch might cast the whole lot of them into a week of eating nothing but small bowls of porridge.

He threw a comradely arm around Gafferty and said, "Hey, I mean it's on *me*."

"Oh, no, that's a nice thought, but—"

"Listen, I got myself into a little poker game over the weekend, won a few. It's bad luck to save that kind of money—got to spend it right away."

"Well then," Gafferty brightened, "if I didn't come to help ya, I'd be letting down a friend."

Buoyed, buoyant, loving the little lie because it produced the right effect, Potter took Gafferty to lunch as if he were an important client and Potter was able to write it all off to Olney and Sheperdson. It added to his good feelings, making him in fact think back with fondness to his hard-drinking hard-dealing PR life in New York; not with regrets, but a certain nostalgia. He regaled Gafferty with tales of those days, intrigues and deals, promotional schemes that earned him raises and others that backfired, and when at 3:15 he met his public relations seminar he simply carried on, knowing, as one always knew when it happened on stage, that he had them in his pocket.

He went home and had a long singing shower before his date, bellowing to himself, arrogantly off key:

> I want to hold your ha-aa-and,
> I want to hold your hand . . .

When Potter picked up Marilyn after her class, she seemed somewhat distraught, as she had on the phone. At first Potter wondered if it meant anything, was some sort of bad response to him, but before going off on that tack it occurred to him that just about anyone would be a little harried after working all day in an insurance office and spending an hour and a half attending a class on Existentialism. He had arrived early and paced around outside the building. It was one of those old Boston buildings that seemed like a combination Church and Armory, with a large lecture hall on the ground floor. Potter peeked in the door, and that peculiar color and odor of Night School seeped out; a dim sort of yellowish, faded light, and the smell of chalk and musty, much-used books. Potter glanced briefly at the backs of the students; some slumped, some with their coats draped over their shoulders, some shifting restlessly, some leaning forward, intent upon the learned drone that might, magically, reveal some secret, open some door, release something inside the mind or soul. Existentialism. It was one of those subjects that somehow held out the promise of easing the pain, or explaining a better way to deal with it. It supposedly dealt with Despair, and yet there was about the word a taunting aura of Hope.

Potter learned over dinner that Marilyn's nights were not all filled with dates, though indeed she had dates, but the interior part of her week was filled with activities. Monday night was pottery class. Tuesday after work she saw her shrink. Wednesday was Existentialism. Thursday she took an advanced psychology course in deviant behavior, which could count toward an advanced degree if she ever decided to go for one. She might sometime, since you couldn't do much with only a B.A. But she really hadn't figured out what she really wanted to do yet. She was groping. She admitted that. She had only been divorced for six months, around the same time as Potter.

All this was difficult to absorb, because Marilyn was still very nervous, and the restaurant was so loud it was difficult to hear anything. Potter had taken her to Jimmy's Harborside, wanting to do something special. The food was good, but it was so large and crowded, Potter felt as if he were in a Greyhound Bus Station. In the middle of sentences, the loudspeaker would blare out, but instead of calling destinations of buses the voice called out names of parties to be seated—"Mr. Gill, party of four—Barron, party of two—"

Potter drove badly on the way home, taking a couple of wrong turns, and once bursting into a torrent of obscene curses at a car honking behind him when he was a split second late in taking off at a traffic light. He apologized to Marilyn.

"Boston drivers are the worst," she said. "They're crazy."

She sounded tired. Potter wondered if he had blown the whole thing. It wasn't going like the smooth, intimate evening he had imagined. It occurred to him that maybe he was trying too hard. He had put so much expectation into their date; it was like a football player getting too "up" for the big game, and fumbling it away. He wondered if Marilyn was doing the same thing.

It was better when they got to her place. She lived in The River House, a large, modern-style building on the flat part of Beacon Hill, and her living room window provided a slanting view of the Drive and the River. You could hear the steady hum of traffic.

Marilyn had done a lot with her apartment. As in most modern buildings the rooms were just boxes, blank and anonymous, defying any effort of an occupant to make it seem particular or personal.

Marilyn had helped to humanize it with a lot

of plants, large plants, that defied and contradicted the nature of the building; they were alive. And individual. Some bushy, some slender, some heavy and formidable.

The furniture wasn't schlock modern or slick Scandinavian, but had the character of age, though it wasn't precious antique stuff that you had to be fearful of sitting on. Marilyn had collected the pieces from secondhand furniture barns in New Hampshire and Vermont. Potter admired the effort, and the energy that had to go into it, the determination to make a human, comfortable haven in a barren place.

"This is really nice," he said. "Your apartment."

She had given him a Scotch on the rocks, which added, as always, to his sense of security. She had a brandy in a large snifter, which she cradled in her hand, tilting back and forth.

"It gave me something to do, when I really needed it. Suddenly being alone, after—seven years."

"Yeah, I know. No matter how bad the marriage was, and how much you think you'd give anything to be free, it hits you like a ton of bricks. Being alone again."

"Yes. It isn't that I wanted to go back to my husband. I had no regrets. It was just the—emptiness."

"Yeah, exactly. I felt the same way."

"How long were you married?"

"Well, about four years, officially. But we

lived together off and on for more than five. It was one of those—uh—" Potter grinned, "dramatic sort of relationships."

"The Real Thing," Marilyn said, smiling.

"Yeah."

"I know. I mean I know because mine wasn't like that. My marriage. I had an affair like that before, and I was convinced I wanted a nice, quiet, stable relationship."

"What happened?"

"I got bored. I thought I was going to die of boredom."

Potter sighed. "Well, it's one thing or the other."

Marilyn got them another drink.

They exchanged the stories of their marriages. They were both very benevolent to their former partners, giving them the benefit of every doubt, stressing how much was their *own* fault. And yet, each told some plain facts, that made the other understand.

"Of course, she was under great pressure at the time, with her modeling," Potter explained after telling of the night his wife, dead drunk, set the curtains on fire in their apartment.

After Marilyn told of the occasion she discovered her former husband, Hank, at a neighborhood Christmas party fucking a divorcée under the ping-pong table in the basement, she quickly added that "Of course, that's a way of getting attention, and the poor guy wasn't getting much attention from me. I was really a bitch, I guess.

I didn't mean to be. I was just so bored. And I couldn't hide it."

Potter understood.

Marilyn understood. She slipped off her boots, and tucked her feet up under her ass. Her sheer knees blinked at him.

Potter was really turned on by her, but he didn't want to push things. It had been so long since he had really wanted to be with anyone—to talk to them and also to fuck them—that he wanted to nurture it, as he had promised himself he would, wanted to savor the anticipation of their first going to bed, not half-smashed on their first evening out, but fully conscious, slowly, exploringly. He wanted a contemporary version of a "courtship"—that is, not screwing till the second date. But he didn't think about it in that mechanical or perfunctory manner. He wanted something that he thought of as "real." He pictured a room with sunlight in it.

He glanced at his watch. It was almost one.

"Listen," he said, "you probably have to get up at some ungodly hour. I really should go."

A look passed over her face as if he had slapped her, and he realized he hadn't yet said anything about meeting again, and hurriedly asked if she could go out Saturday night. And maybe they could do something on Sunday, too. Take a drive or something. To the country.

"That would be nice," she said, with a noticeable lack of enthusiasm.

"Really, I'd really like it," he said. "I'd really like to be with you."

"Well," she said, "what's wrong with right now?"

"Right now?" he asked.

He knew damn well what she meant; he felt like a judo wrestler who is suddenly thrown in the position that he uses on other wrestlers. But he had less defense for it.

A man couldn't say "Why don't we wait?" A man couldn't say "I really like you but I'd like to get to know you better." He couldn't give any of the woman's answers for not doing it. It would make it seem he wasn't a man. It would make him be suspected of being in fact like a woman—effeminate . . . a fag. Or afraid. Fag. Fraid. Fraid. Fag.

Invited to perform, a man had to perform. Or not be considered a man.

Potter closed his eyes a moment, sloshed down the rest of his Scotch, and pulled her to him. Doing his duty.

It wasn't exploring or tender, but angry and biting and struggling and mean. That could be nice too, but it just hadn't been what he had in mind. But he threw himself into it, and she responded in kind.

When it was over, he tried not to think. There was no sunlight in the room; only the luminous glow of the electric alarm clock.

4

Marilyn invited Potter to her place for dinner. She had chilled a pitcher of martinis, and made some guacamole for an appetizer.

Potter was appreciative. The little things. You wouldn't find one of your new generation chicks chilling a pitcher of martinis or making guacamole. They'd hand you their stash of grass and some papers to roll a joint with, and later you'd have to send out for pizza and beer.

He was glad he brought Marilyn the dozen roses. The old-fashioned gesture seemed to genuinely please her, and so pleased him in return. He would never have taken roses to a young girl now, fearing the gift would be scorned as trite, or worse, that cutting roses would turn out to be some obscure ecological offense that would brand the giver as another despoiler of the environment, like General Motors or Dow Chemical. It was nice not to have to worry about all that shit. With Marilyn, he could relax. Be himself. Enjoy. And without any skulking kids underfoot, either."

From the stereo came the familiar, sophisticated tinkle of the Modern Jazz Quartet.

They dined by candlelight. Thick lamb chops, spinach, and baked potato with lots of butter and sour cream and chives.

"This is terrific," Potter said. "It's better than any restaurant."

"I like to cook. Especially when it's appreciated."

"My appreciation overfloweth."

"The last couple years I was married, Hank was usually soused by the time we sat down to dinner. God. He was always spilling things. I might as well have fed him from a trough."

"Yeah. I know how it is. Sometimes Jessie got too loaded to cook. Then we'd both just drink. *That* was fun."

"I think it's really important—eating nicely. It's sort of what keeps you civilized."

"Absolutely. It doesn't have to be fancy or anything. Jessie could cook some real gourmet stuff, but nine times out of ten she'd tell you how it hadn't come out right, and start apologizing all over the place, and then you couldn't enjoy the food. You had to keep saying how great it was, and reassuring her at every other bite. You can't digest that way."

"No. Or if the other person's depressed."

"Oh, brother. I'd rather have a hot dog with a smile than crêpes suzette with a lot of sighs and moans."

"It's worse than eating alone, almost."

"That's hard too, though."

"I make myself do it. When I first left Hank and moved in here I got in the habit of coming home and just nibbling on a piece of cheese or eating tuna out of a can or something and I started feeling just lousy. So one night after work I bought a lot of groceries and fixed a beautiful meal for myself, with flowers on the table and the good silver, and I sat down all alone and ate it. I decided I would do that at least once a week, and I've stuck to it. And other nights I cook something, even if it's just a chop and a vegetable."

Potter pictured Marilyn, alone, going to the store and buying groceries, coming home alone and setting a nice table, and eating her dinner.

"You know," he said, "you're braver than I am."

"Braver?"

"Yes. I mean it. To make a meal just for yourself, and put flowers on the table, and sit down and eat all alone. That takes courage."

Marilyn lowered her eyes a moment, took a deep breath, then smiled. "Well, let's not think about it. Right now, we're together."

She reached her hand across the table and Potter took it in his own and held it very hard.

"This is nice," he said.

"Yes. It is."

As Marva Bertelsen put it, they were "an item" now. They invited the Bertelsens to dinner at Marilyn's house, Potter pouring martinis and playing the gracious host, expansive and cheery, happy to be able to entertain Max and Marva for once instead of the other way around, feeling he wasn't a mate-less orphan kid now but a man with a fine woman he admired, an adult joined with another adult in a kind of union, however tenuous or short-lived it might turn out to be. Now it was fine. Marva said she'd never seen Marilyn look so glowing, or Potter so relaxed. Max nodded his benevolent approval. When they left, Max patted Potter on the back and Marva squeezed his hand and said, "We're happy for you."

That night Potter and Marilyn made love, long and tenderly. Toward the end, they exchanged the magic words.

"I love you."

"Oh, I love *you*."

They stayed up late, sipping brandy, talking and laughing and touching.

"Oh, Phil," she said, "I hope it will stay this way."

"It will," he assured her. "We've both been through enough crap for a while. We deserve this —a good time. Together."

Monday night Marilyn went to her pottery class, and Potter picked up a fat sandwich at Elsie's Delicatessen in Cambridge and took it home to have for supper with a cold beer. He was alone for the evening, but not lonely. He

felt self-contained, and amiable. It wasn't bad
being alone when you knew another person was
out there, a person you'd been with and wanted
to be with again, and would be. Both Potter
and Marilyn decided it would be silly to start
spending every night together, that in fact they
could have a better relationship by not trying
to absorb each other's life, but having each other to look forward to, so that meeting and being
together would be all the more enjoyable.

Potter settled down with a book of Shakespeare
criticism, hoping he could glean some observa-
tions that would add new interest to his own
teaching, enrich his own commentary on the
plays. Around nine o'clock the phone rang, and
he assumed it was Marilyn returned from her
class—though it seemed a little early for that.

It was Jessica.

She said she was fine, all was well with her,
but she had some serious matters on her mind
that she wanted very much to talk over with Potter and wondered if she might run up on the
shuttle tomorrow and have dinner with him.

Potter, trying to sound very natural and calm,
said of course, he'd look forward to seeing her.

When he first hung up, he felt on the brink of
panic. Just when everything was starting to go
well, Jessica was going to parachute into his life
and wreak emotional havoc. But after he had a
drink and lit a cigarette, he felt better about it.
She wasn't going to ruin things with him and
Marilyn, that was his own affair and she couldn't

upset it if he didn't want her to, if he didn't allow her to interfere. In a way, he was thankful she hadn't called until now, when he really did have a new relationship going, one that he wanted to preserve. If he'd been alone and at loose ends he'd have been far more vulnerable to sinking back into the old emotions, the old maelstrom, in which they had whirled so long and dizzily, so passionately and destructively. But now, with the knowledge of Marilyn, he felt strong, and much less susceptible to his former wife and lover.

When he first saw her, standing at the door of his apartment, he felt as if someone had struck a sudden blow to his stomach; it was as if a loved one had come back to life, and the memory of all they had shared hit him with the force of a cannonball, so that for a moment he was slightly dizzy, and had to consciously blink back an unexpected rush of tears. He managed to smile, usher her into the room, and get his insides together.

Jessica herself seemed very composed. She had brought a fifth of Tanqueray gin, and a carton of Winstons. Preparation for conversation. As it turned out, she hadn't been able to get things together till later than she anticipated, and had just made the four o'clock shuttle. It was almost dark when they got settled in Potter's living room. He put an old piano rag record on the stereo. Neutral. Nothing sentimental.

"You look very well," he said.

"Oh? Thank you. I've been fine."

"I'm glad."

"How are *you*?"

"Oh, I'm fine too. You know. Getting along."

"That's wonderful."

Potter shrugged. He sipped at his Scotch, concentrating on moderation. He was glad she was wearing a pants suit, and that she had worn her hair tied in the back, with a demure velvet ribbon. Sedate. They would talk. They would be Friends. He was perfectly prepared to graciously put her back on the midnight shuttle to New York. A kiss on the cheek; a pat on the shoulder; a handshake or a hug.

After her third drink, Jessica began telling about this terribly nice man she was seeing. He was on Wall Street, but very sensitive. Widely-read. The most amazing thing—he didn't drink. He worked out every day at his Club.

"What is he," Potter asked, "some kind of health nut?"

Jessica laughed. "You'd probably think so."

Potter poured himself a new Scotch. "Really," he said. "I didn't mean to be a smart ass. As a matter of fact, he sounds like just the kind of guy I always said you should have."

She smiled. "Like *you* should have the hearty, healthy milkmaid with apple cheeks."

"Maybe in my next life," Potter said. "No kidding, though, this guy sounds fine for you."

He felt a warm glow, really genuine, as he would for a troubled sister who had finally found

Mister Right. He was glad for her, and proud he could feel glad. Maybe it only meant he was "over her," and yet he hoped it meant, if that, something more, too; that perhaps it indicated, on his part, a new sort of . . . maturity?

Jessica coughed, and lit a new cigarette.

"Tell me more," Potter asked, with warm good feeling.

"Well. He wants to marry me."

"Oh?"

"Can you imagine that? Marry *me*, a worn-out divorcée?"

"Come on. Don't badmouth yourself."

"Well—"

"Really. You're a lovely person. A beautiful woman."

"You don't have to say that."

"I know I don't *have* to say that. I'm saying it because it's true."

"You're very kind."

"I'm not kind, goddamn it!"

"I seem to be upsetting you."

Potter took a deep breath. "I'm sorry," he said. "Listen, this is terrific, really. Tell me more about the guy. No kidding. He sounds like what you deserve, after me."

"You don't have to badmouth *your*self, you know."

"I'm sorry. Come on. What are the plans?"

Jessica stood up, slightly swaying, and said, "I plan to get another drink."

"Fine," Potter said. He looked at his watch,

while she went to the kitchen. It was after seven. As soon as she finished this drink, he should get them to dinner. Civilization showed signs of crumbling. How goddamn shaky it always was. Always turned out to be. Apparently composed again, Jessica took a swallow of her new drink, and smiled. "Well," she said, "what do you think?"

"About this guy? Wanting to marry you?"

Jessica lowered her eyes.

"Listen," Potter said, leaning forward, intent, wanting to say it just right, no hooks or slices, all heart and maturity, "I want you to know I think it's terrific. I think from what you say about this guy he's really right for you, he could make you happy. If he doesn't drink, you probably won't drink. As much. It sounds like he's stable, but not just a dummy. It sounds like a wonderful opportunity for you to have a real life, a contented kind of life. I am honestly happy for you."

She mashed out her cigarette, and took out a new one. "You approve then?"

"*Yes.* For godsake, yes. You have my blessings. A hundred percent."

Jessica finished off her drink. Tears blossomed at the corners of her eyes.

"Jessie?"

She bit at her lip.

"Jessie—What is it? Are you happy?"

She sniffed, and pulled a wad of Kleenex from her purse. "I'm sorry," she said, trembling.

"What? *Why?*"

"I knew it," she said, sobbing and choking.

"Knew *what?*" Potter asked in a hoarse whisper. "Knew *what?*"

Her mouth twitched in a caricature of a smile and she sobbed, "You don't love me. You never did. You never loved me at all."

Most of Potter's feelings of "maturity" escaped from him in a long sigh; silently, mechanically, he put a pan of water on the stove to boil for instant coffee.

He phoned for a delivery from The Leaning Tower of Pizza, and made Jessica eat some. He had no more to drink until he got her in a cab and out to Logan in time for the last shuttle, trying vainly to assure her that he had loved her more than anyone in his life, that he wanted her to be happy, and that this new guy sounded just wonderful and that was why he approved.

When he described the whole thing the next night to Marilyn she sighed, and said, "Now she probably won't ever marry the guy."

"But what the hell could I have done?"

"Cried a lot and said that you still loved her and would shoot yourself if she married this man."

"What good would that have done?"

"She'd have probably married him."

Potter turned that over in his mind, then let out a long sigh. "Jesus," he said. "Yeah. I guess you're right."

Marilyn stroked his head, comfortingly, and

said how glad she was that their relationship was rational, that they didn't have to play those games with each other.

"It's great," he agreed. "It really is great."

As a special treat, Potter invited Marilyn to
come to his place for Sunday Brunch. On Saturday night they were going to have dinner with a
married couple who were friends of Marilyn
and go see Truffaut's *The Wild Child,* and afterward to the Jazz Workshop on Boylston Street,
where Stan Getz was appearing—a ghost, Potter
felt, from his own collegiate past of Fifties cool.
A real Night On The Town. After all that so-
cializing Potter thought it would be nice if they
could be alone together the next day, and so proposed to cook up a wonderful brunch of omelettes for just him and Marilyn. They would
laze around and read the Sunday papers in cozy
comfort.

Omelettes were the only thing Potter could
cook, the only thing anyway that required "ingredients." He could boil knockwurst and fry
eggs and hamburgers, but the only thing he
could really cook was an omelette. He learned
during his marriage. In one of those periods
when they both were Trying, Potter decided he

would make a ritual of being the cook on Sunday. He studied Jessie's Gourmet Cookbook, examining the diagrams of omelettes as well as the recipes, and practiced intently. The real moment of fulfillment came when he carefully *flipped* the heating face of the potion over on top of itself, with the goodies lying sequestered in between. He learned to make every kind of omelette, and delighted in inventing some of his own. He made up names for them. The one he made with leftover Chinese water-chestnuts and almonds in the center and lots of soy sauce on top was the Mao Tse-tung omelette. That sort of thing.

Jessica claimed to love them. She even ate all of her "Sweet Georgia Brown" omelette, which Potter had stuffed with canned peaches and cooked in brown sugar and brandy.

They always washed the omelettes down with a lot of chilled white wine, which helped a lot.

The omelette tradition lasted three or four months.

It was one of their better efforts.

"Can't I help?" Marilyn asked when Potter was about to prepare the omelettes.

"No," he said indignantly. "You have to go out in the living room and read the paper."

"Well, I was just trying to be helpful."

"I know," Potter said, trying to control his temper. He kissed her on the nose. "The thing is, you're supposed to just *relax*."

She shrugged, and went to the living room.

Potter went busily about his preparations, but couldn't help being a little annoyed that Marilyn wasn't sitting back and reading the Sunday paper. She just smoked a cigarette and looked out the window, and occasionally paced around the room, like she was nervous.

Potter tried to concentrate on the omelettes. He was just doing cheese this time, nothing too fancy or outrageous. Just plain cheese omelettes, and a very nice chablis.

They ate in the living room, on the coffee table. Potter played a Vivaldi record. The sound of order, tradition. Sunlight streamed in the room, as if Potter had ordered it. He felt expansive.

"How's that for an omelette?" Potter asked.

"Oh—it's fine. Just fine. Really it is," she said in an unconvincing abstract voice.

Potter wondered if he'd put too much Tobasco into the mix.

He swigged from his glass of chablis, and tried to concentrate again on his own omelette. It seemed quite fine to him, but you never knew about other people's taste; some people simply liked things bland. A little too much Tabasco could put them off entirely.

Marilyn picked her way through about a third of her omelette, then put down her fork. There were tears in her eyes. Jesus. Potter knew he hadn't put *that* much Tabasco into the thing.

"What is it?" he asked.

She shook her head. "Nothing."

Potter took a deep breath, and exhaled very

slowly. Trying for calm. He lit a cigarette. Marilyn wadded her paper napkin and dabbed at her eyes.

"I'm sorry," she said.

"But why?" he asked gently. "Why are you sorry? Why are you sad? Isn't everything OK?"

"Yes," she sniffed. "It's fine."

"So?"

"So—I don't know. I guess that's it."

"That everything's fine?"

"Yes—I mean—no. It's that it has to end, sooner or later. Sooner or later it won't be fine. It'll be lousy, and it'll end."

"Well, I guess everything has to end," Potter said. "But Marilyn. For godsake. Why spoil the beginning by thinking about the end?"

"I don't know," she said. "I don't mean to."

They sat for a long time, while the music played on, and then finally it stopped and the needle slipped onto the black interior circle of the record, scratching.

Potter had to make himself lift off the arm of the player.

Marilyn blew her nose, and forced a smile. "I'm sorry," she said.

"It's OK, really it is."

"No, it's my fault for thinking that way."

"Goddamn it, will you just forget about it!"

"You don't have to yell at me!"

Potter closed his eyes, and breathed deeply. "I'm sorry," he said.

"It's OK. I'm sorry too."

"OK," he said.

"OK," she said.

Potter decided that instead of meeting Marilyn after her Existentialism class Wednesday night, it might do both of them good if he just went out on his own, and he arranged to have a beer with Gafferty. The beer became many beers.

"Why is it," Potter asked, "that a man and a woman can't just get along?"

"Trouble in paradise, eh?"

In the first flush of his affair with Marilyn, Potter had told Gafferty he had found just the woman he was looking for.

"Nothing big, yet. Just the old warning signs."

"Ah, well. Maybe it'll all blow over. I've ridden out many a storm myself."

"Jesus, I guess so. That must really be rough. I mean, with nine kids, you can't just walk out."

"Oh, you can take a walk all right, but you damn well better hike back pretty quick."

"Jesus. I don't see how—well, with me anyway, I don't think I could take it."

"Ah, well. We take what we get. And get what we ask for."

"But why is it always so goddamn fucked up and complicated?"

"But man, why did we ever think it would be otherwise? Didn't the Old Testament tell us? Didn't the Greeks tell us? Haven't all the wise folks down through history told us? Isn't that what all art and philosophy and literature is about? The *why* is, why are we surprised?"

"Maybe it was going to movies and reading magazines," Potter said. "At an impressionable age. Remember, when you and I were growing up the stories all had happy endings."

"I was fortunate enough to be reading the Irish poets, even then." He raised a finger for attention and recited:

> All men live in suffering
> I know as few can know,
> Whether they take the high road,
> Or stay content on the low. . . .

"Yeats," he said.

"That's your favorite, isn't it?" Potter said. "Yeats."

"Ah, he's my man."

"Is that who you did your thesis on?"

Gafferty's head jerked back, as if Potter had taken a swing at him. "My *thesis*," he said.

"You know—your Ph.D."

Gafferty let out a long breath. "Ah, you don't know then."

Gafferty belched, and called for another round.

The fifth round.

He explained to Potter how he had first tried to do his thesis on Yeats, then O'Casey, then Synge, failing each time, crossing the adviser each time because he couldn't bring himself to treat his subjects with the required academic attitudes of distance and dissection. He kept writing lyric appreciations of the men and their work, which were judged to be "fine as far as they went" but they never went far enough into the sort of sterilized, surgical, symbol-seeking operations that were wanted.

"I couldn't do it to them," he said. "So I figured maybe I could do the deed on a writer I didn't love. For the last three years, I've been trying to write a proper thesis on Pope."

"Why Pope?"

"Because I find the bastard dull. Always have. You see, if I'm to grind out a dull exercise I feel I might have a better chance with a subject I think is matching."

"How's it coming?"

"Lousy. It's so dull, I can't hardly make myself work on it. But I work on it anyway every weekend. Made a little study in the basement, and I go down there regular, like spending time in jail."

"Jesus. What happens if you don't finish?"

"Ah, my friend. Then I don't teach much longer. Not in a college, anyway, not likely."

Potter damned the injustice of it all, and they had more rounds. On the eighth round, as Potter began to reel, Gafferty glanced at his watch and jumped out of the booth.

"Jesus, man, speakin' of trouble, I'm an hour late for dinner already. And got me a forty-minute drive yet."

"Shit, I'm sorry. Listen, blame it on me."

Gafferty smiled, and said, "Thanks, but it

doesn't work that way. That easy."

"No, I guess not."

Potter felt too bloated from the beer to want to eat anything, so he went home and drank Scotch and sodas. Around ten, he opened a can of cashews, for sustenance. He didn't put on the TV or the phonograph, but sat in a kind of trance, thinking of Gafferty's plight with academia, and realizing he hadn't faced up to his own. The present year of teaching was like a joyride, but soon, if he wanted to continue, if he wanted to make it a permanent thing, he would have to face up to working for his own academic union card, his own advanced degree. That would mean going back to school and taking courses, writing papers, eventually grinding out a thesis.

He couldn't imagine doing it. Nor could he imagine doing anything else. He took the bottle of Scotch to bed with him, sipping on it, like medicine, till he finally blotted out.

The electric buzz of the alarm clock, a steady, insistent, one-note harangue, woke Potter to a clammy grey morning. Thursday. He had no classes, but had to go in for office hours. Student visitation. When the term began he had scheduled his office hours on the days of his classes, M-W-F, because he had to go into Gilpen anyway, and it left the other days completely free. But when he discovered this "freedom" led to late, troubled sleep and a yawning vacuum, he

changed his office hours to the "Free" days, which
meant that he had to get up and dress and go out
into the world. Even if no one came he had to
be there, sitting in his office.

It was on the fifth and top floor of the walk-up
building, a floor that had once been used for
storage but had been remodeled into makeshift
offices. They were furnished with anonymous
grey metal desks and khaki metal bookcases that
you put together with screws. Potter had scotchtaped a poster of Humphrey Bogart on the wall.
It was the best he could figure out, for decora-
tion. The lower left-hand corner of it had come
unstuck, and curled upward. Potter meant to
tape it down again.

He took up a styrofoam cup full of hot black
coffee from the cafeteria, and set it on his desk.
From the bottom right-hand drawer, he drew out
a pint of Cutty Sark, and splashed some into the
coffee. He took a few sips and then went to the
bookcase. Only two shelves had books, and they
were mostly texts—ones that were used in his
courses, or ones that publishers sent in hopes of
having some teacher put them into their curricu-
lum. Book salesmen "called," like guys who sold
aluminum siding for houses door-to-door.

Potter pulled out one of the freebie texts that
a salesman had left. It was called *A Drama
Casebook*. He opened it, and the smell of fresh
paper struck his nose like a perfume. He flipped
through the book, seeing fairly soon it was composed only of the shreds of plays, with long, ac-

companying "exercises," tests and questions and "study proposals." Most of the textbooks were like that. Collections of snippets of real things, and made-up crap strung after them like tin cans tied to a dog's tail.

Potter closed the book, and slipped a little more Scotch into his coffee.

Traffic quarrelled below on Beacon Street, slowed by rain and fog. Potter went to the window and swiped a clearing of moisture he could see through. To other townhouse buildings across the street. He sat back down, wishing to hell a student would come. Any student. No, preferably a girl. Not for any sexual fantasy, just for comfort. There was some kind of comfort that Potter could feel in the presence of a woman, a girl, that not even his best male friends could give him. No doubt it was some other goddamn aspect of Male Chauvinism. He'd never admit it to the militant Lib girl in his PR seminar. He would swear to her it was all the goddamn same to him; otherwise she'd have his balls.

There was a rap on his half-open door, and Potter said brusquely, "Yes, come in."

He couldn't help smiling, with pleasure and relief. It was Rosemary Korsky.

"You busy?" she asked.

"Absolutely sunk in work, tied up with phone calls from New York and Washington, students bugging me and a couple of big producers pleading to get my opinion on their new shows. *How-*

ever. Miss Korsky, for you, I will gladly put it all aside."

"Yeah?"

She grinned and sat down.

Potter started to take a sip of his doctored coffee, but instead pushed the cup aside. Miss Korsky gave him enough of a glow.

He wasn't even quite sure why.

She was attractive, but certainly no great beauty. Dyed light-blonde hair with the darker roots showing where it parted in the middle. Not even long, it just came down to her neck and then curled back upward, like Doris Day. She wore too much makeup, partly no doubt because of what seemed a semi-bad skin. A nicely proportioned body, but nothing to send to Atlantic City. She dressed nicely, wearing mostly sweaters and long skirts and boots, nothing flashy or ostentatious for this flair-conscious time. Nor was it her brilliance or even any interesting, off-beat turn of mind that caught Potter's imagination. She was a solid B student who answered test questions with methodical, information-filled persistence, done in a clear, well-trained hand that was easily readable.

And yet, she was one of the students to whom Potter realized he was talking when he lectured. When, one Wednesday during the third week of classes she was absent for the first time, Potter was rattled and grouchy, and let the students free twenty minutes early.

"Crummy day," Miss Korsky said.

She plunked her lapful of books on the cold cement floor and wriggled out of her coat, letting it fall on the back of her chair. She was wearing a plain maroon sweater with short sleeves, and she rubbed her hands vigorously up and down her forearms.

"Ah," Potter sighed. "Miss Korsky."

"What?"

"Nothing."

He smiled. "What can I do for you?"

Miss Korsky activated a wad of chewing gum that had evidently been put to rest temporarily behind a molar, and slowly, contemplatively, began to mash it around in her mouth.

'Oh, I was wondering, sort of. About this paper you want us to write."

"The thing on Symbolism?"

"Well, that—" She turned to the rain-streaked window.

"Yes?"

"And—"

"Yes?"

Her brown eyes looked straight into him and her mouth made a partial smile that expressed a kind of sorrow, and an unfeigned weariness that is not usually associated with young people, not because it isn't common among them but because their elders would rather not see it there.

"I guess I just didn't want to go out into that yet. Outside."

"It's pretty mucky," Potter said.

"Oh, I don't just mean the weather. You know.

The world, I guess. The whole thing that's out there."

"Yes," Potter said.

He found himself, much to his surprise and embarrassment, fighting back tears. He cleared his throat, and managed to look straight at her. "I know just what you mean," he said.

"I know you do."

They sat for some time in a comfortable, communicative silence, listening to the radiator gurgle, and then a class bell rang, and Miss Korsky put her coat on. Potter stood up. "I'll walk you to the subway," he said.

"Thanks."

They walked, heads down against the rain, to the Arlington Street station, and Miss Korsky stopped at the entrance, smiled, and said, "Thanks again."

Potter put his hand on the top of her head, very lightly. "Be okay," he said.

"You, too," Miss Korsky said, and then descended quickly into the dank entry of the trains.

Potter walked swiftly away, as if going somewhere, and then slowed down, allowing the tears to come because they were hardly discernible from the rain, and no one could tell he was quietly crying, nor could he have explained that he felt quite warm, and good, because he had somehow experienced a blessing. That visit. That hour. That day.

"We need to get away," said Marilyn. "Take a trip somewhere."

Potter thought how often he had heard that advice, or given it himself, when things were going wrong. It was supposed to be a cure-all for failing relationships, like taking Vitamin C for a cold. He didn't mention that, however, not wanting to take a defeatist attitude. He simply asked, "Where?"

"Well, I was thinking—how about someplace New Englandy. Vermont, maybe."

"Vermont?"

"Why not? It's supposed to be beautiful. We could see the leaves turn."

Potter glanced out the window, and back at Marilyn. "Honey, they've already turned. In fact, they've fallen off."

"Not all of them."

"It's almost the first of November, for Christsake."

"Well, then we ought to go right away, before it snows."

Potter tried to examine the logic of this for a moment, but saw a maze that would lead nowhere but a fight, and so agreed to drive up to Vermont for the weekend. He tried, genuinely, to sound enthusiastic about it. He even convinced himself that it might really help. Perhaps the change of scene, the novelty of sleeping in a new and different place, strange and remote, might help revive his steadily waning desire for Marilyn. An old familiar syndrome was setting in. The excitement of novelty was gone, and Potter had begun to notice little flaws in Marilyn he hadn't originally seen: the slight but sure sag of her breasts, the lack of a real curve to her calves, the corns on her toes, like reddish sores. One of her lower back teeth was slightly discolored.

He drank more before taking her to bed. In an effort to recharge desire with variety, they had stopped going to the comfort and familiarity of the bed itself, but fucked on the couch, on the living room rug, on the cold linoleum of the kitchen floor, and once, standing up, in the closet. He had gone down on her, and she had gone down on him, and they had gone down on one another together. They had done it at her place and at his place, and once they did it in the Bertelsens' upstairs bathroom during a cocktail party.

They were running out of places.

They would try Vermont.

Vermont looked just like Vermont should

look. What leaves remained were deep red and gold, and Potter agreed they were beautiful. He agreed that in fact the whole state, leaves or no, was a beautiful area, with its rolling hills and picture-postcard red barns and white clapboard farmhouses, its drowsy little towns and sweeping valleys. It seemed to Potter that in the course of the drive from Boston to the Middlebury Inn he had agreed to Marilyn's endorsements of the beauties of Vermont at least five hundred times.

They arrived a little after four in the afternoon. Marilyn thought the place was charming and that their room, though rather spare, was appropriately quaint. Potter agreed, pulling a quart of Cutty Sark out of his suitcase and bringing the two water glasses from the bathroom.

"Are you starting already?" Marilyn asked.

"What do you mean, 'already'?"

"Well, it's not even five. Is it?"

Potter looked at his watch. "No, it's not five. It's eleven minutes and some seconds after four. And I've been driving for five hours."

"You had a martini at lunch."

"I know I had a martini at lunch. What does that have to do with wanting a drink after driving for five hours?"

Marilyn got out a cigarette. "Never mind," she said. "Go ahead."

Potter set the glasses down on the bureau. "Oh, no. Jesus. I don't want to offend you."

He took out a cigarette for himself, and jabbed it into his mouth.

"Phil, I'm sorry. I just want us to have a good time. I want it to be nice. Let's not spoil it."

"You mean if I have one drink before five that's going to spoil everything?"

Marilyn sighed. "Please? Phil?"

He took a deep breath. "I'm sorry," he said. "Listen. Let's take a walk. OK?"

They walked around the town square and found an old-fashioned drugstore with the curling metal-backed chairs. There was a sign behind the soda fountain that advertised phosphates. Marilyn and Phil both had cherry phosphates, marvelling over the fact that you could still get this wonderful concoction that neither of them had had since childhood. The phosphates confirmed the fact that they had escaped the jangling city, the Pepsi Generation present; that they had gotten away from it all.

They returned to the room a few minutes after five, and Potter pretended to have forgotten all about the booze. He said he'd like to change for dinner, and Marilyn said that was a good idea, she wanted to do that herself. Before Marilyn had unpacked her clothes and selected what to wear, Potter had washed his face, doused some Old Spice cologne under his armpits, and put on a new shirt and tie.

"I think I'll head on down to the lounge," he said casually, "and meet you there. OK?"

"Oh—sure," she said, a little surprised to see him ready so soon. "I think I'll take a bath."

"Swell. Take your time."

He was able to bolt down a double dry martini on the rocks and then order a regular-sized one that he was sipping in a casual way by the time Marilyn came down. She was wearing an outfit he hadn't seen before. It was a blue taffeta dress that came down just a few inches above her ankles and had a big bow at the neck. It struck Potter as just the right thing for a formal tea at the Ladies Aid Society in 1955.

"What's the matter?" Marilyn asked.

"Huh? Oh, nothing. I just hadn't seen that before—your, uh, frock."

"Oh, this," she said, looking down at the dress as if surprised it was on her. "I thought it would be Vermontish. You know. Conservative."

"Oh."

She ordered a dry vermouth, and Potter had another martini.

There was only one other couple in the dining room when they ate. An elderly pair. In the heavy silence of the room, the clink of silverware sounded like gunfire.

Potter had a steak and most of a bottle of wine. Marilyn had the New England Boiled Dinner, and Indian Pudding for dessert. She said it was delicious, and chided Potter for having the same old thing he could have had in any restaurant in Boston. Potter mumbled something about freedom of choice being one of the most sacred principles of the New England heritage. While she finished her Indian Pudding he had a cognac.

He couldn't get his mind off her dress. It reminded him of Mamie Eisenhower.

When they went to their room, Marilyn sat in the rocking chair and lit a cigarette. Potter filled up one of the water glasses with Scotch, loosened his tie, and flopped down on the bed.

"It's so quiet," Marilyn said. "So peaceful."

"Yeah."

"No television or anything."

"Nope. Nothing."

Marilyn got up and poured herself a glass full of Scotch.

"Why don't you relax?" Potter suggested. "Take off your dress."

Marilyn drew on her cigarette. "You really have a thing about this dress, don't you."

"What do you mean, 'a thing about this dress'?"

"You can't stand it."

"I never said any such thing."

"You don't have to paint a picture."

"I don't know what the fuck you're talking about."

"Don't be so fucking crude."

"Kiss off."

Marilyn stood up and jerked the dress up over her head, ripping it as she pulled it off. "Now," she said, "are you satisfied?"

She started bawling.

Potter belted down the rest of his glass of Scotch and got up and put his arms around her. "Come on," he said. "Please. This is a holiday. A vacation."

"Not anymore it's not! You ruined it, you asshole."

After another ten minutes of sobbing, Marilyn

washed her face, put on a nightgown, took two
Valium, and went to sleep.

Potter took the bottle of Scotch and sat down
in the rocking chair. He felt loggy and his head
had begun to ache, but he was wide awake.
There was nothing to read, or watch; no place to
go. He couldn't even walk down to the old-fashioned drugstore for a phosphate. It would be
closed by now. This was a quaint little town in
Vermont. As far as Potter was concerned, it
might as well have been San Quentin.

Potter and Marilyn both tried to salvage what
they could from their trip to get away from it all.

He took her to see a Buñuel movie at the Orson
Welles Cinema, even though he knew in advance it would bore the shit out of him. Because
she liked Buñuel he pretended to find it fascinating. Afterward he took her to dinner at Casa
Mexico, even though he thought it was a pain
in the ass because they didn't serve cocktails and
you had to bring your own wine.

She made him Baked Alaska, and went to a
Celtics game with him, cheering whenever he
did and trying to learn the names of the players.

He bought her a bottle of Jean Naté bubble
bath, and gave her a bath in it.

She bought a copy of *The Sensuous Woman*,
and gave him a treat the author prescribed called
"The Sylvan Swirl," a sort of glorified blow-job.
She even tried the whipped cream recipe for sexual excitement, but it only made him giggle.

He bought her a new Miles Davis album.

She bought him a new Carole King album.

One night when he knew she'd be tired after her night class, he brought over a sumptuous take-out meal from Joyce Chen's.

One night she gulped a lot of brandy after dinner, and asked, "Would you like me to tie you up? To a chair or something?" He thought it over and said, "No, I don't think so, really. But thanks. Really."

They watched Johnny Carson instead.

It was almost Thanksgiving.

Potter knew it was over with Marilyn, knew that the short course of his infatuation had run itself out. There was nothing he or she could do to revive it, no amount of whipped cream on the cock or gourmet dinners designed to reach his heart by way of his stomach, no amount of booze he could consume to wash away his indifference. But he hadn't had the guts to come right out and tell her. It would be a torturous scene. It always was. He had played it out so many times, before meeting Jessica.

For a couple of days he didn't call her.

One night he just stayed home and watched television. Relentlessly. He settled in the easy chair, put a fifth of Cutty and a glass and a full ice bucket beside him, and just watched, whatever came on, not changing the channels, just letting it come at him, wash over him—the canned laughter, the stupid situations, the news and weather and talk shows. Around eleven he opened a can of vichyssoise, and laced it with Scotch. That was dinner. He fell asleep in his chair watching the late movie, and woke from a nightmare with the test pattern glowing and the static crackling. It was still dark out. He turned off the tube and flopped into bed without taking his clothes off. But he couldn't sleep. Old mistakes, regrets, embarrassments, crowded his mind.

Maybe he should have gone to Law School.

Ginny deFillippo, a secretary at Olney and Sheperdson, whom he tried to make out with after coming back to the office from a drunken lunch at The Ground Floor. She had spit at him.

The time he went home with Stephanie, a girl in his acting class, and fucked her even after she told him she had the clap.

Maybe he should have married Barbara Brickett, the Tri Delt he was engaged to at Vanderbilt. She probably would have been a good wife and mother. He might have settled down and had children with her. They would be teen-agers now.

Maybe he ought to go to Europe. Live in an old stone farmhouse in the south of France.

On what?

Berries. Nuts and berries. And the local wine.

Shit.

He got up, washed his face with cold water, and made a drink. A cold grey light was oozing into the silent street. He turned on the television, and got Sunrise Semester. A black man with a goatee was lecturing on State and Local Government.

Potter listened.

Marilyn pulled her quilted bathrobe around her, holding onto it at the neck, as if protecting herself against a blast of cold wind. "You don't want to fuck me anymore. Is that it?"

Potter wished she hadn't put it so bluntly. He got up and went to the kitchen to put another ice cube in his glass. When he got back he sat down on the far end of the couch from where Marilyn was huddled up, knees drawn to her chin.

"Well?" she asked.

"I wish you wouldn't put it like that."

"How would *you* put it?"

Potter took a drink, and looked down at his knees. His pants needed pressing. "I wouldn't put it so—harshly," he said.

"You mean honestly."

"Goddamn it," he yelled, "I can't help it! I wish I still wanted to. I like you. I don't want to hurt you."

She spoke in the same calm monotone. "Is it always like this?"

Potter closed his eyes. "Mostly," he said. "Sooner or later."

"What happens?"

Potter got up and splashed his glass full of Scotch. He felt she really wanted to know, and he wished he could really explain it—to himself as well as to her. He started walking slowly, aimlessly, around the room.

"It's hard to explain because it doesn't make sense. I mean logically. I first saw you, and right away I was attracted. I wanted to fuck you. Then after doing it a couple of weeks, it's as if the desire drains out. And yet you're the same person."

"Maybe it's the conquest. You just want the conquest."

"No, I swear. Not anymore. Maybe that was true in college, but not for a long time. I think I would know that, and if it was the thing, I'd tell you."

"OK."

"It's more as if—well, maybe this doesn't make sense, but let's say it's like I see a beautiful photograph that's all in color. These beautiful colors. And the longer I look at it, admiring it, the more the colors fade away, and then there is no color in it at all. And no matter how much I concentrate, the colors won't come back into it."

He sat back down, exhausted.

"And the fading process doesn't take very long."

"No. Sometimes just once."

"You mean after one fuck."

"Yes. Other times maybe it lasts a couple months."

"What about your wife?"

"That was different."

"How?"

"Well, the only way I can figure it is that we fought so much and broke up so much and started over so much it was like a new thing all the time. Chaos. Constant chaos."

"So why did it end?"

"I stopped it."

"Why?"

"I didn't want to live that way."

Marilyn lit a cigarette. "Is this way any better?" she asked.

"I'm trying to be honest. Don't get nasty."

"I'm sorry."

"I'm doing the best I can."

Marilyn sighed. "We all are," she said.

After a while they both felt a kind of calm relief at having openly admitted their love affair was over. They were too exhausted and too experienced for any more anger or recriminations. They agreed they did not just want to walk out of each other's life, that they did not want to go back to being alone. They agreed that they needed each other, if only for companionship.

PART THREE

1

They became friends.

"Allies," Potter liked to put it, "because it's like we're in a war. Not against each other, but against the outside world."

As Allies, they arrived at certain pacts and understandings for mutual aid and comfort.

If either of them knew of a party, he or she would invite the other. At the party they would be free to look for new prospective lovers, but they couldn't just go off and leave with a new person. If they met someone they liked, they could make a date or accept a date for a future time and place. At the parties, and to the outside world, they would not discuss the status of their new personal relationship, but let people assume whatever they wanted. Experience had taught them both that it was better to be with a mate in order to catch or attract another mate than to be alone. Alone was undesirable, vulnerable; alone put you in a weakened position.

Either of them could call the other at any time of the day or night, and if they were not otherwise occupied with another person, they would, if so desired, come and keep the other one company. It was a hell of a lot better than phoning up Dial-A-Prayer or the Suicide Prevention Bureau.

They would have dinner together any time they had no other dates or invitations; they would alternate between Marilyn cooking at home and Potter taking them out to a restaurant.

Marilyn suggested that after a while, if they both felt like it, they might even have a friendly fuck from time to time.

"Entirely possible," Potter agreed.

They had formed their alliance just in time to be of aid to one another during the most prolonged and dangerous siege of all single people's personal war to survive. The jingly, tinselled specter of it hung just a few days ahead of them, the annual psychic bombardment that every lonely person most feared and dreaded, from the first sign of turkey sales on through the incessant clanging of carols to the last bleary notes of Guy Lombardo playing "Auld Lang Syne"; the trinity of public trials called Thanksgiving, Christmas, and New Year's, that annual punishing gauntlet known gaily as—*The Holidays*.

Thanksgiving. Silver-bright, and silent. All good citizens were gathered 'round the hearth, ready for the great symbolic bird, trussed and stuffed, to be laid legs up on the family table and ringed with bowls of candied yams, cranberry sauce, thick brown gravy, carrots-n-peas, steaming squash, hot gold rolls, bricks of butter, all of it. The nation was prepared for feasting—or pretending to be.

Lone men and women—those who were not taken in like charity cases by benevolent families—huddled out of sight in their own apartments, curtains drawn, TVs tuned to anything that moved and made noise. Stealthily they sloshed rye or bourbon or Scotch into tall glasses, punctured cans of butterscotch Metrecal for the quickest necessary nourishment, or slipped frozen Mexican TV dinners into ovens for half-hearted soggy sustenance. All stores were locked and dimmed, and those loners who had not made previous arrangements for provisions of at least some simple snack that would get them through the day were doomed now to run this holiday's gauntlet with whatever might be found in their cupboards—a long-forgotten tin of sardines, a can of Chef Boy-ar-dee Spanish rice, an abandoned box of stale Cheez-its; or perhaps, rooting in refrigerators, they might seize as gratefully as rats on some spoiled hunk of Liederkranz, the carcass of a barbecued chicken not thrown away because a few edible glimmers of white meat remained to be gnawed, and for a side order, the limp savings of an oversoaked salad left from a week before. Such scraps now appeared as treasures, as royal fare to starving stomachs, for they could, taken together, provide enough sustenance to keep the lone prisoners of social scorn

alive in their isolated cells until the next blessed-
ly non-holyday allowed them to mingle anony-
mously with the rest of the world, as if they were
a rightful part of it.

But if there were not enough scraps to sustain
them inside their own private lair, if their bellies
pushed them beyond pride, if their ill-tended sys-
tems trembled toward an absolute need for food
at any emotional cost, they had no choice but to
walk the plank of the empty sidewalks (past the
warm lighted windows where the righteous were
stuffing themselves with stuffing) to the most degrading and torturous punishment society saved
for those who lived alone. Heads bowed in shame
and the hope of avoiding recognition, they had
to enter one of those plateglass (the better for
others to watch them squirm), strobe-lit dun-
geons of the human heart, whose windows displayed, with a wicked pretense of jollity, cut-rate
imitations of the Great Feast: "Special! Turkey
Dinner With All The Trimmins! $1.85."

The victims carried their plastic trays laden
with plastic imitations of food that mocked the
real feast—gristly gravy over watered potatoes
and razor cuts of some failure of a fowl that
seemed to be bleeding the congealed blood of
cranberry. They carried it alone to a lone table
to bolt it down, hoping no one would know they
were reduced to this un-holyday indignity. Their
eyes were kept glued on the gluey grub before
them. There wasn't even a newspaper for dis-
traction because papers didn't appear on holi-

days, leaving the paper-less loner to suspect that all printers and reporters and editors and vendors were safe and happy in their glow of a home, kindled by the warmth of their kin, while only the outcasts, the derelicts, the failed family-less futile loners were condemned to such places on days like this. No wonder there were so many suicides on holidays. Better, they figured, to stick your own head in the oven for roasting than to sit before the world an acknowledged nonentity eating your holiday meal with all the trimmings in the lit fishbowl of social infamy, displayed like a punished pilgrim in the public stocks.

Potter and Marilyn had been spared the more medieval tortures of the occasion by an invitation to spend Thanksgiving at the Bertelsens'. Marva called Potter to invite him, and she added, "Marilyn, too—that is, if you two are still an item."

"Who said we weren't?" Potter snapped.

"Why—no one, Phil. No one at all. It's just that I haven't heard from either of you in a while, and I didn't know—how things were."

"Well, things are just fine."

"Gee, I didn't mean to upset you."

"You didn't upset me. I'm not upset in the least."

He tried to lower his voice, steady it, not give away any more than he already had. Marva's sixth sense for sniffing out other people's personal problems had somehow picked up the scent of some change in his relationship with Marilyn, and he had no doubt helped confirm her suspicions by his irritable reaction.

"This is very nice of you, Marva. I'm sure we'd both love to come."

"Wonderful. We'll look for you around noon. Dinner will be three or four."

"Fine."

"It's just a family thing, mainly—the kids and us, and Max's father's coming up. Maybe a few others who don't have anywhere to go."

"Like me and Marilyn?"

"My, but we're sensitive today!"

"Sorry, Marva. Listen, it sounds swell. Be seeing you Thursday."

Potter picked up Marilyn a little after eleven. He hadn't eaten breakfast and thought he might have some toast and coffee at her place, but Marilyn had mixed a batch of martinis, and he didn't want to turn one down after she'd gone to the trouble. Alcohol, he rationalized, had calories, therefore it must have food value. Martinis were no doubt a nourishing breakfast.

They each had two, and arrived at the Bertelsens' with a fine glow.

The Bertelsen kids, eleven-year-old George and nine-year-old Daphne, rushed to the door and started tugging at Potter and Marilyn's coats, vying for the honor of carrying them to the bedroom.

"They're all wound up," Marva explained, "because of Thanksgiving."

"Of course," Marilyn smiled.

Potter nodded his own understanding, as the kids' yelping pierced to his brain.

Max, calm and gracious as always, was in the living room pouring champagne for the guests already assembled. There was his aged father, a bony little man who was Harvard Law School, Class of '13; Phyllis Merton, a fortyish woman who had recently lost her husband to a teen-age hair stylist; Phyllis's daughter Lucille, who was in her freshman year at Goddard and evidently hating every minute of it, to judge by the doomed expression she wore; Seth Ramikanandra, an economist from New Delhi who was studying at the Harvard Business School; and Raymond Cloudweather, a genuine American Indian on scholarship at Brandeis.

Potter was impressed, as always, by Marva's ability to assemble just the right crowd for the right occasion. She would never have brought this group together for a cocktail party honoring some literary or academic figure, or to raise support for a political candidate. Yet in an odd way it was just right for Thanksgiving, perfectly fitting that particular holiday's mystique, which called for a huddling together of stray souls who somehow have survived their circumstances thus far, and need to be stuffed and reassured before being sent on their way again out in the cold. The divorced lady and the Indian-Indian were pretty standard staples at such gatherings, but the American Indian was a real plum, a coup for Marva. You could always dig up sad divorced ladies with depressed daughters, and in the Cambridge-Boston milieu Indians from India were a dime a dozen, almost interchangeable as far as Potter could tell, with their gleaming little teeth and shiny bronze skin, their immaculate Western attire and clipped English accents, speaking inevitably of weighty world matters, as if participating in some endless, marathon version of Meet The Press. But a real American Indian—that was hard to find, and the demand was overwhelming. Now that every serious intellectual household had its copy of *Bury My Heart at Wounded Knee,* the trapping of a real Sioux or Pawnee descendant as a dinner guest was a real achievement, especially on Thanksgiving. The irony of it all, the attempt to make social reparation—it was perfect.

Cloudweather seemed, like the few other American Indians Potter had chanced to meet, more inscrutable than any Oriental. Silent and contained, he answered questions politely, monosyllabically, his expression set and rarely altering. He sat stiff and upright, sipping a glass of apple juice. He had refused champagne, and Potter wondered if he thought of it as "firewater." Potter was then ashamed of himself, and tried to strike up a conversation with Cloudweather, hoping to put him at ease.

"How do you like Brandeis?" Potter asked him.

"Very well," he replied.

Phyllis Merton, grasping at this straw, turned to her glum daughter with feigned brightness and said, "Brandeis. You thought of going there. Didn't you, Lucille?"

"No."

"Oh. Maybe I'm thinking of Barnard. I know there was one that started with a 'B.' That you were thinking of applying to."

Lucille shrugged.

"Maybe it was BU," Marilyn offered.

"That starts with a 'B' all right," Potter said. He swilled down the remains of his champagne, feeling the need for harder stuff. Marilyn gave him a sharp poke in the ribs with her elbow, a signal to behave.

"How's your teaching going, Phil?" Max Bertelsen asked.

"Oh, just fine," Potter said.

Ramikanandra turned toward him with an expression of polite interest, and asked, "At where are you a professor, sir? Harvard or MIT?"

"I'm not a professor, I'm an instructor," Potter said. "I teach at Gilpen Junior College."

"So? I fear, from my ignorance, it is not an institution with which I am familiar."

"It is one of many institutions of higher learning that exist in the greater Boston area besides Harvard and MIT."

"Doubtless, I'm sure," said Ramikanandra with a broad smile of condescension. Potter itched to put the little foreign bastard in his place, but luckily Max's father cut in. "Anyone mind if I go turn on the game?" he yelled at the room in general.

"Of course not, Father," Max said. "Anyone

who wants can go watch the game—we won't be eating for a couple of hours. TV's in the library."

"Oh!" Phyllis Merton said. "Is there a game on? What game is on?"

Max's father looked at her as if she were insane. "There's always a game on Thanksgiving Day," he said. "The Thanksgiving Day Game."

"Of course," said Phyllis, "the Thanksgiving Day game. I've heard of that one."

Marilyn finished off her champagne and whispered quietly but fiercely in Potter's ear, "Get me a real drink, for godsake."

Potter got up, excused himself, and went to the kitchen. Marva was fussing around, and, from the looks of things, getting in the way of the cook. The kids were there too, peeking into pans, sticking fingers into pots. Potter poured himself a giant Scotch, and got a glass of gin and ice for Marilyn. He couldn't find any vermouth, so he just dropped an olive in, to give it the respectable look of a martini.

When Potter returned to the living room, Ramikanandra was discoursing on the Gold Standard in his sing-song, bright-toothed monotone, and Potter slipped off to the den to catch a bit of the Thanksgiving Day Game. Max's ancient father was waving his fist in excitement. He turned to Potter and told him the Packers were leading the Lions 7-3. It turned out Max's dad was a big Packers fan.

"That Lombardi, he's a real man. One of the last real men. Should have gone into politics. But look at that ballclub of his."

Potter was somewhat confused, since Lombardi had died the past August, and had left Green Bay to coach at Washington that year before that; but he figured the old man merely meant that the Packer club was still part of Lombardi's heritage.

"Look at that Hornung, will ya!" the elder Bertelsen croaked with delight. "Look at 'im go!"

Potter moved closer to the screen, wondering exactly what the old chap was looking at. Hornung had retired some years ago. Perhaps they were showing a re-run.

"But they better watch out for the Lions' Bobby Layne—oh, he's a sly one!"

Potter finally realized that Max's old man was watching the game that was being played live that day, but inserting coaches and players of the past; he had them on the right teams, but in the wrong era. Mr. Bertelsen was about a decade out of synch.

"Send out Don Hutson for a long one!" the octogenarian urged, thus plunging back another decade.

Potter edged his way from the room and into the kitchen for a stiffer drink.

By the time the party was seated around the groaning holiday table, Potter and Marilyn were well-sloshed, but the booze had not made them any merrier. Marilyn reported privately to Potter she was suffering a pounding headache over her left eye. Potter, wishing he had had toast instead of martinis for breakfast, felt an overall nausea, and had passed from human hunger to a savage starvation.

Just when the assembled revelers were about to dig in, little Daphne Bertelsen banged her fork on her plate and cried, "No, nobody can eat yet!"

"What's the matter, dear?" Marva asked.

"It's Thanksgiving."

"Yes?"

"So we have to go around the table and everybody tell what they're thankful for."

"Oh, no," Marilyn whispered, pressing a hand to her left temple.

"We've never done that before, dear," Max said.

"But we're *sposed* to," little George said.

"Who said so?" Max asked.

"Miss Mallory told us at school."

"Yeah! We learned it in our room too," shouted Daphne.

"Well, we don't observe that custom at our house," Max explained firmly.

"Then it's not Thanksgiving!" Little Daphne began to sob.

"All right, all right," Marva said. "I'm thankful for having such a fine young son and daughter."

She looked to her right, where Phyllis Merton gulped from her wineglass, forced a smile, and said, "Well, let me see—I'm thankful that, in spite of everything, in spite of all that's happened this past year, I'm thankful that even though—

even though Roger left me for that—that scrawny little nitwit—"

But before she could finish, her face melted, like a wax figure in a furnace room, and she burst into tortured tears.

Little Daphne, evidently pleased that ritual was being observed, pointed a fork toward Marilyn and said, "Now *you!*"

Potter quickly said, "Marilyn and I are thankful we didn't have to eat at the Hayes-Bickford Cafeteria today."

Max, in one of his rare shows of force, told the kids in a tone not open to dispute that "We are going to eat now, and we'll have no more questions or you go straight to bed."

Lucille Merton stared straight ahead, seemingly oblivious to her mother's tears diluting the gravy, and said, "This is a crime. Eating all this food. There's Vietnam, and the ghettos, and we all sit here stuffing ourselves."

No one replied, or acknowledged the statement. Somehow the meal was got through.

Later, while Potter and Marilyn were sprawled across her bed in their underwear, drinking double Alka-Seltzers, Marilyn said, "Well, anyway, it's over. We survived it."

"Yeah," Potter said. "One down. Two to go."

2

December, with its long, slate-colored days and sudden snowfalls, brought a more secret and somber tone to the city. Muffled and bundled, heads bent forward, citizens seemed like spies, moving back and forth on appointed missions, possible and private. Codes, in colored Christmas lights, blinked from windows of stores and homes. Shadows fell, cathedral-length.

Potter took to hanging around school longer, postponing the trip back to Cambridge and his still unfinished apartment with its liquor boxes full of books, its accumulating piles of magazines and papers, laundry and dishes. Like his life, his apartment seemed to be in a perpetual state of disarray.

Even though he and Marilyn were friends, and saw one another quite often, Potter felt essentially alone again, having no lover. He found it harder to activate himself out of apathy the way that Marilyn did with her therapy and evening classes, her tutoring of ghetto children, her initiative in getting tickets to plays and concerts and going with one of the girls from the office, "making an evening of it," as she said.

Potter decided he should have more friends. He enjoyed drinking with Gafferty, but that always had to end early so Gafferty could get back home to his wife and baseball team of a family. He didn't want to go alone to the Bertelsens' at this stage, knowing Marva would try to pry out new information about him and Marilyn that he didn't feel like discussing now.

Dean Hardy had asked Potter to look up a fellow Communications instructor named Ed Shell, whom he felt he would have much in common with, Shell being a "promising young film writer" and Potter a former man of the theatre. Though the Dean assured Potter he and Shell were sure to "hit it off," Potter was not so confident of that when someone first pointed out Gilpen's promising young film writer. Shell was wearing bell-bottom trousers, cowboy boots, a button-down shirt with a rep tie, and a tweed jacket with leather elbow patches, giving him the incongruous look of a man who dressed the top part of himself for the Fifties, and the bottom half for the Seventies. Besides that, Shell had a dour, frowning kind of seriousness about him that Potter found unattractive. He reasoned, though, that he was committing the sin of snobbery, of judging by appearances, and he ought to give the guy a chance. Besides, he had nothing better to do.

Potter agreed to go have a drink at Shell's

place, even though he lived in Somerville, which was unfamiliar territory. Somerville began at the edge of Cambridge—the poor, un-Harvardy edge. It had a large contingent of Portuguese and Italians, interspersed with students, hippies, teachers, dropouts, the underground Bohemian set who had come to the area because of low rents and proximity to Cambridge.

"Welcome to the pad," Shell said when he opened the door.

It reminded Potter of the temporary living quarters of his own starving-artist days in New York. It was one small room, with a kitchenette and bath. The room had peeling flowered wallpaper, and a large poster of Orson Welles. There was a mattress on the floor with grubby striped sheets flung over it, and scattered debris—a partially empty cup of yogurt, an overflowing ashtray, one dirty sock, a tattered copy of an old *Esquire*, an empty pack of True Menthols, and a can of Colt 45, tipped over and leaking the last of its contents.

"Get you a beer, man?"

"Sure," said Potter.

He picked his way over scattered and piled pages of what must be movie scripts, and sat down cross-legged on one of the pillows that evidently served as chairs.

Dedication, Potter thought; *Dreams.*

It made him feel very old.

"It looks like you're very productive," he said when Shell brought him a Colt 45.

Shell sat down on a pillow across the small room, and said, "Seventeen scripts. So far. Working on the eighteenth."

"Jesus. That's a lot."

"When one hits, a lot of 'em will hit. Ones that've been turned down'll get done."

"I guess that's the way it works."

"It's a matter of time. You have to wait it out, and keep working."

"I know."

Till you can't wait any longer, till it's gone and drained out of you, Potter thought.

Shell assured Potter that he wasn't just daydreaming, having acquired an M.A. in Film at Boston University, and written-directed-produced a four-minute film on a waitress at a hamburger drive-in that won honorable mention in a national contest for film students sponsored by a nationwide motel chain. The award had brought him fifty dollars, a free night with meal of his choice at any of the chain's motels throughout the land, and a confidence that he had what it takes to make it big in film.

"My last script," Shell said, "this director who's very hot now was dying to do, but he couldn't get a producer. One before that, this very highly regarded producer was hot about, but he's committed to a three-picture deal with a particular studio, and they just had a big turnover in management, and so the whole project got fouled up."

"Damn, that's too bad."

"It's just a matter of getting it all together. It's bound to happen soon now."

"Hell, yes."

"That's why I have to live like this—temporary. Ready to go."

"Go? Where?"

"The Coast."

"Oh."

"I've got a suitcase packed. In the closet."

"Well, that's—uh—very shrewd of you. Looking ahead that way."

When Potter left, Ed Shell gave him one of his scripts to read. Potter was both fearful and fascinated, wondering what it would be like, terrified it would be a hopeless exercise, but dying to know if it just might—by the most incredible chance—be a goddamn miraculous feat of genius.

It was neither.

Potter lay on his bed at home, smoking a cigarette, holding the script on his lap, pondering the thing. The script was called "Karen." It was about a bright young girl who went into social work and was disillusioned by the bureaucracy but still kept her faith in helping people and fell in love with a poor young guy on her welfare route who worked for his old man at a fish market in the Boston harbor. It wasn't anything that would knock you out, and had its share of cliché ideas and situations, but it wasn't all bad either; it wasn't as bad as a lot of stuff Potter had seen on the screen or on television. As far as he could tell, it could perfectly well be done, would help fill up time and space for a number of people, would bring money and satisfaction to Ed Shell, who would have with its production confirmed his image of himself. And it could just as well go begging, lost, undone, for all the justifications of it that could also be made, and Ed Shell could end up—how many years later—waiting for the call to the Coast, keeping his suitcase packed. But you don't keep your suitcase packed forever. Potter knew all about that. If it didn't happen, the day would finally come when Ed Shell would unpack that suitcase. Potter would just as soon not be around to see it or know about it.

It occurred to Potter, though, that even if Shell had to someday unpack his dream, in the meantime it gave a shape and purpose to his life, helped him get through the day. The value of a dream was that, like booze or religion or dope, it filled you up for a while.

Potter's next evening was empty. Marilyn had a date with a guy from her Existentialism course who had asked her for coffee after the last class, and had sprung for an invitation to dinner. She had high hopes for this one, a lawyer who was taking the course to "broaden his horizons." Potter thought that sounded a little hokey, but he didn't want to disillusion Marilyn in advance. Besides, he wished her well and hoped something nice might come of the date. A lawyer who wanted to broaden his horizons might just turn out to be her Mister Right.

When Potter complained about his own lack of companionship for the evening, Marilyn suggested he try going to a bar called The Pub, where she said it was possible for nice men to meet nice women; it wasn't a hooker place or anything. She had been there herself a couple of times with girls from the office, and sometimes they'd made a connection with a couple of guys, perfectly decent sorts, just wanting to meet people.

With no other prospect for the night but television, Potter went.

There were a lot of little tables, but he headed straight to the bar. After his eyes adjusted to the dim light of the place, he swung around on his barstool, casually, and gave the place a quick survey. Most of the girls were in couples; some had one or two men already joining them or trying to join them. But one girl, at a table way back against the wall, sat alone. Potter peered at her through the gloom, and she stared right back. He looked away, looked back, and she still was staring straight at him. No mistaking it. He finished off his drink, and went over to her table.

"May I sit down?" he asked.

"Sure."

"Would you like a drink?"

"Thanks. I have one."

The girl's coat was folded on a chair, and a pile of books, along with a notebook, sat on top of it. She didn't look like a student, though; a little too old, a little too carefully dressed. She wore tiny pearl earrings, a fashionable pants suit, and hornrimmed glasses.

"Are you a student?" Potter asked. He figured if she wasn't, the mistaken assumption would be flattering.

"I take some courses. Twice a week, I come in to town."

"You live out of town?"

"In Framingham."

"Oh—that's sort of a suburb, isn't it?"

"I guess."

"Isn't that kind of—inconvenient? Unless you're married?"

"My husband's dead," she said quickly.

"Oh. I'm sorry."

"I'm taking a course in poetry writing."

"Oh? That must be—uh, interesting."

"I just started. But I like it. I like to be able to express myself."

After two drinks she agreed to have a drink at Potter's apartment. She wouldn't go in his car, though, but insisted on following him, in her own. It was a station wagon. Potter feared she might just lose herself in traffic, on purpose, but she stuck on his tail, and pulled up behind him across from his apartment.

He put on classical guitar, and got them drinks. She took off the coat to her pants suit, and Potter saw that she had enormous breasts. He found it hard to believe his good fortune. Going to a bar and picking up a woman who seemed to be reasonably intelligent and pleasant, and also was blessed with unusual physical endowments. He was beginning to feel a warm glow of good feeling, when the woman said suddenly, "There's something I have to tell you."

Potter braced himself.

"I'm a terrible liar," she confessed.

"Oh?"

"Yes. For instance, I've lied to you already."

"You have?"

Potter mulled over the possibilities. She had said she was twenty-eight; maybe she was really thirty-one. Maybe it was something as silly as that.

"You remember I told you my husband was dead?"

"Yes," Potter said, "you did mention that."

My God, he thought, *did I bring home a murderer? The Suburban Strangler?*

"Well, that was a lie," she said. She paused, fixing her gaze intently on Potter, and said, "My husband's not dead—I just wish he was dead."

"Oh," Potter said. "Well, that's quite a difference."

"Yes."

Potter lit a cigarette. "Well, I'm awfully sorry," he said. "I mean, I'm not sorry that your husband's not dead—I don't even know him. I'm sorry you *wish* he was dead. Since he's not."

Potter was aware his response was complicated, but he doubted there was any graceful way for commenting on this particular situation. "Maybe you could get a divorce?" he suggested.

"He'd never do that. He'd kill me first. He swore he would."

"Oh."

"He's very violent."

"I see."

Potter became more sober as the information began to sink in. It occurred to him that if this lady's husband would kill her for trying to get a divorce he might easily kill her for sleeping with another man. Or in fact, while he was at it, might just as well kill the other man.

"Under the circumstances," Potter said, "maybe the wisest course—I mean, for now—uh, would be for you to just, uh, go back to your husband."

She shrugged. "Mind if I finish my drink?"

"No, not at all. Take your time."

The woman who wished her husband was dead left around ten, and Potter poured himself a drink—he had waited to make a new one until she was gone, fearing if he got too sloshed the allure of the lady's beautiful body might overcome the rational fear of her killer husband.

Marilyn called around ten-thirty.

"What happened?" Potter asked.

"It was awful," she said. "You'll never believe it."

"I'll believe it," Potter assured her.

He went to her place to hear all about it, sorry her latest hope had been blitzed, but glad he had somewhere to go and someone to talk to.

Marilyn was huddled up on the couch with a drink.

"Is that a martini you're having?" Potter asked.

"Just gin."

"Oh. What happened?"

"He wanted to dress up."

"Dress up? You mean in a tux or something."

"No. In *my* clothes."

"Oh."

"And I thought he was a regular guy."

"Well, it takes all kinds."

"Yeah. And I find 'em."

"Well, buddy, maybe a class in Existentialism isn't the best place to look. Maybe you should switch to American Government. Or Business Administration. Something solid."

"Fuck."

Potter told her about the woman who wished her husband was dead.

"We're just not meeting the right people," Marilyn said.

"Yeah. But maybe it'll change. Maybe we'll meet a whole new group of terrific people."

They both started laughing. It wasn't a light or happy sound. It was the laughter of comrades who are fighting together in a long and wearing campaign that has come to seem hopeless, like a misguided medieval crusade that has gone too far to turn back.

Despite the way things had been going, Marilyn had high hopes for the party she and Potter went to that Saturday night out in one of the Boston suburbs. Potter couldn't keep the goddamn suburbs straight, either by name or geography. There was Lincoln and Sudbury, Lexington and Concord, Newton and Weston and Marlboro. Potter had no idea of the relative position of any of them to Boston or to one another. He was accustomed to the basic grid of Manhattan, and was utterly confused by the complex sworls of roads and streets, expressways and turnpikes, routes and highways and bypasses that twisted and curled out of Boston in all directions.

Marilyn drove.

"Why is it you think this one's going to be so good?" Potter asked as Marilyn gunned his car along the twisting country roads.

"Well, I only know the hostess, I don't know any of her friends. Or her husband's. She just got married a few months ago, so they must still know a lot of single people. Since I don't know any of the people, the odds are better, that's all. You know. It might be a whole new group of terrific people."

"It's possible, I guess."

The people at the party were "new" but not different. Potter and Marilyn agreed about that when they got back to her place.

"Driving all that way for nothing," Potter said.

He had loosened his tie, unbuttoned his collar, and was sprawled on the couch with a drink and a cigarette. Marilyn had kicked off her shoes, and was rolling down her pantyhose. "What about that redhead you had in a corner?" she asked.

"Oh. Her."

"What was wrong with her?"

"Nothing, I guess. She's a nurse at Mass General. She wishes they would bring back *Dr. Zhivago*. She thinks it's the most beautiful movie she ever saw."

"So?"

"So nothing. I got her number, just in case."

"In case you feel like fucking her."

"In case they bring back *Dr. Zhivago*. Shit. I don't know."

"You bastards."

"What?"

Marilyn picked up her shoes and pantyhose, went into the bedroom and came back wrapped in her old blue terrycloth bathrobe and a pair of red wool socks. When they were lovers, she wore a Japanese mini-kimono. Potter belched, and rubbed his stomach. He felt as if he and Marilyn had been married twenty years.

"What's this 'bastard' shit?" he asked.

"You guys. You can always get laid."

"*What?* You mean you can't—as easy as I can?"

"Yeah, sure. To some married man."

"So?"

"So what's in it for me?"

"So what's in it for me fucking that redhead to the theme music of *Dr. Zhivago?*"

"Fuck. At least you can take her out in public, go to a restaurant, have a good time. You don't have to sneak around like a fucking criminal."

"Shit, Marilyn, every man in the world isn't married."

"Every good one is."

"Thanks a lot, buddy."

"Oh, I don't mean that. I don't mean you. I mean every good one's married, or divorced and bitter, or divorced and looking for some fucking nymphet teen-age bride."

"Not every man is."

"Yeah? Well tell me how many are looking for someone their own age when they're thirty-five or so. Huh?"

"Well, I don't know."

"Don't know, my ass. You and Dr. Shamleigh."

"What have I got to do with your goddamn shrink?"

"I'll tell you what. You're both men, that's what, and you won't admit the truth. And I'm not talking any Women's Lib bullshit, either, the stuff about who opens the door for who and whether you wear a bra and how you should light your own cigarette. I don't want to run for President, either. All that's very well and good, but it's not the part where we really get screwed."

"What part is that?"

"You guys can keep getting older, and keep getting younger women. But we can't keep getting younger men, or even men our own age after a while. We're like cars—we go out of style. The year of our make becomes obsolete, outdated, undesirable. And it's even worse than cars, because there's more new women coming onto the market every year than there are new cars."

"Maybe—uh—you have a point."

"You're goddamn right I have a point. And that goddamn Dr. Shamleigh keeps asking me why I keep messing around with married men, like it's some neurotic, sick compulsion or something, when the fact is I rarely *meet* any others. And when I do rarely meet them, either they have a twenty-year-old girlie, or they—well—they—"

"They turn out like me," Potter offered.

"They don't last, is all. Mostly they don't even start."

"Yeah. Well, shit. What can I say?"

"Nothing."

They both sat for a while in silence, drinking and smoking.

"I've got to get some sleep," said Marilyn. "I'm going to take a Phenobarb."

"When did you start on those?"

"Week or so ago. At least the shrink's good for that. Prescriptions."

"Yeah."

"Listen, are you going to stay tonight?"

"Well, I'd like to, but I know I can't go to sleep for a while."

"Well, OK. But listen, it's hard enough getting to sleep—will you try not to wake me up when you get in bed?"

"Sure, but—you know, I can't help it if I toss and turn."

"Well—maybe if you concentrate—"

"No, hey, why don't I just sleep on the couch?

I don't want to wake you or anything. But I
hate to drive back home. I don't much want to
be alone tonight."

"I know."

Marilyn got sheets and a blanket and pillow,
and made up the couch.

"Thanks," Potter said.

She gave him a good night kiss on the forehead. Potter stayed up drinking, chainsmoking,
and flipping through old magazines whose articles and stories failed to hold his attention very
long. When the windows began to fade from
black to grey, he slipped out of his trousers, folded them over the back of a chair, hung his jacket
over it, and shoved himself into the bedding, still
wearing his shirt and shorts and socks. He
mashed the pillow over his head, hoping to muf-
fle light, and noise, and memory.

Potter sat in his office hoping no students
would come. He'd drunk himself to sleep again
the night before, and he felt as if he'd been
stomped by a street gang. He sipped at a cup of
coffee and tried to immerse himself in the box
score of a Celtics game. Concentrating on the
details, the names and numbers, helped him forget about the ache in his back, the throbbing in
his forehead.

Both sensations were brought back sharply by
a sudden rap on the door.

"Come in!" he said sourly.

"Did I disturb you?"

Miss Linnett's dreamy grey eyes looked moist and innocent.

"No, no," said Potter, "sit down."

She did, crossing her long, lovely legs and tugging her leather miniskirt the four or five inches that it reached down her thighs. She wore the mini-est miniskirts of any Potter had seen, and her twisting around in them and tugging at them during class often made him forget what he was saying, had said, and wanted to say.

"What can I do for you, Miss Linnett?"

Miss Linnett twisted a strand of her long, yellow hair, and launched into a long explanation of why she wouldn't be able to hand her paper in on time. Potter didn't really hear the details. He wondered if she had a boyfriend. A lover. Maybe many lovers. Maybe she was a real swinger. Maybe she had a crush on Potter.

Maybe she just wanted more time to do her paper. Or have it done for her. Maybe she wanted an A.

Potter gave her the extension she asked for. He would probably give her the A, too. After all, if she distracted him in class she also inspired him.

But, once again, he determined to stick to his hands-off-students policy. He was proud of this principle, but it was getting increasingly difficult, in fantasy if not yet in practice.

Potter did not stand up to walk Miss Linnett to the door when she left his office. He feared she might notice his embarrassingly noticeable hard-on.

3

As he watched the number of shopping days till Christmas dwindle, Potter found himself dreading the end of school. It was not just the specter of Christmas itself that he feared in his present condition, but the space of empty time, the two weeks of days without classes or office hours, opening before him like a deep and treacherous pit through which he must fall in order to land at the start of another new year and the relieving resumption of duties.

On the last day of classes before the vacation break, his PR seminar turned into an impromptu party. The students had got together and bought him a fifth of Cutty Sark for a Christmas present, a gift that indicated their knowledge of the bottle he kept in the drawer of his office desk and also their evident appreciation of his class. Potter was moved, feeling like a premature version of Robert Donat in *Goodbye, Mr. Chips*. He thanked the class, and, in the spirit of the occasion, proposed that instead of taking home his gift he share it with all of them right then and there. This daring proposal was greeted with cheers, and the peppy little Miss Patterson quickly brought back from the cafeteria a dozen styrofoam cups and two bags of Fritos.

It was a nice feeling. The pleasant anticipation of the students for the season almost upon them relieved Potter's own apprehension, allowed him to share the warmth. They spoke of ski trips and parties, of going home to Schenectady or Cleveland, of hitchhiking to Florida. Halligan, the veteran who was waging a losing battle against his girlfriend's marital offensive, admitted with a nervous grin that he was getting engaged over Christmas. There were hoots and cheers.

Ted Featherstone, an engaging young guy who had announced in the second session of the seminar that he was interested in public relations as it could be applied to selling things like peace and brotherhood, population control and universal health care, had come to class dressed in his usual outfit of Levi's and motorcycle boots, and was also carrying a large rucksack.

"Where you heading?" Potter asked him.

"Oh. This commune where some friends of mine live."

"Going there for Christmas?"

"For the Winter Solstice. That's what they celebrate."

"How do they celebrate it?" Foster B. Stevenson asked with an obvious edge of contempt. "Get stoned?"

Featherstone shrugged. "Some do, some don't.

On the actual day of the Solstice, people from neighboring communes come over and they have a real feast."

"What do they live on, Rich Daddy money?" Halligan asked.

"Nope. Some have jobs in a neighboring town. Their farm's over in the western part of the state. It seems real remote, but there are towns around. Also, they raise their own vegetables, of course. And some are musicians, they bring in a lot of bread. Like 'The Sandman.' You know, the guitarist? He signs all the profits of his albums over to the farm. If they can't make a mortgage payment, he gets a gig."

"What do the women do?" asked Myrna Seely, who was one of the few Women's Movement activists at Gilpen.

"Everybody does their own thing," Featherstone said.

"Yeah—and I bet I know what *their* own thing is—cooking and washing the goddamn dishes and all the rest of the menial shit."

Featherstone only smiled, refusing to be drawn into battle.

Myrna finished off her drink and left, and the room broke up into groups of twos and threes. Potter had more Scotch and questioned Featherstone further about the commune. Potter had never been able to imagine himself living communally, for he cherished his privacy as much as he despised his loneliness. But he had always had a fascination about such experiments, understanding as he did the need of people to huddle together, any way at all, for mutual warmth and sustenance. Featherstone spoke of his friends' commune in glowing terms, and said they even had "this older guy" who lived there, who used to be an architect, as if this would make the whole thing seem more plausible to Potter. After a few more Scotches, Potter accepted an invitation to visit the commune that very weekend, along with anyone he wanted to bring. Featherstone drew him a map.

Potter tried to convey his enthusiasm about the commune visit to Marilyn that night, but she seemed reserved, suspicious. Besides, she had lined up another party for them to go to on Saturday.

"Jesus," Potter said, "it'll just be the same."

"Well, what'll the commune be?"

"Different," he said.

"Well," she said, "I guess that's something."

On the way to the commune, Potter and Marilyn stopped in a supermarket to buy some supplies. It seemed only right that they get into the spirit of the thing by bringing food and drink to share. But once in the supermarket, Potter was confused about what would be appropriate. Marilyn picked out a big roast she thought would be nice.

"But what if they're vegetarians?" Potter asked. "A lot of them are—I mean a lot of people who live on communes are, I don't know if these people are, but they might be."

"You should have asked."

"Well, it's too late now."

They walked slowly up the aisles, staring vacantly at the bright rows of cans and bottles and jars, all of which seemed too fancy and commercialized to be suitable for a commune.

"If they're vegetarians," Marilyn said, "I guess we have to bring vegetables."

"If they're vegetarians, they probably grow their own. Besides, you can't just take people a bushel of carrots."

"Well, what the fuck *can* you take?"

"There's no need to get excited. Try to be cooperative."

Marilyn closed her eyes and sighed. "OK," she said. "I'm trying. What about fish? Do fish count?"

"Hey, that's great. I think you're right. I think fish is all right."

Potter purposefully pushed the empty cart to the fish section, and looked down at the selection, frowning. "These are all frozen," he said.

"What did you expect? This isn't Fisherman's Wharf."

"Is it all right for them to be frozen?"

"What the hell do you mean is it 'all right'?"

"I mean, doesn't freezing them add some harmful chemicals or something that they couldn't eat?"

"By God, if we can eat them *they* can eat them."

She started hurling packages of frozen haddock into the cart.

"That's enough!" Potter said.

There were more than a dozen packages of the stuff.

"OK," said Marilyn. "What else? What about bread?"

"They probably bake their own."

"Maybe they don't need *anything*."

"Wine," Potter said. "I'll get some wine. They might just have dope. They don't like hard liquor, but I think wine is OK."

He bought a gallon of Tavola red table. It seemed very earthy to him, and therefore hopefully acceptable.

According to the map, the commune was a dilapidated brown small house with a garage whose roof was caving in. Potter was not so much surprised at the deteriorating nature of the place, if that was indeed the right place, as he was by its proximity to the world it was presumably trying to escape. It wasn't far from the supermarket in town, and once here, you could see at least three neighboring farmhouses. Potter had imagined something hidden away, far from towns and main roads, far from anything.

It was the place, though.

A girl in a dirty blouse and torn jeans came to the door.

"Hi," said Potter, with his best smile. "My name's Potter."

The girl only stared at him.

"Is Ted Featherstone here? He asked me to come."

The girl turned in toward the room, and yelled, "Ted!" then walked away. Potter and Marilyn still stood outside, shivering. Featherstone appeared, looking a big groggy and pulling a T-shirt over his head.

He looked at Potter blankly for a moment, then rubbed his eyes and said, "Oh—hey—yeah."

"Well, I found it," Potter said.

"Far out."

"This is my friend Marilyn."

"Hey, yeah—c'm in."

"Thanks."

Potter handed Featherstone the supermarket bag filled with frozen haddock and the gallon of Tavola.

Featherstone looked inside the bag. "Far out," he said. "Listen, just sit down anywhere. I'll get some glasses."

Potter and Marilyn took off their coats, and looked around the room. There was one old chair with the stuffing coming out, but it was occupied by the sprawled body of a large, red-haired young man reading a comic book. There were pillows scattered over the bare floor and Potter and Marilyn each grabbed one and sat down. Featherstone came back with jelly glasses filled with wine. A girl walked in from the kitchen, and climbed up a rickety ladder to what was evidently a sort of dormitory floor above, with bedrolls.

Featherstone lit up a joint. "Wow," he said, "you came."

"Yeah, we really came," said Potter.

He didn't dare look at Marilyn. He was hoping things would pick up. Several other people passed in and out, glanced at them, and walked on, as if they had merely noticed a couple of spots on the floor.

"So this is it," said Potter.

"Not everyone's here right now—Roger, the older guy I was telling you about, had to make a run into town. He ought to be back."

Potter inhaled furiously on the joint, wishing to hell it would stone him out of his skull, but it only led to a coughing fit, and he passed it to Marilyn, who puffed delicately, and drank more wine.

A tall, frail-looking guy with thick glasses came out of another room and Featherstone motioned him over. It was The Sandman himself, and, true to his image, he looked as if he was still half-asleep. When introduced to Potter and Marilyn, he nodded and yawned.

Roger, the older guy, came back from his run into town with a carton of Camels and some frozen orange juice. That made Potter feel better about the frozen fish. Frozen must be OK. For all Potter knew, frozen was beautiful.

The fish, however, were never mentioned again. Dinner was pumpkin-and-cucumber soup, and homemade dark bread. Four people, including The Sandman, sat at a round table. The others crouched or knelt on the floor.

"Let's have some sounds, man," The Sandman said, and the girl in the dirty peasant blouse put on a record. It was some kind of Rock, and blared out any other possibility of sound, which was actually a relief to Potter since the only other sounds were primarily those of snoring and farting.

Roger, the older guy, nodded at Potter and Marilyn when introduced but didn't look them in the eyes, as if he didn't want anything to do with people who were vaguely his own age. Right after dinner The Sandman summoned Featherstone into the back bedroom, which it turned out The Sandman had all to himself. He seemed to have all the rights and privileges of leadership except for the lack of a title and the pretense that he was just one of the others. Marilyn went back into the kitchen to ask if she could help with anything, but the dirty-bloused girl and a tall, rather pretty blonde said no, they were going to leave the dishes till tomorrow.

The dirty-bloused girl deigned to come out and sit by Marilyn and Potter on the floor.

"How long have you been here?" Marilyn asked.

The girl shrugged. "I wanted to go to South America, even found out about a job on a freighter, but they wouldn't take me on, just because I was a chick."

"That's too bad," Marilyn sympathized.

"You know it. I mean, it really shits when a

chick can't ship on a freighter."

"Damn right," said Potter, shaking his head.

He and Marilyn had more wine.

Featherstone and The Sandman came out. Featherstone sat down by Marilyn, but The Sandman explained he had to get back in that room, there was a little problem.

"What's wrong?" Potter asked.

"It's Andy," said The Sandman.

"Andy's just been here a couple months," Featherstone explained, "and he's not used to it yet. He isn't into anything yet, you know, like creative, so he just sits around and looks out the window."

"What's happened to him—or happening?" Marilyn asked.

The Sandman yawned, and scratched at his head. "He's having what used to be called 'a nervous breakdown.' "

"Oh," said Marilyn.

"What's it called now?" Potter asked.

The Sandman smiled. "He's freaking out."

"That's a shame," Potter said.

Featherstone stood up, and said, "Listen, I ought to go back and rap with him, along with Sandman. Whenever you want to crash, there's plenty of room up on the dorm floor. Take any bedroll. If it's someone else's, they'll find another one."

Featherstone and The Sandman disappeared.

"Listen," Marilyn whispered, "let's get the hell out of here."

"What? Drive all the way back to Boston?"

"We can go to a motel."

"*Where?*"

"Anywhere. There's motels everywhere. Thank God."

"You can't just do that," Potter said. "I mean, we can't just leave."

"The fuck we can't. You think any of these creeps would know the difference, or care less?"

"Well. I ought to tell Featherstone."

"To hell with the little fart. He's busy playing medicine man."

"Well. Maybe you're right."

They snuck out quietly, jumped in the car, and gunned their way back to the highway, giggling and cursing. They found a Howard Johnson's motel, checked into a room with a color TV, and ordered club sandwiches and beers from room service.

The next time Potter saw Featherstone he apologized for having to leave without saying goodbye, and Featherstone said he understood, it was nobody's fault. The Sandman had figured out that the bad vibes that led to both Potter's departure and to Andy's freaking out had been due to a full moon in Sagittarius.

"There's something I have to tell you," Marilyn said.

They had recovered from the commune trip, and were lolling around Marilyn's apartment Sunday afternoon, talking of the coming events of the great holiday season.

"Jesus," Potter said, "not *you!*"

"What's wrong?"

"Everytime a woman says, 'There's something I have to tell you,' it's bad news. It's the clap, or it's going into the convent, or it's Aunt Tillie's coming to stay for a month and of course she doesn't know I have lovers. The last time I heard that, it was the woman who told me her husband wasn't dead she just wished he was dead."

"God, you don't have to get so—overwrought."

"I don't, huh? OK. Then just tell me what the thing is you have to tell me, and we'll see how overwrought I have to get."

Marilyn got up to make herself a new drink. "Want yours freshened?" she asked solicitously.

"Now I *know* it's bad," he said.

"Don't be silly."

She fixed the drinks, sat down, and looked at Potter with a tenuous smile.

"I'm waiting," he said.

Marilyn lit a cigarette.

"I'm waiting for the worst, so you might as well hit me with it," Potter said.

"Listen, Phil, you're making a big commotion about nothing. All it is—the only thing is—I have to go away for a few days."

"Away? Where? For what?"

"Well. You remember my mother. In Florida?"

"You mentioned you had one there."

"Well, she's very old, and she isn't well, and she wrote this really pathetic sort of letter begging me—really begging me—to come down and visit her."

"I thought you hardly saw her anymore."

"I don't, hardly. That's just it. I haven't seen her for a couple of years. More than two. She's all alone down there, and if she dies and I haven't seen her it will really be terrible. Dr. Shamleigh said if that happened I'd feel horribly guilty, I'd probably go into some deep depression."

"That asshole."

"I know he is, but he may be right about this. It's just for a few days, and then it will be off my conscience."

Potter's eyes narrowed to a squint. "*Which* few days?" he asked.

"Well," she said lightly, not looking at him directly, "I thought I could leave on the twenty-fourth and get back on the twenty-sixth. It's just two nights and three days, altogether."

"It's Christmas!" Potter screamed. "It's Christmas and Christmas Eve! You bitch, you goddamn bitch! I thought we were allies! I thought we were friends!"

"We *are*, Phil, we *are*—"

"And you're leaving me alone on Christmas and Christmas Eve, two of the worst fucking times of all, two of the hardest days of the whole rotten holidays!"

"You think it's pleasure for *me?*" she yelled back. "You think I'm going to have it easy getting through Christmas in a fucking trailer park with my hysterical, alcoholic mother rolling herself around in a wheelchair, and singing Deck the Halls and all that crap? Getting soused and crying about my father gone to the great Christmas in the sky?"

"OK," he said. "OK. I'm sorry."

He sat down beside her on the couch, and they put their arms around each other, comforting.

"You'll make it through," she said. "I know you'll make it."

"So will you, kid. Listen, I got confidence in you."

4

On the day of Christmas Eve, Potter didn't want to leave the house. He had the Bertelsen party to go to at six, but he didn't want to risk wandering around Cambridge or Boston before that. The pitch of the season would soon reach its jolly crescendo of wassail and song, before the stone silence of the holy day itself. This was the last chance for shopping and bustling around on merciful missions and the streets would be full of cheerily fake Dickensian characters with long, colored scarves and clown-red noses. The street-corner Santas would be jingling their bells to hell and gone, those bells that were tuned to penetrate your skull and harangue your brain with their silver insistence to *give give give,* and the shivering Salvation Army combos would be bleating their baleful brass versions of the carols, managing to make a dirge out of "Joy to the World."

Potter had a container of low-fat peach yogurt and a cup of Tastemaker instant freeze-dried coffee for his noon breakfast, and turned on the daytime soap operas. He had started watching

the soaps on television the Monday after vacation began. It was the first time in his life he had
resorted to this, and he drew the venetian blinds
shut in the living room and kept the volume low,
fearing someone would find him out. He figured
it was the ultimate degradation. But of course
it was not. Whenever you think you've found
the ultimate degradation, you soon find ways to
elaborate on it, new refinements and improve-
ments to add. Potter started sipping Scotch and
sodas while he watched, and used the commercial breaks to run to the kitchen for freshening
the drink or getting more ice. But this still left
many commercial breaks in which he had nothing special to do, and his mind would begin to
slide back to reality. To combat this, Potter took
to keeping the *Globe* crossword puzzle in his lap,
so that whenever the story was interrupted by a
commercial, he could immediately focus his
mind on the puzzle. But after a few days of doing this, he discovered he was finishing the puzzle too fast—that is, before the last soap was finished—which allowed his thoughts to go free
again during the remaining commercials. He
solved this new dilemma by going to the big
magazine stand in Harvard Square and buying
up a bunch of Crossword Puzzle magazines. He
slipped away surreptitiously with them, hiding
them beneath a Boston *Globe,* as guilty as if he
were carrying hardcore pornography.

Potter was at first surprised to find he *liked* the
soaps, that he found them far more credible than

any of the dramatic series on nighttime television; their slow, nagging pace of problems and misunderstandings and high-strung, headache-y conflicts were far more typical of daily life as he knew it and saw it around him than the adult evening TV dramas or the quick-image flashings and clean resolutions of the hip new movies.

The episodes he watched on the day of Christmas Eve made him a confirmed fan forever. They seemed to him the only honest portrayals of the whole, hidden horror of the season.

On one of the shows, a troubled young college student went to the home of his favorite professor and his wife, confessing that he didn't have the guts to go home and visit his parents for Christmas. The professor and wife urged him to brave it, saying how much it would mean to his parents, how hurt they would be if he didn't come. Suddenly a strange smile crossed the face of the troubled young man, and he said, "Well, maybe there is a way. A way that would give me the courage to do it." The prof clapped him on the back, and the sympathetic wife smiled syrup at him. In the next scene the young man sat alone in the living room of his fraternity house. A knock came at the door, and the student let in a suspicious-looking man with dark, slicked-back hair and the collar of his overcoat turned up. The student took off his jacket, and rolled up his sleeve. The pusher got out his works and gave the young man a fix. A Christmas fix. The young fellow smiled beatifically.

He could make it home for Christmas now! Over the river and through the woods.

Potter laughed out loud, and got himself a new drink. He sat at the tube engrossed all afternoon, as the real traumas of the holiday were enacted. Deserted wives wept at piano bars while listening to "White Christmas," husbands explained to lonely mistresses they had to hurry home to the wife and children, idealistic interns tried to comfort patients whose cases were hopeless and later cried their hearts out to lovesick nurses. Young married couples argued bitterly over whether the in-laws who tried to stop the wedding should be given a day of amnesty on Christmas and forgiven with a visit, while unwed mothers shoplifted dolls for their deserted little babes and amnesia victims in far-off flop-houses were stricken with flashbacks of former happy holidays in lives whose location they could no longer place.

When the whole marvelous show was over in the waning hours of the afternoon, Potter took a long, hot shower, singing "Deck my balls with boughs of holly," feeling quite appropriately mad for the spirit of the day. He vowed he would be a glowing guest at the Bertelsen party. He would not let Marva get under his skin with the inevitable questions about where Marilyn was, and why, and whether she and Potter were still an item even though she'd gone away and left him on Christmas.

"Merry Christmas!" Marva said, giving Potter a mistletoe peck on the cheek, then peering around as if someone might be hiding behind him.

"Where's Marilyn?" she asked with concern.

"In Florida," Potter said, steeling himself with a studied smile.

"*Florida?* By herself?"

"With her mother. Her mother lives in Florida."

"Oh! How long is she there for?"

"Just a few days. Till the day after Christmas."

Marva took Potter by the arm, leading him toward the bar, obviously still concerned about Marilyn's absence and the possible hidden meanings of it.

"I'll have a Scotch and soda," Potter said to the man tending bar.

"We haven't seen you for ages," Marva said. "Why don't you and Marilyn come for dinner when she gets back from Florida—I mean, if you're still—"

"We're 'still,' " Potter said.

"It's a shame she had to leave you at Christmas," Marva said. "I'd have asked you for dinner, but it's been so long, I thought you and Marilyn probably had other plans. But *you* could come, Phil. I won't hear of you being alone on Christmas."

"Oh, thanks. But I can't."

"But what will you do? You can't just sit at home!"

"Oh, I'm not. I'm leaving early in the morning for Maine."

"*Maine?* All by yourself?"

"Well, I'll probably drive up by myself, but there's plenty of people coming to this—well, I don't know how you'd describe it," Potter said mysteriously, trying hard to improvise.

"What do you *mean?*"

"Well, this guy I used to work with in New York has a sort of estate on an island off the coast of Maine, and he's invited a whole bunch of people up—show people, you know—for a big bash on Christmas Day. You know."

"No, I don't think I do!"

"Well, you know how show people are. They like things a little—uh—*different*. And this place is so isolated, anyone can do whatever they want."

"Phil, it sounds like some kind of orgy or something!"

"Well, you never can tell."

"An orgy, on Christmas?"

"I didn't call it an orgy, Marva. You did."

"Yes, but—"

"Really, I don't think I'd better say any more about it," Potter said, trying to sound sincerely apologetic.

He moved off quickly into the guests, leaving Marva with her inflamed imagination. He nodded to the Harvard couple he'd met at the same dinner where he met Marilyn, waved to Max through circles that gathered aound him, avoided the rival bachelor Hartley Stanhope, and went toward a frail, nervous-looking woman who seemed to be shivering in a corner.

She turned out to be an old college friend of Marva's who taught Medieval history at Connect-

icut College for Women, and had come up to
Boston for the holidays, to stay at the Bertelsens'. Another of the lost sheep Marva had gathered to the fold. She was tiny, and prim, and
her mouth kept twitching. Potter found her appealing, and after her initial shyness wore off a
bit she displayed a sharp wit, skewering the Harvard contingent. She shared with Potter an aver-
sion to eggnog, preferring straight Scotch, which
he felt was an immediate bond between them.
Besides, beneath her hesitant and birdlike demeanor he sensed a sexual magnetism and responded to it, like picking up a wavelength.

He had just invited her to go out somewhere
for dinner with him, when he saw Marva motion-
ing wildly to him from across the room. Potter
excused himself, and went to Marva, who was
all in a lather.

"Do you know who that is you're over there in
the corner with?"

"Her name, she told me, is Melissa Vander-
bush. Isn't that right or is she really someone
else?"

"Phil, don't be funny now. Melissa is a very
sensitive person and she's had a terrible time
this year."

"I'm sorry to hear that."

"Her husband is in the Institute for Living."

"The Institute for Living?"

"In Hartford. You know. It's one of those ex-
clusive booby hatches. Like McLean's and Aus-
ten Riggs."

"That's too bad."

"Melissa's all at loose ends right now, and I feel responsible for her while she's here."

"Fine. What do you want me to do about it?"

"I don't want you to do *anything* about it. That's the whole point. She's very vulnerable right now, and she just isn't the type for a one-night stand."

"It sounds to me like that ought to be her own business. It certainly isn't yours."

"Phil, she's my friend."

"The trouble with you, Marva, is you think that being a friend of someone allows you the license to meddle in their private life and act like you were their shrink and their minister and their welfare worker. I'm sick and tired of it myself, and I imagine your friend is too, and if she isn't yet she will be. She's an adult and I'm an adult and what we do or don't do is no fucking business of yours!"

Marva backed away and put her hand to her cheek, as if she'd been struck, and for a moment looked at Potter with a frozen expression of horror while he stood, hot with his own fury, and she suddenly broke into tears and rushed to the stairs. From across the room Max saw her and followed. Potter went to Melissa and said, "Listen, let's get out of here."

They had dinner at Stella's and she sympathized with his explosion and assured him Marva'd get over it; she had been like that in college. . . .

They went back to Potter's and started necking as they wrestled out of their coats and without a word went straight to bed. Potter was excited but apprehensive. He kept thinking he had to be very gentle and careful and solicitous, as if she were a scared virgin. With that in mind he eased himself into her, cuddled her small shoulders close to his chest, and very slowly and discreetly began moving in and out of her, with the rhythm and feeling of a lullaby. Suddenly she cleared her throat, sighed, and in a voice that was deeper and steadier and firmer than he had till then heard come out of her mouth, she said, "Move it around, will ya?"

Potter did his best.

He woke in the night to find her gone, and, on the back of a cocktail napkin, in prim handwriting, a thank-you note, as if for an afternoon tea.

The silence of all the Sundays of the year was gathered into the great holy hush of Christmas Day. Outside, nothing stirred. The day was sharply cold, the sky grey and featureless. Potter woke around ten, straggled to the living room, and poked his head out the door, surreptitiously, looking up and down the empty town, trying to get the lay of the land. Later, armed bands of children would make small sorties into the street and over the frozen yards, menacing strangers with shiny pearl-handled revolvers and glistening M-16's, bright new bazookas and bows and arrows. The greatest supplier of arms in the

world had made his annual distribution of wea-
ponry the night before, bestowing on eager little
children replicas of every instrument of death
devised by man from the hatchet to the armed
helicopter. Peace on Earth! Bang-bang, you're
dead!

Potter closed the door, drew the blinds, and
went in the kitchen to make a cup of instant coffee that he doused with Scotch. After he drank
it, he would call his parents. But first he had to
open their packages. He wished they hadn't sent
things this year. Opening presents by yourself
seemed like dancing alone in an empty room.

He got a steak knife to cut the heavy cord of
the outer wrappings, and, sitting on the floor,
tore open the box and ripped through its contents in a kind of controlled frenzy, wanting to
get it over with. There was a wide, striped tie
of a style he would never wear. A new Norelco
razor with a note that said "Try it." They knew
he always used a double-edged blade razor. A
desk set with a barometer inlaid in it. A barometer. Now he could tell if a hurricane was coming.

He stacked the gifts in a pile, and put them in
an empty bureau drawer in his bedroom. He
wadded up the bright wrapping paper, stuffed it
into the cardboard box, and put the box outside
by the garbage can. That part was over.

He poured a Scotch over ice, lit a cigarette,
and made the call.

Potter thanked his parents for the gifts. They

kidded about the electric razor. His father said
he shouldn't be so old-fashioned. Potter promised to try it.

His father thanked him for the leather comb
and brush set.

His mother thanked him for the elegant cologne, and the handsome appointment calendar.

They both thanked him for the box of bran-
died apricots sent from a gourmet store in Cambridge.

Potter assured them he was having Christmas
dinner that afternoon with a nice family.

His mother said he ought to call his sister, and
he assured her he would, as soon as he hung up.

As soon as he hung up, he made a new drink.
He was glad they hadn't asked about Jessica. He
was glad that they weren't the kind of parents
who focussed all their emotions on him, tried to
live their lives through him. They had their own
lives. His father, a long-time State Department
man, was now a Washington consultant to a
large manufacturing firm with many overseas
outlets. His mother was as socially active as ever, engrossed in benefit balls and worthy causes,
garden parties and afternoon teas. When Potter went into the theatre and vowed it would be
his career, his father did not protest, but rather
lost interest in him. His mother was excited for
a while by the possibility of the glamour that
might ensue, but when it became obvious that
such glory was not to be, she too lost interest.
Besides, they both had Sunny, his sister, who had

turned out more as they had hoped and expected. Sunny, who was four years younger than Potter but always seemed like his older sister to him, had married a brilliant Philadelphia lawyer and was the mother of three children. That took a lot of the pressure off Potter.

He loved his sister, but he didn't want to call her. Her husband thought Potter a ne'er-do-well and Potter in turn thought him an insufferable snob, but that was not the real issue with his sister. Sunny had believed in his theatre dream, and when he gave it up she was disillusioned, disappointed in him, in a way that no amount of pretense could cover over. Seeing one another made both of them sad, and so they rarely did. Each Christmas, she sent the standard picture of the growing kids; he in turn sent them presents and a United Nations Christmas card.

Those exchanges made, he didn't see the need to call.

He had done his Christmas duties. It was almost noon.

Potter packed a small suitcase with his toilet gear, a bottle of wine, a bottle of Scotch, a fresh shirt, socks and shorts, a brand new crossword puzzle magazine, paperback copies of the three James Bond books he had not yet read, a pack of playing cards, a pair of dice, a pound of corned beef and two dill pickles, a half-dozen onion rolls, a frozen Sara Lee cheesecake, and an LP album of Great Moments in Sports.

He put on his overcoat and a heavy scarf,

tossed the packed suitcase in the back seat of his car, gunned the motor, and set off to spend his Christmas.

He did not know a soul in Maine, and had no intention of going there. When he faced the dilemma of being alone on the big day, he recalled a friend in New York, a bachelor who proposed that all single people could solve the Christmas dilemma by going to the apartments of other single people in different cities; that way when someone asked what you did for Christmas, you could say "Oh, I went to Denver," while your friend in Denver could say he went to New York. Once in the apartment in the different city you could simply close the door, watch TV, or do whatever you wanted. No one would know, and it would sound as if you'd had a glamorous out-of-town holiday trip.

But Potter didn't want to spend the money to actually leave the city, so he'd asked Marilyn to leave him the key to her apartment.

There, behind locked doors and closed curtains, he spent the afternoon and evening of Christmas drinking, eating corned beef sandwiches and slices of Sara Lee cheesecake, doing crossword puzzles, playing solitaire, throwing dice, reading James Bond, listening to Great Moments in Sports, and successfully preventing any sight or sound of Christmas from creeping into his consciousness. A little after midnight, stuffed and soused, he sprawled across the bed. Like the marathon runner who falls across the finish line, he was proud of his accomplishment, deeply relieved, and totally exhausted. He would tell everyone he spent Christmas in Maine.

Potter had a shaker of martinis waiting for Marilyn when she got home from the Christmas visit with her mother, and she bolted the first one down like a soft drink.

"Trip was that bad, huh?" Potter asked.

"I don't even want to talk about it yet. Tell me about yourself, or someone else. Anything else."

Potter filled her in on the scene with Marva, saying he was sorry now that it happened and yet in a way he figured it was bound to come, sooner or later, the way Marva kept nosing into everything.

"She means well," Marilyn said. "I mean, after all, she's how we met. She's always taking in strays and fixing people up."

"Yeah, but then she wants to know every intimate detail about their relationship, as if that's her price for getting them together in the first place."

"Listen, there's worse things."

"I guess," Potter said.

Marilyn didn't feel up to cooking so they went to Felicia's, and after some wine and a soothing lasagna, Marilyn felt more relaxed and was able to talk about her trip.

"My mother wasn't so lonely after all," she reported.

"Hey, that's great. Isn't it?"

"Yeah. I suppose. It was sort of depressing, though. I didn't know whether to laugh or cry. She has to be in a wheelchair, but she has this boyfriend, two trailers down from her, and evidently they're having a torrid love affair."

"Well, that's encouraging. For all of us, I mean. How old is she?"

"I'm not really sure. She says she's sixty-three, but I know that's a lie for the benefit of the boyfriend, I guess, although I'm sure, he must be in his seventies. There's another old gal after him, too—it's a regular triangle. Mother was all upset because he'd taken the other old lady to church the Sunday before, but she evidently is winning because he took her and me to Christmas dinner."

"So, what's wrong with all that?"

"Just that it's the *same*—like it's the same crap you and I go through now, except it's done in wheelchairs in Florida, in trailer camps. I could picture you and me there in thirty years, hobbling and wheeling along in and out of bedrooms, getting pissed off because our lover went to church with a rival Senior Citizen."

"Jesus," Potter said, "I guess it never ends."

"Evidently not. As long as you can breathe and propel yourself from one bedroom to another."

Potter and Marilyn decided to go formal on New Year's Eve. He bought a ruffled shirt to go with his old tux, and she revitalized a long, green velvet gown she had worn for somebody's wedding. Though neither of the places they were invited required formal dress, they both agreed that getting all decked out would help lift their morale. Potter cited the precedent of those nineteenth-century British officers dressing in their finest white uniforms for cocktails in some Godforsaken outpost of empire. Chins up, stiff upper lips, all that sort of thing. Marilyn thought it a fine idea, and added to her outfit a pair of huge, dangling earrings that looked like Christmas tree baubles. Potter bought a bottle of some bargain domestic champagne for just him and Marilyn to begin the evening on, and she made up a batch of fancy hors d'oeuvres featuring cream cheese and caviar. Sitting on her couch, they grinned and clicked glasses.

"Here's to the New Year," Marilyn said, "in which both of us will find fulfillment beyond our wildest dreams."

"Nothing can go wrong," Potter said.

They giggled, and drank.

To further insure their having a good time while ushering in the New Year, Marilyn brought out a tiny white round pill for each of them.

"What is it?" Potter asked.

"It's the latest thing Dr. Shamleigh prescribed. To make me feel better."

"I mean what's it called?"

"Ritalin. It's an upper."

"That's a new one on me. There used to be a lot of Dex around in New York, PR people, show people. But I kind of got off it."

"It's hard to get now. They just passed some kind of law making it harder to get any kind of amphetamine."

"What's in this stuff, then?"

"God knows. All I know is, it's supposed to be the latest thing."

"The latest thing in uppers."

"Yeah."

"How do they make you feel?"

"Nervous," Marilyn said, "but nice."

"Anything with 'nice' in it, I'll try."

They each took a pill, and washed it down with champagne.

There was only punch at Dean Hardy's party. Potter was pissed off that there wasn't any real, untainted liquor. A hell of a note for New Year's Eve. Marilyn made him eat a lot of cheese fondue, even though he whispered to her he didn't like the stuff.

"It'll line your stomach," she hissed back forcefully. "Just eat it."

So Potter downed the runny goo trying to think positively: *I am lining my stomach.*

The party itself was—desultory. Mostly faculty members who had nowhere else to go. None of the Cambridge-Boston luminaries, not even the grunting Harvard history professor. Guy Hardy kept saying he was sure the Bertelsens would be there later on. Potter wondered if they might stay away to avoid a confrontation with him and Marva.

Communications Chairman Don R. Sample

was there, in his ubiquitous blue serge suit, casting his arid aura over everything. Potter spoke but tried to avoid getting entangled in conversation with him. He chatted for a while with Monica Thistlewaite, a large round lady who worked as a secretary in Admissions. She was of indeterminate age, though surely older than the sort of Alice-in-Wonderland outfits she always wore, with hair ribbons and fuzzy sweaters and plaid jumpers. She was friendly in a desperate sort of way that Potter found both appealing and frightening.

"The punch doesn't have much punch," she said.

"I'm afraid not. And tonight's the time it's most needed."

"It's always needed," Monica said, then gave a high, wild kind of giggle. Potter smiled. It was New Year's Eve all right; everyone on the edge of cracking.

The highlight of the occasion was Harriet Hardy spilling a meticulously arranged bowl of fruit salad. Harriet was obviously smashed, though it couldn't have been from the innocuous punch, pinkishly sweet and laden with bobbing strawberries.

Potter joined a few other gentlemen who had fallen to their knees in a gallant attempt to retrieve the pieces of fruit that had flown about the room, splaying over the carpet in what seemed to Potter marvelous abstract designs. He found himself grinning as he pushed himself to and fro on his knees, plucking stray chunks of grapefruit from the rug.

The Ritalin was working.

Harriet's condition made it even more delicate a bit of diplomacy for Potter to explain that they had to leave and go on to the party of a friend of Marilyn's who lived out in Lexington.

"It's not even time to sing 'Auld Lang Syne,' " Harriet protested when Potter said they had to be getting on, much as they wanted to stay.

"It's not New Year's Eve if you don't sing it," Harriet insisted.

Potter proposed they sing it right then. He could see no other way out.

"Oh, Jesus," Marilyn whispered.

"Should old acquaintance be forgot . . ."

Potter started, but no one joined him. Harriet began to cry. "It's too early," she sobbed.

"I'm sorry," Potter said.

Guy Hardy came to the rescue with bluff gregariousness, helping lead Potter and Marilyn to their coats, trying to avoid another crisis, holding Potter hard on the elbow, squeezing it in knowing camaraderie, wishing him a fine and prosperous New Year.

Walking down the block to the car, Potter and Marilyn heard the first isolated blasts of holiday horns.

"Oh, God," Marilyn sighed, "it's beginning."

"Courage," said Potter.

The car was like a freezing compartment. The fan that would eventually warm them

blew arctic air in their faces when Potter turned
the engine.

Marilyn's teeth started chattering. "Fuck," she
said.

"Courage."

"Where the hell did you get all this sudden
courage?"

"If I had to make a wild guess, I'd say it just
might be your Ritalin."

"Yeah. That helps."

Potter had been determined to drive, in order
to practice navigating the Boston suburbs, but
he hadn't yet mastered their intertwining mys-
teries. He got lost on the way to Lexington, and
couldn't find a gas station open. Finally he came
to a streetcorner phonebooth, and Marilyn, shivering and cursing under her breath, called her
friend to get further directions.

They finally got to the party a little past
eleven-thirty.

At least it was warm inside, and there was
real booze. There were crêpe paper streamers of
many hues, and bright red paper bells. In the living room a monster-sized TV showed Guy Lombardo emanating from his traditional stand at
the Waldorf Astoria. The dining room had been
cleared of furniture, and darkened for dancing,
with Frank Sinatra crooning from a stereo. Potter smiled at everyone, and got a huge tumbler
of Scotch for himself, and gin for Marilyn.

Couples gathered around the television to
laugh at the couples shown dancing to Guy

Lombardo in the Waldorf ballroom. It seemed to Potter that if the cameras were reversed, the couples at the Waldorf might as justifiably turn and laugh at the couples in this suburban living room who were laughing at them.

The great moment came. Midnight. The end of the year. Beginning of a new one. Potter looked around for Marilyn, and saw she was being expertly kissed by a tall, balding man of distinction. Potter shrugged, and started to sing, joining his voice with the others who weren't still kissing.

". . . I'll take a cup o' kindness yet, for—"

He felt a tap on his right shoulder.

He turned and saw a blonde woman smiling at him. Her eyes were wide and glazed.

"Happy New Year," she said.

Before Potter could return the greeting, the woman reached her hands up and clasped them behind his neck, her eyes closing as she moved her mouth onto his. Her tongue licked out and explored his teeth. After a moment, Potter pulled away and looked at the woman, to make sure whether he had ever seen her before. Maybe she was some long lost girl of his youth whom fate had catapulted into his arms as a special treat for this New Year's Eve.

"Hi," she said.

He had never seen her in his life.

"Hello. I'm Phil Potter."

She shook his hand. "Let's dance, Phil."

She led him into the darkened dining room.

The host had rigged up a kind of homemade
light show for the dancing room, and balls of
different colors floated across the walls. Potter
and the woman clasped one another and began
tilting to the music, not really dancing, just
swaying in place. Potter had a full-fledged erection. He nibbled at the lady's ear lobe, and said,
"I didn't catch your name."

"I didn't say it."

"Is it a secret?"

"It's Carol."

"Carol."

She pressed into him harder, swaying, and
whisper-singing along with the music, "I get
along without you verree well . . ."

Potter felt he had been transported back to his
college fraternity game room. Dancing to Sinatra
and having a hard-on. And he was thirty-four
years old. He had thought it would be different.
He didn't know how or why it should be, he had
just assumed it. As in so many cases, he was
wrong.

He went to get himself and Carol another
drink, and they sat down together on a velvet
love seat in the dancing room. Potter noticed
Marilyn drift in with the balding man of distinction. He exchanged winks with her, through a
green ball of color.

Carol rubbed her hand along his leg.

"I like you, Carol."

"I can tell," she said, running her fingers
lightly over the top of his taut prick.

"Where do you live?" he asked her.

"Where do *you* live?"

"*I'm* not coy," he said. "I live at Thirty-four Ellery Street, Cambridge. Ground floor, front apartment."

"Write it down for me, will you?"

"Sure. But where do *you* live?"

"Out in the sticks," she said.

"Which sticks?"

"Suburban sticks."

"There's a lot of them."

"They're pretty much the same."

"Well, I don't know about that."

"You don't? Well, I'll tell you sometime, Phil."

"When?"

"Wednesday. Any Wednesday."

"Only Wednesday?"

"What's wrong with Wednesday?"

"Nothing. Jesus. Wednesday is a fine time."

"Write it down for me. Where you live. Now, before we forget."

Potter went to the bathroom, and wrote down his name, address and phone number on the back of an old parking lot stub. He handed it to her and she stuck it down her cleavage, without looking at it. Just like in an old movie.

They danced again, and she undulated against him. He wondered if he could maneuver her up to some empty bedroom. But he didn't know the house, or the host and hostess, and he dismissed it as too dangerous. He didn't want a scene. He wondered how Marilyn was doing with her man of distinction. They weren't in the dancing room anymore. Potter felt a light tap on his shoulder, like the gesture of someone who wanted to cut in.

"Sorry," the man said.

Potter broke away, smiling awkwardly. "Quite all right," he said.

Carol smiled at the man and asked if he wanted to dance.

"I want to go home," he said.

"Do we have to?" she asked. "This early?"

"It's late enough," the man said firmly.

Oh, shit, Potter thought, standing up straight and trying to collect himself, trying to look casual and friendly. The last thing he wanted was a New Year's Eve brawl with some chick's jealous date.

"I'll get our coats," the man said, and left the room.

Carol leaned up against Potter and kissed him, but he gently pushed her away. "You better go on with your date," he said.

"Oh, him," Carol said. "He's not my date."

"Then how come you have to go home with him?" Potter asked.

Carol shrugged. "Tradition," she said.

"What kind of 'tradition'?"

"The regular kind. He's my husband."

"Oh," said Potter, backing away from her. "Well, that makes sense, then."

Carol smiled. "Does it?" she asked.

It turned out that Potter guessed right about

Marilyn's bald guy being a man of distinction. When they got back to her place she told him the man was a leading psychiatrist in New York City. Furthermore, he had a wife and four children there. Furthermore, he had a date with Marilyn and she intended to keep it. He was charming and brilliant and wealthy.

"And married," Potter said.

"And bored with his wife," Marilyn said.

Potter told her about Carol, who was evidently bored with her husband.

"Well," said Marilyn brightly, "we did pretty good. We've both got dates for the New Year."

"Yeah, but with married people."

Marilyn, weaving, shucked off her gown. "Don't knock it," she said.

"Shit. It just means trouble."

Marilyn burped, unhooked her bra, and turned to Potter with a look of tired but firm conviction.

"Trouble," she said, "is better than nothing."

PART FOUR

1

Potter got a call from Carol at four on Wednesday afternoon.

"Would you like to meet me?" she asked.

"I thought you were coming to my place."

"I think I'd like it better if we met. Someplace. To have a drink."

Potter took a deep breath. He wondered if he now was going to have to talk himself into something that he thought was already agreed upon. This seeming change of the ground rules annoyed him, but still, he was curious. Besides, he had nothing better to do, and he'd been looking forward to the event. If it led to trouble, maybe Marilyn was right, that trouble was "better."

Than nothing.

That was even more likely to kill you than an angry husband.

Nothing.

"OK," he said. "Wherever you say."

It was a sort of cocktail lounge on top of the Wursthaus restaurant in Cambridge. He had often been to the Wursthaus, but he never knew it had this little cocktail lounge overhead. Not too dark, not too light, not too populated. He wondered if Carol went there often. On Wednesdays.

"I guess I was pretty drunk," she said. "When we met."

Jesus. He wondered if the whole thing was going to be an apology, an explanation of an embarrassing misunderstanding.

"I guess we both were," Potter said.

She ordered a daiquiri. He ordered a double Scotch on the rocks.

She was wearing a grey suit, and proper pearl earrings. She looked as if she were on her way to some kind of legal meeting.

"I have three children," she said.

"Oh?"

"Two girls, twins. And a boy."

He didn't know how he was supposed to react to this information.

"That must be nice," he said.

"Sometimes."

The drinks came, and she looked down into hers for a while, as if it might reveal something.

"Do I look that old?" she asked.

"No," Potter said quickly. "How old do you mean?"

"To have three children."

"Jesus, you could be twenty for all I know. A person twenty could have three children. Especially if two were twins."

He figured she must be somewhere in her early thirties.

"Thanks," she said.

He didn't want to say "You're welcome," so he said nothing and took a swig of his drink.

"I said Wednesday because that's when my husband goes to Providence. He teaches an art course there. On Wednesday and Thursday. But Thursdays I have dance class."

"So that leaves Wednesdays."

"Yes," she said, "that leaves Wednesdays."

She started sipping her daiquiri then, and telling how her husband had a girl he stayed with in Providence, one of his art students, and how for the children's sake they had agreed not to get a divorce, and not to ask questions of one another's private life. They didn't talk much about anything anymore, and didn't sleep together anymore, and yet they weren't angry toward each other. They just didn't feel anything, one way or other.

With the second daiquiri she told how he once had dreamed of going to New York and making it as a painter and then he got her pregnant and it was twins for godsake and he took that as a sign and got a job as a commercial artist and when she urged him to keep up his real work, the work that he loved, he got the part-time job teaching at the Rhode Island School of Design, in Providence. After he got the part-time job he got the studio, and after he got the studio he got the girl to go in it.

"I still like marriage, though," she said. "In the ideal. But I guess it never happens there—in the ideal."

"Not many things do," Potter said.

She smiled, and he liked her.

They each had two more drinks, and Potter asked if she'd like to have dinner. She looked very tired.

"No thanks," she said, "I don't have time for dinner."

"Well, can I take you someplace then?"

He meant to her car or a bus or a train, however she was going home.

"How about your place?" she asked.

Afterward, he took her in to Boston, to the underground parking garage beneath the Commons, where she'd left her car. They squeezed hands, and didn't say anything.

That Saturday, he got a letter from her. It was on pale blue stationery, with her married name and address engraved on the back of the envelope. He opened it, apprehensively, wondering if she was going to cause trouble after all, wanted to get involved in some big, complicated affair, or was angry or sorry about what happened, or wanted to blame him or her, or what. Before he took the letter out of the envelope he poured himself a drink. He sat down on the couch, and pulled from the envelope the single piece of blue paper, bordered in white. It said:

Dear Phil,
     It was beautiful beautiful beautiful beautiful beautiful beautiful beautiful . . .

The beautifuls covered both pages.

Potter showed the letter to Marilyn.

"It's beautiful," she said, smiling. "What are you going to do about it?"

"Nothing, probably."

"Why not?"

"I don't know. It just doesn't seem like that kind of thing."

"You aren't going to see her again next Wednesday?"

"I doubt it."

"*Why?*"

"I want to stop while I'm ahead, maybe. While everything is beautiful."

"Is that all?"

"I don't know. I really don't know. I just don't want to go on with it."

Marilyn sighed, then shrugged. "Men," she said.

"Don't 'men' me," Potter said.

"I'm sorry. Besides, I shouldn't complain about men right now. I found myself a terrific one."

"The distinguished shrink. How did it go?"

"He stayed over in Boston two extra nights. With me."

"And?"

"And he wants me to go away with him."

"How far away?"

"The Virgin Islands."

"Great. You'll probably have a good time."

"I want more than that."

"How much more than that?"

"Marriage."

"Come on."

"I'm serious."

"But why? Why a married guy who has a family?"

"Well, let's see. We had beautiful sex. And a wonderful time. He's warm, and wise, and he's wealthy. He's been married sixteen years, and he's bored with his wife. He hasn't slept with her for several years."

Potter wondered if any husband in America was sleeping with his wife.

Marilyn stood up and started walking around the couch. "Besides," she said, "why the hell shouldn't *I* have a townhouse on the Upper East Side, and a summer house on Martha's Vineyard? And servants, and money, and clothes, and —and—"

She turned around to face Potter, with tears coursing down her cheeks. "And," she said sobbing, "four children!"

Potter put his arms around her, held her tightly as she cried, and rubbed the back of her neck.

"I know," he said, "I know."

He got her to take a shower, and a tranquilizer. He gave her a backrub with Isopropyl, and took her to dinner at the Athens Olympia. She ate hearty, consuming a leg of lamb and rice and a Greek salad, and two baklavas for dessert. When they got back to her place they had brandy and sodas, and Marilyn seemed in good spirits again. She talked of the coming trip to the Virgin Islands, of how she had always wanted to go away like that in the winter to some sunny place. Then she fell silent.

"What is it?" Potter asked after a while. "What are you thinking about?"

"The Game," she said.

"What game?"

"The one we all play. With each other. Me and Herb, even though we just met. You and that woman. The woman you aren't going to see next Wednesday."

"What about her?"

"I was thinking about that letter she wrote you, the one with all the 'beautifuls.' "

"Yes?"

"She wrote the wrong letter."

"What do you mean?"

"If she wanted to see you again, she should have written, 'Dear Phil, it was terrible, terrible, terrible, terrible, terrible, terrible . . .' "

"Shit," said Potter, but he couldn't help smiling a little.

"Don't give me that," Marilyn said. "I'm right."

Potter didn't say anything. He didn't move. Without meaning to, he realized he was holding his breath, trying not to think.

Marilyn leaned toward him and spoke, quietly, insistently: "I'm right," she said. "Aren't I right? Wouldn't you have dragged your ass all over New England to see her again? If she'd written it was terrible, terrible, terrible?"

"Shut up, goddamn it!"

He slapped her.

She drew back, holding her hands on her face, her eyes wide and bright and wild with fright, not of what he would do, but of what she understood from what he did.

Potter shook his head violently, as if trying to come out of a spell. "I'm sorry," he said.

Neither of them spoke for a long time, and finally Potter placed his hand on top of hers and, without looking into her eyes, spoke to her very quietly.

"You're right, of course. It's always The Game. And you have to play it with your wonderful Doctor if you really want to get him."

"I know, I know, but I hate it. I just want to tell him I love him, and be able to enjoy it."

"That'll be the end of it."

"I know, damnit, but it's so hard, to be coy and scheming and say things you don't mean and keep thinking all the time about keeping him hooked, unsure—and thinking up new strategies and all of it. It's all so hard."

"Listen," Potter said. "I'll help you. I'll be—like an advisor."

Marilyn thought for a moment. "OK," she said. "I'll try anything."

"OK. It's a deal."

"A deal."

They shook on it.

The new issue of *Time* magazine had a picture of actress Ali MacGraw on the cover, and a story on "The Return to Romance," which explained how the fantastic success of *Love Story* as a book and now as a movie indicated a vast movement among the populace away from cynicism and toward sentiment. Potter read it with special care, not only because of his natural interest in the subject, but because he had to teach it.

Before the vacation break he assigned his Communications students to buy the issue of *Time* that appeared the week classes resumed, and read whatever happened to be the cover story. The exercise was part of the course's attempt to make students conscious of the style and techniques of persuasion used by the different news and information media.

"All I know is, it made me cry," Miss Korsky said.

"You'd cry at anything," Mr. Stevenson said.

"Wait a minute," Potter said. "Wait a minute. Miss Korsky, you mean to say the article in *Time* made you cry?"

"No, no. The movie. *Love Story.*"

"I don't see what's so romantic about dying of cancer," Mr. Stevenson said.

"Wait," Potter said, "we're not discussing the movie of *Love Story*. I mean we're not supposed to be. We're supposed to analyze the article in *Time.*"

"I think it's right," someone said from the back of the room.

Right. Wrong. Good. Bad. Pass. Fail. Potter

had hoped for a more detailed analysis. How
could he wrench from the class some subtlety
of observation, make them see some shades of
distinction?

"Let's look at the article itself," he said. "Let's
try to see how it moves from describing the success of *Love Story* to more general assumptions
about the society."

The class went blank and silent for a moment,
all heads downturned toward the magazine.
Pages riffled. Someone blew his nose. Potter
found himself making an almost audible grunt,
as if pulling oars, trying to psychically pull some
specific responses from them.

"Now listen to this," Potter said, *"carefully.
Time* quotes this NYU professor who says, 'The
mood today, particularly on campus, is toward
personal relationships rather than politics, love
rather than action. Not by accident does this
mood coincide with the Nixon era.' "

A roomful of faces stared at Potter, blank or
quizzical.

"Well," he said, a note of desperation beginning to creep into his voice, "do you agree with
that? You're students. He's talking about *your*
mood. Is he right? Do you feel that way?"

"What does he mean, 'love rather than action'?" Miss Korsky asked.

"Good point!" said Potter, pouncing gratefully on anything specific.

"What do *you* think he means?" Potter asked,
proud of his Socratic technique.

"I don't know."

"Try," Potter pleaded.

Miss Korsky, responding to Potter's need, tried. "Well," she said, "I'm not sure what *he* means, but I don't agree. I mean, it sounds like you have to choose between love and action, like you can't have both. A lot of actions are done out of love. Aren't they?"

"Yes, absolutely," Potter said beaming. "I think the statement is a contradiction. You see, I want you to be aware of what these articles say—don't just take them in but *question* them, decide for yourself how valid the statements are."

Potter made a kind of game out of looking for other contradictions in the article and the class got into the spirit of it, actually interested, actually—Potter hoped—learning something.

Toward the end of the hour, Mr. Halligan even found what he felt was a contradiction in the caption of one of the color photos that accompanied the article. The photo was of the actress Sarah Miles, demurely dressed and posed in a pastoral scene. Miss Miles was quoted as saying, "I'm a romantic to the end. I think people are sick and tired of all the sex stuff. They want a story. Life is so hard to live anyway."

"I don't think it follows," Halligan said. "I mean to say that people are tired of sex and life is hard anyway. Wouldn't it be harder if they didn't have sex?"

The class giggled, and Potter smiled.

"I guess so," Potter said, and, surprising himself, added, "I'm not really sure anymore."

Potter counted the class a success; it had even made the teacher think.

2

Gafferty had something on his mind, something
he wanted to discuss in private. When Potter returned from his afternoon seminar Gafferty was
waiting in his office, twiddling his fingers behind
his back and examining the shelves of textbooks
with feigned interest, as if he hadn't seen them a
thousand times. He suggested they take a stroll
over to Jake Wirth's. It wouldn't be crowded
now, they could doubtless have a booth to themselves.

On the way out of the building they ran into
Ed Shell, who asked if he could join them for a
beer. Gafferty made an animated apology, saying
right now he had a little business to discuss with
Potter, but by all means, without fail, the three
of them had to go together for a real drinking
session sometime, sometime soon. Shell, obviously
miffed, said "Sure, sure," and went off brooding
down the hall.

Potter and Gafferty walked across the Commons purposefully, not speaking, the weight of
whatever was Gafferty's private business holding
them silent. It was brutally cold, and the sky

had a dark, purplish cast. The aura of the afternoon was Icelandic.

They entered Jake Wirth's puffing and stomping and rubbing their hands, and Gafferty headed for a booth. There was an old man eating knockwurst, and a couple of others sipping shells of pale gold beer, but otherwise the place was deserted. An ancient waiter in a frayed tux took their orders for steins of dark, and Gafferty shifted his bulk around in the booth, as if trying to burrow into a solid position.

Potter waited.

"The thing of it is," Gafferty said, "I'd like to use your apartment sometime."

"My apartment?"

"Sometime, that is, when you wouldn't ordinarily be there. I mean, I don't want you to have to go out and sit in some bar just on my account, but if there's some particular time, an hour or so, when you wouldn't be being there anyway and it wouldn't be inconveniencing anything for me to—uh, have the use of it, at such a time."

"Hell, man, you can use my apartment any time you want. You know, it isn't any luxury pad or anything, it's just an ordinary apartment. It's a mess most of the time, but Christ, yes, of course you can use it."

"No luxury?" Gafferty laughed. "Ah, man, it'll be luxury indeed compared to the little office I have at Gilpen, with the door locked but people passing by it down the hall and occasionally someone pounding and pressing their face against the frosted glass, trying to squint through it. Luxury? Ah, I presume you've some kind of bed, and even a pallet on the floor is luxury compared with the cold steel desk."

"Desk?" Potter asked, not getting the picture, "you sleep on your desk?"

He imagined poor Gafferty, exhausted from staying up till all hours doing battle with his thesis, maybe from waking in the night to the bawling of little kids, rising at dawn to drive in to Boston, teaching his classes, counseling his students, preparing lectures, grading tests, and finally, sapped of all strength and lightheaded from lack of sleep, sprawling over the hard, unyielding surface of his long grey desk, dozing off fitfully, only to be jolted awake by the pounding fists of impatient students.

"Not sleep, exactly," Gafferty said. "Ah, Phil, you see, the matter is—damnit, man, I've a girl."

Potter sat for a moment with his mouth dumbly open and then started laughing, not at Gafferty or the news that he had a girlfriend, but at his own obtuseness. A grown man asks to use his apartment and he thinks the poor bastard wants to take a nap.

"Sure, I know, it's a comical thing, a man in my circumstances, mind you I don't want to change my circumstances, but—"

"No, no, I'm not laughing at you. It's me. I'm a fool."

"Nothing of it, you only assumed that I was happy with my wife and family, and mind you, that is a *correct* assumption, I love them all, wife and kids, but after a time—"

"Jesus, man. You don't have to explain. Or least of all, apologize. Listen, you can use my place whenever you want."

"Oh, it's a hell of a thing to ask, I know, but I can't afford the price of a proper hotel room, and my girl—well, she lives with her parents. More's the shame. A student, of course. The old, old story. Me the dirty old man, you know, the leering professor, and a young girl—"

"Cut it out," said Potter. "If you want to confess, see a Priest. Jesus. You're only human."

"There's those that would think otherwise," Gafferty said, scratching madly at his head in a kind of anguish.

"Fuck them. Listen. You can use my place whenever you want. Just let me know in advance. Sometimes I spend the night at Marilyn's, and you could stay all night at my place. Or even—hey!"

"What?"

"Marilyn's going away for the weekend. She'll probably leave me the key, and I can stay at her place. You could have my apartment for the weekend."

"*Weekend*," Gafferty whispered. "My God, man, that's an eternity."

Potter smiled, happy to have the power to grant such a miracle to a friend. "It's yours," he said.

Marilyn told her boss that her mother was ill in Florida and got a four-day weekend from her office so she could fly to the Virgin Islands for the tryst with her new married man shrink-lover. Potter went shopping with her and picked out a new bikini that Marilyn thought was outrageous but which he assured her was just the ticket. He also advised that she get a pair of tiny-heeled black mules with dainty puffs of feather on the toes.

"Why do I have to have them?" she asked.

"Because," said Potter, "you can't go slinking around the bedroom in your old red sweatsocks."

"OK, if you say so."

"I say so."

Potter took her to the airport, and they arrived early enough to have a drink before boarding time.

Marilyn ordered an extra dry martini straight up, and some of the mercury-colored liquid drooled out over the rim of the long-stemmed glass as she brought it, trembling, to her lips.

"Relax," Potter said. "Be cool."

"I'm a nervous wreck."

"Well, then you'll wreck the whole thing. Try to see it as a wild time, leading to nothing else. A thing in itself. Then it *will* possibly lead to more. If you go down thinking about Future Plans, you'll blow the whole thing."

"OK. I know."

"And you've got to stop shaking."

"I know—oh, shit!" she grabbed for her purse, and started thrashing frantically through its contents.

"Don't tell me you forgot your pills."

"Not *those* pills, damnit. My Valium."

"Oh, no."

Suddenly she plucked a small bottle out, clutching it gratefully. "Thank God," she said.

Potter smiled. "Now you'll be tranquil."

She unscrewed the top of the bottle, slipped a small yellow tablet onto her tongue, and swallowed.

"Don't worry," said Potter. "You'll knock 'im dead."

"Well," said Marilyn, "I don't want *that*. Let's just say—delirious."

"Atta way, babe. Now you're getting it."

"You think?"

"Absolutely."

Under the table, he crossed his fingers for her.

Potter got up early the next morning, put out the garbage, washed the dishes, straightened up the worst of the debris, and put clean sheets on the bed. He hadn't spent as much time tidying up the apartment since the Sunday he had Marilyn over for the omelettes. He felt almost as much anticipatory pleasure in the thought of Gafferty's illicit weekend there as if it were an affair of his own.

He had packed a small valise to take to Marilyn's apartment for the weekend, where he had no plans more passionate than grading the final tests of his two Communications classes. He had no dates or invitations to dinners or parties, and decided it would be a good time to get the grading out of the way. He also promised himself he would do a better job on the finals than he did on mid-terms, which he graded far into the evening while drinking, later realizing that scores and comments grew higher in proportion to the higher he became himself. This time he vowed every paper would be graded under the same harsh and equal stimulus of hot black coffee.

He drove into Gilpen to pick up the blue books he had stacked on the desk in his office, and, while retrieving them, he suddenly laughed out loud, thinking of Gafferty and the girl humping away on one of those desks. He started stuffing the blue books into his valise, giggling to himself, imagining the face of Dean Guy M. Hardy, Jr., if he were to ever walk in on such a scene, when suddenly, in mid-giggle, Potter stopped frozen. A new and horrendous thought flared in his mind.

What if on just such a desk as this the dastardly cad Gafferty had been humping away on one of Potters own favorite students, one of those special girls for whom he felt a mixture of nobly subdued lust and virtuous protectiveness? Gafferty had only said the girl was a student, he hadn't said *what* student.

What if Gafferty was fucking Miss Korsky? The innocent Rosemary Korsky! Or maybe Miss Linnett, Amanda Linnett, the wispy, ethereal, fragile, long-haired blonde who made his second Communications section a joy to instruct on the scattered occasions when she chose to attend? What if, even now, that dirty old man Gafferty was mounting one of those angels of Potter's imagination, on the clean sheets of Potter's own bed? He felt his cheeks burning, and his heart knocked against his chest like a Nazi pounding on a victim's door.

Potter slumped down in his chair, pulled open the bottom desk drawer and grabbed the pint of Scotch, put it to his mouth with trembling hands and gulped a fiery swig. He breathed out, belched, and slammed the bottle on the top of the desk.

Gafferty, you sonofabitch.

At school Monday, Gafferty looked wan but glowing, like a man who has come back tired but happy from a strenuous vacation. Potter had gone back to his apartment late Sunday night and found the key under the mat, as prearranged. There were no traces of Gafferty's frolic with his student lover, except for a certain scent to the sheets, a musky kind of perfume. After Potter's first Communications section Miss Korsky had come up to ask him a question and he found himself leaning close to her and inhaling deeply, seeing if possibly the scent of the sheets matched her own, but he couldn't really tell. In his second section, he looked for Miss Linnett with more eagerness than usual, but she didn't appear. He wondered if perhaps she had been so exhausted from a weekend of sexual cavorting with Gafferty that she couldn't drag herself to class. But her absence probably meant nothing, she cut classes so often.

Potter had hoped to have a drink alone with Gafferty and perhaps pick up some clue to the identity of his girlfriend, but just as they were debating where to go Ed Shell trapped them again, and it was impossible this time to slough him off without permanently injuring his feelings.

Gafferty drove them into Cambridge and at Shell's suggestion they went to Cronin's, an old-style collegiate bar-restaurant, the type with fading pennants on the wall. Potter found it depressing, but kept his mouth shut. Shell related a complex story about one of his scripts that might get financial backing from a group of young bankers in Tallahassee, Florida, who wanted to get into movie production, but Potter just nodded, all the time catching glimpses of Gafferty's face, trying to read something in it. Finally, Shell excused himself to go take a piss, and Potter asked quickly, "How was the weekend?"

"Glorious," Gafferty said, rolling the word around as if tasting it. "Glorious."

"The place was OK? You find everything you needed?"

Gafferty joined the thumb and forefinger of his right hand into the "OK" sign, and twisted his face into a gigantic wink.

You lecherous bastard, Potter thought.

"Terrific," he said. "Listen, anytime you and —uh—your girl—"

He let that hang for a moment, in the slim hope that Gafferty would fill in her name, but the red-faced old fucker just kept staring at Potter with his shit-eating grin, so Potter continued, pretending he hadn't intended at all to worm out the girl's identity: "Anytime you and she want to use the place, just give me a little notice."

"You're a friend in need, for sure, man."

Potter was tempted to just blurt out the question—*who the hell is it, what's the name of this student you've been fucking on your office desk and in my own bed*—but part of his personal code of honor dictated that you didn't ask people such things, whether they were men or women, you didn't pry into matters that were not your business unless the other person volunteered the information. If he came right out and asked he'd be as bad as Marva Bertelsen.

Shell returned, and asked if Potter and Gafferty would like to come with him to a meeting of what he implied was a small, elite, highly, intellectual group of film buffs who met at one of the Harvard houses on Monday nights and watched a private screening of a movie that they then discussed. Gafferty said he had to be home for dinner or there'd be a big commotion, and he gave a secret, knowing look to Potter. Potter gave a quick wink back, as if in chummy collaborative approval.

Marilyn wouldn't be getting in till the next day, and since he had nothing on for the evening Potter said he'd go with Shell to the film buff meeting. Potter asked if it was all right to stop in Harvard Square so he could pick up a bottle of Scotch to take along, if the buffs wouldn't mind that.

"Sure, anything you like. It's all very casual."

The more that Shell stressed the casual nature of the thing, the more Potter realized what a big deal it was for him. Just getting together with some of the gang over at Harvard. What ho. Jolly good. Nothing to it.

Potter bought a fifth of Black and White, which he'd contribute to the group. He didn't like seeing any kind of movie without being able to have a drink in his hand, and alcohol became all the more imperative if he was to sit through one of those arty jobs, probably foreign with subtitles or foreign and dubbed and all out of synch.

Much to his surprise, the movie being shown was an American comedy of the 1930s with Cary Grant and Katharine Hepburn. He and Shell arrived just after it had started, and sat down on the floor near the door. There were about a dozen people in the room, some on chairs or a couch, a few others cross-legged on the floor. Potter slipped into the kitchen, which fortunately was lighted, and made his necessary drink.

The plot of the movie revolved around a leopard, called Baby. It was quite funny, and the in-

tellectual audience guffawed and snickered and
giggled just like a regular Saturday Matinee
crowd at the Bijou. When the lights went on
there was even a bowl of popcorn passed around,
and beers were flipped open.

Potter soon learned, however, that this seeming light comedy bore historical and artistic implications far beyond its humor and entertainment value. It was *Bringing Up Baby,* directed
by Howard Hawks, who had been rediscovered
as one of the foremost directors. Hawks was
heavy now, and his films thus merited the kind
of dissection and analysis that literary critics
lavished on the *Duino Elegies.* Lighting was discussed, and camera angles, editing, sound ef-
fects, dialogue. There was even a heated debate over whether the two leopards in the movie
were played by the same leopard, or by different
leopards. The leopard or leopards came in for
praise, and someone realized that it was probably
the trainer who deserved the credit for the leopard performance.

"I wonder," someone asked, "when the first
animal trainer came to Hollywood."

"That would be a fascinating line of research," said the host, a guy named Chip Strider,
who was Senior Tutor of this particular Harvard house.

Potter could envision it: a whole Ph.D. thesis
on the first animal trainer who came to Hollywood, and his influence on the art of the film.
Potter had consumed three good Scotches, and

he could not resist raising his hand.

"Actually," he said, "the first animal trainer who came to Hollywood was Joseph R. Scrotz, a Russian émigré."

All heads turned toward him, in respectful attention. He couldn't just say "Hey, fellas, I was only kidding." He had to carry it on.

"Scrotz," he said, "had worked throughout Europe with the old Budapest Circus, but came to this country for political reasons after the 1917 Revolution, and signed with Ringling Brothers. He was retained by Von Stroheim to work on a silent version of Kipling's *Mowgli,* which was never released, but his value was obvious and he stayed on with the old Mecca studio."

Ed Shell was surprised, and the others were impressed by Potter's apparent familiarity with arcane film history. Chip Strider said he *must* come to dinner at the House sometime.

When Marilyn returned from her Virgin Island idyll, she was nicely tanned, and perceptibly radiant—more so than Potter had ever seen her. She gave him a hug, and a bottle of Appleton Brothers Rum. "Herb said this was the best," she explained.

"It must be then. Here—let's break it open. From the way you look, we can celebrate."

They settled down on her couch with the rum Herb said was the best, and Marilyn purred her account of the wonderful beach house where they stayed in St. Thomas, the gourmet meals in town, the moonlight walks at the edge of the surf, frozen daiquiris for breakfast, fucking that matched the mood and the scenery, hand-in-hand rapport, sharing the same kind of humor and pleasures, swimming in the waves, peaceful silences, watching the great liners dock on their winter cruises.

"But that wasn't the best thing," she said.

"Oh?"

Marilyn grinned, poked a finger in her drink, and rolled her tongue on it, licking at the rum. "He mentioned it," she said. "I never brought it up. He did."

"It?"

"Marriage."

"He asked you to marry him?"

"I didn't say that. I said he brought it up. Marriage."

"How do you mean, 'brought it up'? In general? A discourse on the future of the institution?"

"He said he'd give anything to be able to marry me,"

"He might have to, when he's finished with alimony and child support."

"He's aware of all that. It will be difficult, naturally. It will take some doing. And, of course, some time."

"Of course. Did he say how much?"

"You said I shouldn't press him. I just let him talk."

"OK, fine. When do you see him again?"

"Next weekend."

"How? Where?"

"He wants me to come down to New York. He'll get me a hotel room, and be there with me as often as he can get away, without anything looking suspicious."

"Mmmm. He's footing the bill, of course."

Marilyn stretched, smiled, and said, "Of course."

"Mmmm," Potter said. "So far, so good."

"No," she said. "So marvelous."

"I stand corrected."

"Phil?"

"Yes?"

"What do you think my chances are? Realistically?"

"Goddamn it, I'm not Jimmy the Greek and I'm not making odds on people's lives!"

His anger was not so much because of the question as because of his fear that the odds on Marilyn's dream would not be reassuringly high.

3

"The odds are," Gafferty said, "that the first party is for the losers, guys like me who don't have their Ph.D."

"That's ridiculous," Potter said, "Ed and I are invited to the second party and neither of us have our Ph.D."

"Ah!" Gafferty whispered, leaning forward, "but Dean Hardy no doubt thinks you both have the capability and drive to go on and eventually *get* the degree, even though you don't have it yet!"

"Wait a minute," Shell said, "if the first party is for the losers, why would they be invited *first*? If you ask me, the second party is for the people the Dean considers second-rate."

"No, no," Gafferty argued, "he wants to have the party for the losers first so he can get it out of the way, fulfill his obligation, and then be free to enjoy entertaining the people he likes at the second party."

Hunched over a small table in the corner of the school cafeteria, Potter, Gafferty, and Shell

were chainsmoking, nervously dropping unfinished cigarettes into half-filled styrofoam cups of
coffee grown cold, and joining in the general
speculation that was sweeping the faculty about
the meaning of the two separate cocktail parties
Dean Hardy was holding during the semester
break. Like Kremlinologists, the teachers analyzed the hidden meanings of all that the Dean
did and said, and special significance was placed
on the invitation lists of his social functions, on
the assumption that these provided pertinent
clues to who was In and who Out. The fact that
over the break he was giving *two* parties, inviting
all faculty members to his home, but on separate
nights, had given rise to a frenzied examination
of the implications of which people were attending which party.

Much to the chagrin of the avid theorists, it
was casually pointed out by someone from the
science department that the guest list of the
first party was made up of all those faculty members whose last names began with A-L, while the
second list consisted of those from M-Z.

Potter asked Marilyn to come to the party with
him, though he warned her it wasn't likely to be
a lot of laughs; he was asking her as a friend to
give him support and comfort in getting through
it. With her own secret love affair going full
force, Marilyn was in a good mood and happy to
oblige.

The party was pretty much as Potter imagined
it would be, with one significant surprise. He

knew it almost as soon as he entered the living room; there was someone out of the routine faculty context. He picked up the presence of the unidentified person without even looking at her, like a blip on a radar screen. Somewhere in a corner of the room, in a corner of his vision. He didn't even look right away. He preferred to wait, and savor the suspense.

"Yes," he said, grinning in agreement with whatever it was Harriet Hardy had gushed at him. He hoped it was something he was supposed to agree with. He got a cutglass cup of punch for himself and Marilyn, feeling some of it trickle stickily down his hand as he ladled it out, trying to avoid the armada of floating strawberries. It was another one of *those* kinds of parties.

Blip.

The girl had glossy brown hair that curled under and up just at her neckline, and she wore a silver bar in it, the way girls used to do. The plain black dress she wore with a simple silver pin was the sort of ornament Potter associated with girls of his own era who were considered "sophisticated." She tilted her chin up as she exhaled from her cigarette, as if she had learned to smoke by watching old Debutante movies.

"She's cute, isn't she," Marilyn whispered.

Potter felt himself blushing. "Huh? Who?"

"The girlie," Marilyn said.

"Jesus, have you started reading my mind? I've hardly even looked at her."

"Reading your mind on occasions like this is like watching a wide-screen movie with stereophonic sound."

Potter sighed. "That obvious, huh?"

"Well, I know you. Maybe it's not so easy for everyone else."

"I wonder who she is. I can't imagine our Dean inviting a student to this thing."

"Find out," Marilyn said. "I'll mingle."

Potter began edging around the room toward the girl, trying not to be obvious, stopping to exchange greetings with his colleagues and their wives, mouthing the required rote, but never letting his target get out of the edge of his private radar screen.

Blip.

He moved up just as she was fishing for a match, and flipped open his trusty Zippo.

"Thanks," she said, taking an excessive drag.

"I haven't seen you before," Potter said with concerned interest. "Are you at Gilpen?"

"Am I what?"

"A student. At Gilpen."

"Oh, no. I'm sorry. I always forget the name of it. Where Dr. Hardy is."

"Gilpen Junior College."

"Yes, of course. No, we're friends of the Hardys. My family."

"Live here in Boston?"

"They do. I'm at Barnard."

"Ah. Home for semester break?"

"Sort of."

Potter glanced around the room, in what he hoped was a casual manner. "Your parents here?"

"They're in Bermuda."

"Oh. That's too bad—I mean that you're not there too."

"Not really. Under the circumstances."

"Circumstances?"

"Just family—uh—hassle," she said, shrugging elaborately.

"I didn't mean to pry."

"I know."

He offered to get her a punch, and surveying the room, was flashed an understanding wink of approval by Marilyn, who was being solicitously attended by a couple of Business Administration teachers.

The girl's name was Trevor Marshall. A family name. They called her Trevvy. Her father was big in Electronics. Her mother was Virginia society. While they were in Bermuda, Trevvy was staying alone in the family townhouse on Chestnut Street. She said she'd love to have dinner with Potter the next evening.

Back at his apartment with her after the Veal Piccata at Stella's, Potter learned that Trevvy's family hassle had resulted over her having to have an abortion just after Thanksgiving.

Potter was surprised. "I wouldn't have thought —uh—that you'd have to have one," he said.

"I was pregnant," she explained.

"Yes, but I mean—I thought that nowadays—"

"I'm allergic to the pill."

"Yes, but there are so many—uh—"

"I forgot my foam."

"Oh. Well. I guess that can happen."

"It happened," she said, "to me."

She started to sob.

"I'm sorry," Potter said.

He held her, comforting. She clung to him. Very hard.

Then they were on the floor.

They were undressing one another and Potter suddenly stopped and said, "Listen—I hate to mention it, but do you have—uh—your—"

"Emko," she said.

She stood up, pulled the dress over her head, picked up her purse, and went to the bathroom.

When she strolled back, nude and graceful and composed, her perfect small body decorated only with the pale imprint of the area where last summer's bikini had been worn, Potter almost tackled her. He had a kind of erection he had almost forgotten about. There are erections and erections. And then there are erections. There are ones that just barely earn the title, that barely are able to get you inside. Then there are nice stiff ones that feel strong and powerful. And then, sometimes, occasionally, the same old prick outdoes itself, seems to swell beyond its own capacity, grows gloriously super-stiff and majestic, attains the proportions of heroism, and brings to its owner the experience of grandeur.

That was the kind of hard-on he had.

Hot out of his mind, thinking of nothing but

his prick, he rolled on top of her on the floor, starting to force it. She gently pushed him a little bit away, gave a gentle nibble at his ear lobe, and whispered something.

"What?" he asked.

"Take a slow trip," she said.

"Oh—sure—I'm sorry," he said, relaxing a little, feeling embarrassed, thinking to himself, *"And a child shall lead you."*

He saw her the next night, and the next, hoping and thinking that in spite of the fact she was only twenty something might really come of this. She was so damn sophisticated, maybe the age difference wouldn't matter. Maybe he would go down and see her in New York; she could come up to visit him in Boston. Maybe this would turn into something.

Sometimes, talking to her, he felt she was really forty years old.

Other times he thought she was ten.

She cried a great deal.

The fourth time he was with her she asked if he wanted some acid and he explained very carefully and with what he hoped was tolerance and understanding that he didn't want any himself, it was not his own thing, he had enough problems with his head already (he was conscious of saying "head" instead of mind, trying to speak her language), and after that she said it was a shame because she had just taken some herself an hour before. He shouldn't worry, it was a wonderful kind, called Shimmering Rainbow.

The names of the alleged different brands of

acid sounded to Potter like the brand names of scented soaps.

He told her she was a goddamn little fool.

She became mute, and then hysterical, claiming she saw the Devil on his ceiling.

Angry but scared, Potter stayed up with her all night, trying to be reassuring and helpful, trying not to let his anger show.

"I'll probably never see you again," she said calmly when he took her home at dawn after a silent breakfast.

"Don't be silly," he said, knowing she was exactly right.

Dean Hardy called and said he would like for Potter to come by and have a little private chat.

Shit! As if it weren't reckless enough getting involved with a twenty-year-old girl who was suffering the traumas of abortion and acid, Potter had to pick one whose family was a friend of the goddamn Dean of the college where he taught. He figured that's what Hardy wanted to have a private little chat about. His scandalous affair with the daughter of dear friends of the Hardy family.

As it turned out that was not the subject at all, but the matter the Dean did want to discuss was not a whole lot more comforting to Potter.

"Tell me, Phil," Dean Hardy said, tamping down his pipe as he and Potter sat in big leather chairs in his study with glasses of brandy, "what are your plans?"

Potter suffered a sort of multiple déjà vu of all

since he could remember, by his father, his future father-in-law, his guidance counselor at
high school, his troop leader at Boy Scout Camp
Guitche-Goo-Mee, his marriage counselor, his
acting teachers, the head of the PR firm he had
worked for, girls he had slept with on summer
vacations, his CO in the Navy. He wondered if
the "primal scream" might be traced back to the
fact that when a baby came out of the womb a
doctor was there to slap it on the ass and say
"Tell me, kid, what are your plans?" But now
he was thirty-four years old. And still being
asked.

He envisioned a future scene after death,
finding himself in a neat office being interviewed
by a man in a business suit, a man who was
puffing a pipe and leafing through a folder
marked "Potter, Phillip." The man looked up
from the folder and asked pleasantly, "Tell me,
Mr. Potter, now that your life is finalized, what
are your plans?"

"I don't mean anything personal of course,"
Dean Hardy said, "but career-wise."

What it all boiled down to was the inevitable
ultimatum that Potter knew would eventually
come, but not so soon: if he wanted to think beyond another year of teaching he would have to
start work on his Ph.D. Potter said he would seriously consider it because he had found his
teaching experience so rewarding; he would begin to look into the possibilities of his working

toward the degree, and try to have some specific plans in mind that he could report on to the Dean before spring vacation. The Dean expressed his delight and offered his full cooperation.

The idea of going back to school at his age, of listening to lectures and writing papers, of sucking up to professors, of writing an interminable thesis, was about as appealing to Potter as the suggestion that he go into the desert, remove all his clothes, pour honey on his genitals and have himself tied to an anthill.

Back home, Potter got a drink and a notebook. He opened the notebook to an empty page and wrote "Possibilities." Under that he scrawled— "Teaching—grad work." He sat for a long time after that, finished his drink, made himself a new one, then took up the notebook again and wrote "PR—Charlie Bray."

Charlie Bray was a partner in one of the bigger Boston PR firms, a friendly, old-fashioned sort of a guy whom Potter had invited to come and talk to his PR seminar in hopes of pepping it up, getting the students turned on by a successful, practicing PR guy who was right here in Boston. But Charlie didn't produce the desired effect. He had made a long, rambling talk, building up to a dramatic bit about how hard it was to define Public Relations, but how through his many years' experience he had come up with an answer, and he was going to reveal it right there, in that classroom. With everyone awaiting a fan-

tastic revelation, a gem of pure insight and shimmering imagination, Bray paused, leaned forward, and as if giving away the secret of the uni-
verse, said, "Public Relations is simply this—
doing good and telling about it!" Potter thanked
him profusely and dismissed the class in order to
spare Bray from embarrassing questions or comments. Bray had taken him for a drink at The
Statler, and, buoyed by his chance to perform before an audience and unaware that he had
bombed, he praised Public Relations education,
praised Potter in particular, and said if he ever
wanted to get back in the field, back in on the
action, there might well be a place for him at
Sondheim and Bray. Potter thanked him, and
tried to seem grateful, but hadn't really taken it
seriously. Now, faced with the conundrum of his
Future again, he wrote down Charlie Bray's
name and then underlined it.

Wearied by his effort at planning for the future he closed the notebook and turned on the
Tonight Show. Potter had watched the talk
shows so often he had come to feel part of them,
as if he were actually an unseen guest just beyond the camera angle. He felt that Johnny and
David and Dick were talking to *him*, Phil Potter, that he was right alongside them in one of
those chairs. He didn't feel he was merely among
the great unknown mass audience, but that he
was a regular insider who knocked around with
Johnny and David and Dick, got drunk with Ed
McMahon, and hung out in Vegas with Doc

Severinsen. It seemed only right that he finally be interviewed himself, in person, on one of the shows. Best of all, the Tonight Show.

He began to see it. First of all Johnny finishing a commercial and saying to the whole world out there watching, "Would you welcome please, Mr. Phil Potter!" Perhaps Doc Severinsen from his personal knowledge of Potter would have picked the Vanderbilt alma mater song, jazzed up, of course, as the theme for his entry, and Potter, cool and smiling, would emerge through the high curtains, parting them gracefully (he hated to see the guests who fumbled their way through the curtains), and would stride to the platform to shake hands with Johnny and Ed and their other guests of the evening —Zsa Zsa and Gore and Don Rickles and Aretha. The men would smile and shake his hand, Aretha would give him a peck on the cheek, and Zsa Zsa would call him "Phil, dahling" and hit him with a smoldering caress that would have the audience screeching and whistling.

"Phil, it's good to see you again." Johnny smiles, tapping his pencil.

"Good to be back, Johnny."

"Now, Phil, for those of our viewing audience —those very few—who don't know all about you, could you tell us something about your career?"

"Well, Johnny, as you know, I'm a failure."

Gasps and giggles from the audience.

"Failure? What does that entail? I don't think I've heard that term recently."

"Well, Johnny, you're right in thinking it's
kind of outdated. You see, 'Failure' was a popular term in the late Fifties and early Sixties—
when I was becoming one."

Laughter. Camera pans to beautiful girls in
the audience who are obviously taken with Potter's clever wit and can't wait to mob him when
the show is over.

"You see, Johnny," Potter continues, "the opposite of 'Failure' was 'Success,' which is now
exemplified by someone like, say, President
Nixon."

The audience breaks up.

"When I first realized that I had a knack for
being a 'Failure,' Johnny, was back when—"

"I'm sorry to interrupt you, Phil, but we have
a message from one of our sponsors. Stay tuned,
folks, and we'll be right back to hear about the
fascinating career of Phil Potter, an old-fashioned 'Failure'—and perhaps he'll tell us something about his plans for the future. . . ."

Applause.

Alpo.

4

With Marilyn going to New York every weekend, Potter set out on a series of haphazard sexual adventures, not out of lust so much as loneliness and boredom. He picked up girls wherever
he could—sitting in Cambridge coffeehouses, waiting in line at his bank to cash a check, eating a
cheeseburger at Brigham's, waiting for the subway,
shopping for records at The Minuteman. He
smiled, cajoled, joked, winked, bought them drinks,
took them back to his place and put on the ritual
records. Once he got them as far as his living room
he was pretty sure of getting them from there into
bed. On rare occasions, however, the living room
was as far as they would go.

The rebuff that hurt most came at the hands
of a BU student whom he picked up at an art
gallery on Newbury Street. He took her to dinner at Casa Mexico in Cambridge, and she agreed
without hesitation to go back to his place for
drinks. About halfway through the first drink,
she wondered if he minded her asking a personal question.

"Of course not," he said, imagining he had nothing to hide.

"How old are you?"

Potter felt the tips of his ears getting hot. He had never had a girl ask his age before.

"Why do you ask?" he said, feigning a casual tone.

"I'd just like to know."

In his own mind, Potter still thought of himself as being twenty-eight. In his twenties, he had never been able to imagine himself being thirty years old. Much less any older. Like most people, he had taken his youth for granted, assuming it would be a permanent condition, imagining against all reason that only people such as his parents got old. But he knew all that was of little interest to the girl.

"*Well,*" he said, trying to smile, "actually, I'm thirty-four."

"*Thirty-four!*"

She looked as if Potter had just confessed to being a transvestite—Communist—child-molester.

"What's so bad about thirty-four?" he asked, more offended than embarrassed now.

"Well," she said, "that is—*getting on.*"

"Jesus. I'm sorry."

"It's not your fault," she said.

"Thanks a lot. That's very generous of you."

"Listen, you don't have to get mad. It isn't my fault either. That you're thirty-four."

Potter knew anything he said would only make

matters worse, so he drank and said nothing. In a little while the girl said she guessed she'd better go. Potter agreed. He sat by himself, drinking, the phrase "getting on" blinking in his brain.

The next young girl he met, he lied about his age.

He said he was thirty-two.

Later he was angry at himself for lying, and for making it such a useless lie. Thirty-two wasn't much better than thirty-four. If he was going to lie he might as well have said twenty-nine, but that seemed transparent to him, like Jack Benny's joke of always saying he was thirty-nine. Besides, he couldn't have borne the embarrassment of being caught trying to "pass."

He began to wonder if he "looked his age." What did thirty-four look like, anyway? There were a few tell-tale grey hairs in the curly black; circles of dissipation under his eyes, but nothing on his face he would classify as an actual "wrinkle." His waistline, which had held firmer than most men he knew in their thirties, was only recently beginning to show signs of spreading. Maybe he should diet. Or adopt a program of daily excercise. Shit. It was degrading, getting older, and he figured it could only get worse. He thought of those businessmen in New York who ordered hamburgers without the bun for lunch, trying to stave off the growing flab. He had always smiled to himself about that, thinking condescendingly that it was in some way a humiliating gesture, eating hamburgers without buns—like having a drink of soda without the Scotch. He should no doubt cut down on that, too, but he knew that would be much harder than foregoing hamburger buns. He had heard people talk of a "Drinking Man's Diet." Maybe he would look into that. Maybe he would have to.

The depression about his age goaded him into more fucking, more indiscriminately, as if he had to get all he could while there still was time. The women were of all shapes and sizes and ages. All they had in common was that none of them were more than a one-night stand in Potter's persistent quest for relief from himself.

He tried, at least, to please them, since nothing seemed really to please himself, including orgasms. Discussions and stories and articles on Women's Liberation had made him more conscious of the woman's right to her own sexual pleasure and, if possible, fulfillment, and with that in mind he attempted to prolong his fucking until there was indication that the woman had come, in some way or other (the great vaginal-clitoral debate, and the widely varying views on it of the women he met, had left him utterly confused on the issue), or until he simply couldn't continue any longer.

But even this effort to please was often in vain. While pumping away in a sandy-haired beautician who had one glass eye and teeth that were smoke-stained a dull yellow, he noticed that the sounds coming from her did not seem to be moans of pleasure, but merely discomfort. He hurried himself to a climax, and afterward, the girl asked, "Are you through now?" in the flat, annoyed tone of a waitress who is anxious to clear off a table and get the customer on his way.

It seemed, during this weird and debilitating period, that whenever Potter fucked he either took too long or he didn't take long enough. When trying to please, he went down on a woman, she complained he hadn't shaved close enough and his beard was scratching the sensitive skin of her inner thighs. Sucking a breast, he was told that his teeth hurt. Trying to go in from behind, he got the wrong hole. Trying a sixty-nine, his partner complained she couldn't breathe. One girl criticized him for being too rough in bed, the next one groused that he was too damn gentle. One lady confided her fantasy was to be fucked by a man with a bag over his head. Potter complied, but he cut out small holes in order to see, and she whined in disappointment that the eye-holes ruined the whole thing.

He seemed unable to do anything right, in bed or out. At a candlelight dinner with a drama student, he said with conviction that she looked quite beautiful, whereupon she banged down her fork and called him a sexist. He said he did not mean to offend her, and that he would not take it amiss if a woman told him he was handsome, or that he looked nice on a particular occasion. She said that was entirely different. He asked why, and she said he wouldn't understand because he was a sexist. Another liberated young lady asked if she could take him out to dinner, because she was "into role reversal." He thought that was swell, but he had expected that being into role reversal meant that after dinner she would take him back to her place and try to seduce him, but the girl explained that she wasn't "into fucking" anymore. He said in that case she wasn't really into role reversal, and she said he was a male chauvinist pig.

He found himself thinking of Jessica again, nostalgically, wondering whether she had found a new love, whether she would ever marry again, whether it would work if she did, whether he had made a mistake after all in breaking with her. Maybe they should have gone to more marriage counselors. Maybe they should have made a real effort to stop drinking so much. Maybe they should have moved to a real house in the suburbs, with a lawn and a fence and a two-car garage. Maybe they should have bought a farm in Vermont, and lived the simple life, healthy and rustic. Maybe it could have been different.

Maybe. The word buzzed maddeningly around Potter's mind, an annoying gnat.

Potter was grateful to Ed Shell for inviting him to a party out in Merrimack, where some friends of his taught in the English Department of a small junior college. It was about forty-five minutes from Boston, and Potter drove while Ed told him of new movie deals hatching, without the slightest hint of suspicion or cynicism. Potter tried to think positively about Ed's chances; about everything. He wanted to stop thinking about his own problems, wanted to be a regular fellow, have a good time at the party, make new friends, maybe find a really exciting new girl and begin a meaningful relationship.

The party turned out to be composed entirely of faculty and faculty wives and girlfriends. No extra women. No music. Just serious talk. Ed Shell, all concentration, plunged into a deep discussion of the continuing relevance of Arthur Miller's *Death of a Salesman*. Potter's own view was that the play was about as relevant now as the foreign policy of John Foster Dulles, the hula hoop craze, and the Single Wing formation. But he didn't want to put a damper on things, and so kept his peace, trying to entertain himself by sizing up the people in the room.

Most of the men smoked pipes.

Most of the women had short, frizzy hair.

At least there was plenty of booze. It was some kind of godawful blended whiskey, but at least it was hard stuff, and that was better than fruit-laden punch.

Potter got himself a second drink, and sat by the only girl in the room who was definitely under forty. She was sitting beside a young teacher, all earnest and corduroyed, who was hotly involved in the *Death of a Salesman* debate.

"Do you teach here, too?" Potter asked the girl.

"I'm a student."

She looked at him noncommittally, neither friendly nor aloof. She was probably as bored as he was. She wore a flowered dress of miniskirt length that exposed quite hefty thighs. Her hair was the color that once was called dishwater blonde, and pulled to the back. She wore no makeup except for powder that muted but didn't really hide a semi-bad skin. Her eyes were light brown, and anonymous.

They spoke of innocuous matters. Potter got them both another drink. Stiff ones. She majored in English, and lived in a rooming house. She liked Chinese food, and Cape Cod.

"Do you ever get into Boston?" Potter asked.

"Every week or so," she said.

"I live in Cambridge, why don't you come by, the next time you get to Boston?"

"Why?" she asked.

"What do you mean, 'Why'?"

"I mean—well, what did you have in mind? What—uh—kind of relationship?"

Kind of relationship. What did he have in mind. Oh, God. Potter thought of saying he wanted to communicate with her soul, or take her for a stroll on the Dunes at the Cape, or go to Joyce Chen's with her for a fine meal, but he couldn't bring himself to play the game, he couldn't through his fog of whiskey summon up any pretense of social nicety, or perform any verbal pirouettes.

"I just want to fuck you," he said. "That's all I have in mind."

She lit a cigarette, and Potter closed his eyes, waiting for the putdown, knowing he had blown it. He sighed, opened his eyes, and found that she was looking, blankly, right into them.

In a calm, pleasant tone, she asked, "Would Sunday afternoon be all right?"

Potter didn't really think she would show, but on Sunday he showered, and sort of half-prepared himself for the possible visit, pushing back the worst of the living room debris. Under the circumstances that shouldn't matter much, but it was reflex action, he supposed, of what one should do.

She arrived a little after two, the promised time.

He offered her a glass of wine, which she politely accepted.

He had a Scotch, and wondered what to say. "Did you drive in?" he asked.

"Yes. I have a '67 Galaxie. It's got almost 80,-000 miles but it really holds the road."

"I have a Mustang," Potter offered.

"How do you like it?"

"Oh, fine. It does just fine."

She finished her wine, and looked at him.

"Would you like some more?"

"Oh—no thanks, I don't think so."

"Well. Shall we go to bed?"

"OK."

The sex was as dutiful as their conversation. Afterward she got dressed, and Potter asked for her phone. She wrote it on the inside of a matchbook, along with the name "Donna." He assumed that was her.

"I'll call you sometime," he said.

"If you want."

That night Potter didn't want to be alone, and he was thankful Marilyn got back early from her latest New York weekend. He took over some Chicken Delight, and told her the story.

"Well," said Marilyn, "I guess it's a dream come true."

"When you tell it," Potter said.

"But not really?"

"No. Not really."

"Didn't it make you feel—sexy?"

"No."

"Well—what *did* it make you feel like?"

Potter thought for a while. "Like death," he said.

Potter vowed that he would stop his random fucking. He remembered in college reading a definition of morality by Ernest Hemingway that said what was moral was "what you feel good after." In that case, the kind of fucking he'd been doing of late was indeed immoral. He felt lousy after it. The depression that followed his fucking the Sunday Afternoon Girl was so overwhelming that he pledged he would not go to bed again with a woman until he met one he really cared about.

Potter knew his vow was a good decision, because God interceded to aid him in keeping it.

A few days after his encounter with the Sunday
Afternoon Girl, he found himself itching a lot,
in the area of his groin. He thought it was probably a nervous condition brought on by his decision to stop fucking for a while, and he put a
lot of talcum on it. The itching got worse,
though, and Potter took long, hot baths, soaking
himself for as much as an hour, keeping the water as hot as he could stand it, stopping just short
of scalding himself. And the itching grew even
worse. It was getting to be an embarrassment.
He could hardly get through a class without
turning toward the blackboard and giving a
quick, furious scratch to the area over his crotch.
He woke in the middle of the night, tormented
with the itching. He wondered if maybe he was
being bitten by cockroaches, or some such thing,
and he bought a can of bug spray and fumed up
his bedroom with it. Still, the itching increased,
to the point that it was becoming unbearable.
Marilyn gave him the name of her dermatologist,
and Potter made an appointment.

Dr. Garson Simpson was a large, ruddy man
who had a muzak-filled office in a posh new
building. When Potter described his complaint,
Dr. Simpson said gruffly, "Take down your
pants." His fingers probed the hairs on Potter's
groin while his tongue clicked reprovingly.

"Oh, brother," the doctor said. "You've really
got 'em. Holy saints alive, you have a *case* of
'em."

Potter, growing panicky, was beginning to

wonder if whatever the hell he had was fatal, or would require surgery or a trip to the Mayo Clinic, or perhaps mean lifelong hospitalization. Was it treatable at all? Would he die of itching?

"What the hell is it?" he asked. "That I've got?"

The doctor stood up, gave Potter a sneering sort of smile, and slowly walked back to his desk, sat down, motioned Potter to a seat, drew out a cigarette, tamped it on the desk, got out a lighter, flipped it several times without results, finally caught a flame, lit the cigarette, took a long drag, exhaled a smoke-ring, lounged back in his comfortable swivel chair, and asked, "Ever hear of The Crabs?"

Potter had heard of The Crabs in high school, he had heard of The Crabs in the Service. Some of his best friends had had The Crabs. It was one of the few miseries you could get without actually fucking someone who had it, but just by sleeping in a bed where a carrier had slept. If you actually slept with someone who had them, you were pretty sure to get them yourself. That pretty much covered Potter's knowledge of The Crabs, but he saw no reason to recount it.

"Yes," he said, "I have heard of The Crabs."

The doctor leaned forward, grinning now.

"Well, brother, you've really got 'em. I mean, you are in*fest*ed with 'em."

Potter wanted to strangle the sonofabitch. From his luckily sketchy experience with members of the medical profession, he had arrived at a firm theory that most of them were sadists, and had the same psychological makeup as cops, but higher IQs, so they had gone into medicine instead of police work.

"I would appreciate it, Doctor," he said, in an even tone of pure hatred, "if rather than dwelling with such apparent delight on the extent of my malady, you would simply tell me—that is, if you possess such information—how the fuck I can cure the goddamn thing!"

The doctor, snickering and shaking his head, slowly made out a prescription for some kind of medicine. Obviously unmoved by Potter's plea to restrict his remarks to medical advice, he muttered loudly, "Never heard of a guy going so long without knowing he had The Crabs. Jesus. Wonder you weren't eaten up alive."

Potter took the prescription and exited without a word, leaving the doctor still shaking his head in joyous wonderment over his plight.

The medicine was called *Kwell*. Potter took the prescription to the Medical Arts Pharmacy in Harvard Square, and handed it to a young pharmacist who read it, moving his mouth, broke into a grin, and told Potter it would take about fifteen minutes. Potter had a double dry martini on the rocks at the Wursthaus bar, and returned to pick up the *Kwell*, which the pharmacist handed him with a wink, and a loud wish of "Good Luck, buddy."

In a way, having the goddamn Crabs was a relief. Potter knew he couldn't, literally, go to

bed with anyone while he had them without passing them on. And he would wish that exquisite
torture on no one—except Dr. Garson Simpson,
who he would gladly have condemned to a regular case of The Crabs throughout the rest of
his natural life.

Much of Potter's attention now was focussed
on the effort to rid himself of his evil itch. The
good doctor had said it usually took about four
days, but in his case it might be a week or more.
If he wanted to hasten the cure, he could shave
the hair on his groin before applying the medicine. Potter shaved. It was messy and almost
sickening, but the act was a kind of penance,
and would prolong the period of his celibacy,
since he wouldn't want to expose his bare groin
to a stranger, and have to go into lengthy ex-
cuses or explanations. Perhaps in the spirit that
a monk shaves his head, Potter shaved his groin.
He also had to buy new towels and sheets, and
change them every day. Fighting the itch provided a temporary focus to his life, a goal, for
which he was grateful.

It also gave him an excuse for refusing Gafferty the use of his apartment any time that week,
any time until he had cleansed himself of The
Crabs. When Gafferty suggested that just the two
of them go to Jake Wirth's after classes for a
beer, Potter knew what he wanted to ask, but
he pretended innocence, and found that he secretly, shamefully got a perverse pleasure out of
knowing he would have to refuse—on humani-

tarian grounds, of course—Gafferty's request to have another romp with his student lover in Potter's bed.

"Ah, that's a shame, man," Gafferty said, then reddening, quickly added, "I mean your condition. Doesn't matter my not getting your place for a while, that's a luxury."

"I guess you'll just have to rough it this week," Potter said, grinning in spite of himself. "On the old desk."

"Ah, well."

"But your girl must be very understanding—I mean to have had to do it that way for so long. Or however long it's been."

"That she is. Oh yes."

The bastard wasn't letting the slightest bit of information eke out. Not even how long his affair had been going.

Potter began casually speaking of students, tests, grades, class response, and then, after a forced yawn, asked, as if nothing could be less important, "By the way. You ever have any students named Korsky, or Linnett?"

"Korsky. Linnett. Let me see. There was a Fred Kautzky, I think. I don't think it was Korsky, though. Why?"

"Oh, nothing really. Just wondered. They're pretty good students. I just thought you might have had them, but if you'd had them I'm sure you'd remember them."

"Ah. No doubt. You remember good ones. Even some of the troublesome ones."

The conversation droned down, and petered out, neither man having his mind fully on it. Potter felt slightly more assured that Gafferty's girl wasn't one of his own favorites, but of course there was always the chance that the clever bastard had only pretended ignorance of their names, that his mentioning a "Fred Kautsky" was only a ploy to make it seem he didn't even connect those names with girls. Thinking about it, Potter grew annoyed, and distracted. Gafferty was saying something he'd missed entirely.

"What?"

"I just said I better be going, and wished you luck getting rid of those little devils."

"Oh, yeah. Right. Listen, I'll let you know when—uh—when it's OK."

"How long does it take," Marilyn asked, "to get rid of them?"

Marilyn was fascinated by the subject of Potter's affliction. She had once had the clap, but never The Crabs, and was interested in all the details. She even wanted Potter to take down his pants so she could look at them.

"You can't see them," Potter said. "All you can see is little red dots where they've nibbled at you."

"Can't you see them scurrying around, like little ants or something?"

"No. They're too small."

"Oh." Marilyn was obviously disappointed.

"I'm sorry I can't put on more of a show for you," Potter said.

"Don't get defensive."

"All right, all right. Let's talk about something else, for godsake."

Marilyn told about her growing dissatisfaction over the way things were going with Herb, her married shrink-lover. It was getting to be a routine, her going down on weekends, hanging around in the hotel room, waiting for him to come at whatever hours he could get away from his wife and family. He could rarely escape on Saturday nights, so Marilyn usually spent those evenings alone watching television, ordering up from room service.

"You're going down too often," Potter said. "You've got to take a weekend off—do something else. You mustn't make yourself so available, all at his convenience."

"But I do want to see him—I want to be with him. I love him, Phil. And he loves me too, I know it."

"OK, but remember our pact? I was going to advise you on strategy. And I'm telling you now, you've got to be more—elusive. Hard to get."

Marilyn sighed. "Play the game, you mean."

"Yes," Potter said, "that's exactly what I mean."

He got up to go to the bathroom, but just when his hand touched the doorknob, Marilyn yelped, "Phil! Wait! You can't go in there!"

"*What?*"

Potter turned around, confused. "What are you talking about? Is there a body in your bathroom?"

"No, I mean—your *things*. The Crabs. Can't

you get them on toilet seats?"

"I wasn't going to sit down."

"Oh. Well—are you sure it's all right? No kidding, Phil, if I got The Crabs, I could never explain to Herb in a million years."

"Look," Potter said, "I'll be very careful. They're not going to climb out of my fly and parachute down to make landings on your toilet seat."

"Well—if you're sure."

Potter, feeling like a leper, pissed very carefully, zipped himself up, and only stayed long enough to get Marilyn's assurance she would take a weekend off, let her lover sweat a little bit. He advised her to be vague, make the guy worry and wonder about her. Reluctantly, she promised.

Potter was glad to get back home to the secure isolation of his own little private leper colony.

Potter was pleased when Chip Strider, the guy he met at the film buff evening, invited him to a dinner at the Harvard House where he served as Senior Tutor. Each house, Potter learned, had a Senior Tutor to counsel the undergraduates who lived there, and also a Master of the House. It sounded quaint and English, like Tom Brown's School Days. Potter looked forward to the evening as the kind of event that would provide high-level intellectual stimulation, and take his mind off mundane cares like curing The Crabs. He hoped he wouldn't be questioned too closely on his film knowledge, and he got himself pretty high before starting out. The Senior Tutor's residence was comfortably medieval, with heavy old wooden furniture and rich, dark wall hangings.

Potter felt at once he was involved in a form of ritual. Everyone had two drinks before dinner, which was fine except for the fact that it would have seemed a terrible gaffe if anyone had wanted one drink or three drinks. But everyone had two. The assembled company was carefully balanced, like a political ticket. There was the Senior Tutor and his wife, both of whom were economists; a lady anthropologist and a black assistant dean; a visting Fellow at the Kennedy Center for Political Study, and an intense young woman biologist; a thirty-ish woman who was writing a study of The Women in Dostoievski on a grant from the Radcliffe Institute. And Potter. He was probably there for his phony film expertise, but he felt he represented the academic world's outcasts and also-rans.

All he remembered from the dinner were Names.

They spoke intimately of Teddy and Henry and Ken, who everyone understood to mean Kennedy, Kissinger, and Galbraith. Not only was everyone on a first name basis with their distinguished contemporaries, but also with the distinguished dead. When the conversation—which ran like a seminar, with one subject discussed at a time—took up American Literature, someone shook his head pitiably over "Poor Red," who turned out to be Sinclair Lewis. There was also intimate chit-chat about Scott and Zelda, "Dos" and Gene O'Neill and Bunny Wilson. Potter was tempted to make some casual mention of "Hank" Thoreau, but restrained himself.

Potter wanted to get out as soon as he could, before making some smart-ass remark he would later regret, and so he took up the invitation of the Kennedy Center man for a ride home. The man was Sid Persons, who was on leave from what Potter gathered was a high-powered consulting firm in Washington to take this year at Harvard.

"I don't really buy the whole academic scene," Persons said, "but it's a nice change of pace."

Potter agreed, and finding Persons an amiable sort, less pretentious when removed from the Harvard Dinner scene, Potter also agreed to have a nightcap at his place. Persons lived in an elegant modern high rise on Memorial Drive, his own one-bedroom apartment finely appointed in a masculine, comfortable club style, with big leather chairs, deep carpeting, and heavy velvet draperies. Persons himself was a big, handsome, club-member looking guy with distinguished greying hair and a sunlamp tan. He put on a record of some kind of string quartet, very soothing, and brought Potter a he-man sized Scotch and soda. Potter quickly, on request, filled in a little of his own background, saying he wasn't really sure if he'd continue teaching or if he did for how long. His plans were all up in the air.

"Ever been married?" Persons asked.

"Once. Just split—less than a year ago."

"Rough. It's always rough."

"You divorced?"

"No—never quite made it down the old aisle. Came pretty close a couple of times, but at the last minute—well maybe you could say I chickened out, or maybe you could say I was wise. At any rate I've never regretted staying single, playing the field. Now I'm a confirmed bachelor."

"Well, it must be nice to know what you want. Know how you want to live."

"You mean you'd do it again? The marriage bit?"

"I really don't know. I just don't have any policy about it. It seems to me like it's hard either way."

"Well, seems to me if a man's tried it—what the hell. Once is enough. No sense being one of those jokers who just keeps trading in wives, going through the same thing over and over."

"True."

"The way things are now, people don't have to try to fit themselves into the old grooves like they used to. Society's opening up. And if you ask me, it's a healthy development. Let people do what they want."

"Hell yes."

"Here, let me freshen that drink."

"Oh—"

Potter was only about halfway through, but he took a big gulp and handed the glass to Persons. Whistling, Persons came back with a Scotch and soda mixed by martini proportions, the soda getting as short shrift as vermouth.

"Hey," he said, "you dig Sinatra?"

"Sure."

"Good. I know he's out of fashion now, but I guess I'm hung up on him from the old days."

Persons put on the Sinatra album of "Songs for Young Lovers."

As always, The Voice made Potter feel mellow.

"I tell you," Sid said, "I still like the old music, but I'm glad we've gotten rid of some of the old ideas, the hangups and prejudices."

"Absolutely," Potter said.

"Some people attack the Women's Movement as being a bunch of lesbians, like it's still some kind of crime. Jesus. If a woman wants to make it with a woman, why shouldn't she? It's a personal matter."

"Of course it is."

"Just the same as if—" Persons paused, as if trying to think of the right analogy, and said with a shrug, "as if, for instance, a man wants another man."

When Persons brought Potter the second drink he had sat down on the couch with him; not close, but close enough so that now as he casually threw his arm up along the back of the couch his hand was resting directly behind Potter's head. Potter didn't move. He was aware of not moving. He was also aware, with sudden clarity and self-reproach that he had, as naively as a virgin schoolboy, got himself into what was almost a compromising position. The "almost" was exactly the distance between the back of his head and Sid Persons' hand. He judged that to be about three and a half inches. He had only to tilt his head back that far to begin what would soon be turned into a passionate embrace by his genial, broad-minded host.

You moron, he thought, meaning not his host but himself.

"I don't mean I go for the Gay Militants parading around in the streets with banners and picket signs," Persons continued, "but if an adult male happens to find that—in addition, mind you, to enjoying women—he enjoys physical contact with another man, I see no reason why it's the business of society to condemn him."

"Of course not," Potter said, shifting slightly so that he was farther from Persons' hand, and facing him more directly. His main concern was to get out of the situation without either leading Persons on any further or embarrassing him. He wanted to convey the feeling that he had no opposition to homosexuality for those who found it pleasurable, that he did not look down on any man, Persons included, if he was a practicing homosexual, *but,* thank you, it was simply not his own thing.

His head now as clear as if he had drunk nothing more than a glass of milk, he politely, respectfully, sincerely, expressed his staunch support of the right of every man to pursue whatever sexual course attracted him but that, perhaps, due to his own middle-class upbringing or some possible lack of imagination on his part, he did not prefer homosexual encounters for himself, which made him no better than those who did, it was simply a circumstance of his own life and nature and personality.

Persons nodded, gravely, evidently with acceptance of Potter's position, but when Potter rose to say he'd better get on home, he had to get up and teach in the morning, Persons suddenly came toward him, embraced him, put his head on Potter's shoulder and said, his voice shaking, *"Please stay."*

"I can't," Potter said. "Please understand. I can't do it. For godsake, man, I'm sorry, but there's just no way. I'm sorry. No shit. I have to go."

He wrenched himself away, not wanting to look back, and ran out into the carpeted hallway and down the stairs, into a cold, slow rain. A cab passed, but he wanted to walk.

He felt exposed and ludicrous, not because of what he had seen of Sid Persons but of what, through him, he had seen of himself. Persons had shown him something he had never looked at before. There had been something hauntingly, teasingly familiar about the whole situation; Persons mixing him the strong and stronger drinks, putting on the romantic music, leading into a personal discussion of sex, casually maneuvering himself into physical proximity on the couch, close but not too obviously close; the seduction pitch made, rebuffed, and then the pitiful plea to stay.

What Potter understood he had seen was simply the same performance he had gone through a thousand times himself, with a woman; but for the first time, that evening, he was privileged to see it through the woman's eyes. What he saw made him feel supremely silly.

Marilyn was in a real stew because her regular shrink had advised her to stop seeing her shrink-lover.

"Why?" Potter asked.

"He says I'm being self-destructive. He says I'm letting Herb take advantage of me. And that it won't lead to anything. Then he gives me that bullshit about how I ought to meet 'eligible men' and he won't believe there aren't any."

"So what the hell does he want you to do?"

"Well, he wants me to end it with Herb, and I said I wouldn't. Then he wants me to go into this 'Assertion Group' thing. It's a kind of behaviorist therapy technique that he says is getting a lot of results now."

"And what did you say to that?"

"I said I'd try it."

"That seems fair enough."

"But Phil—"

"Yes?"

"I don't want to go alone."

"Now wait a minute—"

"I know, I know how you feel about therapy, but it's only once. Just go with me the first time. Then, if you hate it you don't have to come back."

"You mean I'm supposed to be part of it? The therapy?"

"Well? Don't you have any problems?"

"Don't get smart."

"It can't hurt you. Phil? Please?"

The group met in a spare, brightly-lit little room in an office building on Boylston Street. Besides Potter and Marilyn there were only three other people, though the group leader, a bearded young guy named Bill Buford, said there would be more the following week. He explained that the purpose of their efforts was to work on specific problems of behavior by practicing troublesome situations with one another, and then act the same way when the situations arose in real life. He said they weren't into a lot of Freudian self-examination, just clear-cut specific instances of acting in a more productive way with other people.

They all introduced themselves, and told briefly what they did, and a few told what they wanted to work on. To his surprise, Potter had an immediate feeling of community with this unlikely assortment of people, more so than he would have had he met them in "real life," but being together in the room, it was as if by accident they found themselves in the same lifeboat, on a rough open sea, during wartime.

A woman named Adele volunteered to go first. She was tall, well-built, not beautiful but quite attractive, and charming. There was a genuine kind of warmth about her, a feeling that she liked *you,* and so it was easy to like her in return. She wore her hair swept up in back, and piled on her head. She was a legal secretary. She was married, and had no children. Potter guessed her age in the mid-thirties.

She said her problem was that her boss was very disorganized, and just before quitting time every day he gave her all kinds of work to do, and it made her rushed and nervous and she was inevitably late getting home.

Bill Buford asked Potter to pretend to be her boss, and had Adele come up to him and politely explain the problem, and say she would appreciate it if he could arrange things so that she could get the work earlier in the day and be able to finish by five. Potter thought she seemed calm and entirely reasonable, but he made some bogus protests and questions to give her "practice," which she also answered intelligently and convincingly. Bill said she had done very well, and he was sure she could pull it off with her boss. Adele mentioned, as if in passing, that of course this was only a small, surface kind of problem compared to the really complicated things, the deep things that really bothered her.

No one asked what those things were.

Buford called on Joe, a young computer analyst recently up from Georgia, who spoke in a shy drawl about his problems meeting new women now that he was separated from his wife. He kept twisting the wedding band on his finger while he talked. He tried to practice picking up Adele, and Buford pointed out it was bad form to keep twisting his wedding ring, calling attention to it, maybe he should even get rid of it. Joe blushed, mussed his hair, and said "Shee-it."

Potter began madly searching his mind for some kind of situation to practice if called upon. Rebuffing Sid Persons and trying not to make him feel bad? Making Gafferty reveal the identity of the student he was fucking? Nothing seemed suitable. He wondered, also, if Marilyn would try to go into the whole complexity of her affair with the shrink-lover in New York. Would she practice making him swear to get a divorce and marry her? Potter was relieved when Adele spoke up again.

"Do you have another situation you'd like to try?" Buford asked with enthusiasm.

"Well—I don't have any more like the first one," she said. "The thing with my boss—to tell the truth, that was easy. That's nothing compared to what I have going on inside."

"But internal feelings can always be externalized," Buford assured her. "Try to explain what it is you mean. I'm sure we can work out a situation for it."

Adele took a deep breath. "I don't know what's wrong. I'm happily married. I love my husband and he loves me. It's what I always wanted. I never wanted to be a career girl. I don't mind working, but that wasn't my goal. I always thought that if only I found the right man, if I had a good home and a happy marriage, all these things that have made me miserable all my life would disappear."

She paused, and pulled a wad of Kleenex from her purse.

"It's like," she continued, the words tumbling faster now, "where I read once that Dustin Hoffman used to walk around New York and see those theatre marquees and think if only he had his name on them, as the star of a really good movie, everything would be all right and he wouldn't have to worry anymore and he could relax and enjoy his life. I don't know if that's exactly what he said but that was the idea. And then he got his name on the marquee and he walked around New York, and he saw it and saw the crowds waiting to see the movie, and yet it didn't help, it didn't change anything."

Adele poked the Kleenex at her eyes. Tears were flowing down her cheeks.

The room was frozen in a kind of silence that was different than just a lapse, or an interlude, or a break in the session. No one moved or coughed or itched or blinked.

"So now I have what I wanted—my version of the name on the marquee—the love and warmth and the man and the home and all I dreamed of and there's no real reason to be unhappy anymore, no reason to feel anxiety or fright or sorrow or loss but I am just like I always was it isn't any different inside me it is still the same misery and now it's worse because there's no reason for it, nothing to blame it on."

Adele rubbed the Kleenex over her cheeks. Not even the therapist spoke. Potter was grateful that Buford did not attempt to "externalize" what Adele had poured out, into some "real life" situation that she could "practice on."

Everyone in the room had slightly bowed his head, but neither that communal gesture nor the silence that followed it were born of embarrassment or confusion. And yet there was a tangible feeling in the room, a shared emotion, and Potter, wanting to name it for himself, realized it was not a word that appeared in psychology books. Maybe there was no word that covered it at all, but the one that came closest was reverence.

Potter stayed on Marilyn's couch that night. He didn't itch anymore and figured his crabs were gone, but anyway he didn't take his clothes off and anyway Marilyn didn't even ask him about his condition. When they got home they didn't speak at all, they just drank in silence, and then Marilyn hugged him and went in to bed. It rained all night, a torrential kind of rain, and at dawn when it let up, retreating with the light, Potter opened the living room window. A warm, wet wind rushed in, carrying with it the sharp, poignant perfume of grass and fresh earth.

It would soon be spring.

PART FIVE

PART

FIVE

1

Potter and Marilyn decided that the two of them were as much of a "group" as either needed, therapywise. Hearing one another's problems was sufficiently depressing without having to hear about the horrible depressions and horrendous hangups of a half-dozen other poor souls. Marilyn continued to see her own shrink privately, though, mainly because he supplied her with prescriptions for the pills she now used regularly to get to sleep and to wake up, to perk up and to calm down.

Her sessions with Dr. Shamleigh had turned into shouting matches over what she should do about Herb. Dr. Shamleigh said she should give him up and find a nice, eligible bachelor. Marilyn said there weren't any. Dr. Shamleigh said she wasn't looking hard enough. Marilyn accused him of trying to break up her relationship with Herb because Herb was a shrink too, and Dr. Shamleigh was jealous of him having all this good sex outside his marriage. Dr. Shamleigh insisted he was not jealous, that he had no desire to seduce Marilyn but only to help her, though she made that very difficult. Marilyn then suggested that Dr. Shamleigh wanted her to break up with Herb because he was a shrink and his affair with Marilyn made it seem like shrinks were just as fucked up and human as everyone else. Dr. Shamleigh said that was nonsense, he wanted her to leave Herb because there wasn't any "future" in it. Marilyn angrily sputtered that "there isn't any future in—the *future* for godsake, that's a dream." Dr. Shamleigh said Marilyn was losing her grip on reality, partly because of the fantasy nature of the affair, because it took place in the "unreal" situation of secret weekend meetings, and because it was based on the "fantasy" that Herb was going to leave his wife and family and run off with her into the sunset. Marilyn pointed out that even if he wanted to do it Herb couldn't just go get a divorce and sweep her off to city hall, never mind sunsets, all that took time. Dr. Shamleigh said indeed divorces took time, but if Herb was seriously going to do this he could make his feelings known to his wife and thus begin preparations for what would be the long and difficult proceedings that would lead him eventually to marrying Marilyn, if that indeed was his honest intention.

Marilyn broke down one night after one of those sessions and called Herb, sobbing, and told him he had to make a choice between her and his wife, that he had to tell his wife he want-

ed a divorce or Marilyn wouldn't see him anymore. Herb said that was an ultimatum, not a
choice. Marilyn said he could call it whatever
he wanted but she couldn't go on this way. Herb
said he had to have a little time, he would have
to consult Dr. Gumbacher. Marilyn asked who
the hell *that* was, and Herb said it was one of
the most distinguished analysts in the country.
Marilyn asked, incredulously, if a shrink had to
see another shrink before he could make a decision of his own. Herb said this was different because Dr. Gumbacher had been his analyst for
the analysis that all analysts must go through before they can become analysts and analyze other
people, and Herb wanted to get his former analyst's professional opinion on whether the desire
to leave his wife and children and marry a
younger woman was a healthy life development
or whether it had some dark roots in conflicts
that perhaps were left unresolved in his analysis.
Marilyn told Herb that he and his analyst had
better figure it out right away because when she
came down this weekend she wanted a straight
answer or she wasn't coming down anymore.
Herb said in that case she left him no choice but
to try to reach a rational decision about a complex problem involving his whole life in a matter of days, and Marilyn said that was exactly
right because between her shrink and Herb and
Herb's shrink she was going to go to pieces if
she didn't get the thing settled next weekend one
way or other.

"Wow," said Potter.

He had guzzled two martinis while Marilyn paced the room, poured straight gin in her glass, and filled him in on how things stood and why. He poured himself a third, and said, "I guess this sounds pretty feeble, but is there anything I can do?"

She stopped her pacing, turned to Potter, and much to his surprise, said, most emphatically, "*Yes.*"

Usually, no matter how good your intentions, when you ask a friend if there is anything you can do, things have reached a point at which no one can do anything.

"What can I possibly do?" he asked, genuinely not knowing what it might be.

"Come with me this weekend," Marilyn said.

"To *New York?*"

"To New York."

"Look, Marilyn, I'd do anything—"

"Then come."

"But what can I do, if you'll be seeing Herb?"

"I'll only be seeing him part of the time—the time he can sneak away from his happy little home. The rest of the time I'll be alone in an anonymous room that will probably be pretty high up in the Fifth Avenue Hotel."

"OK, but if I come, what do you want me to do?"

"Keep me from jumping."

Herb always put Marilyn up at the Fifth Avenue Hotel because it was down in Greenwich Village, where his wife, neighbors, and colleagues were unlikely to be hanging out. Herb, of course, lived in a swank apartment in the Upper Seventies, off Park. Being, as he was, a Freudian.

The Fifth Avenue Hotel was a good one, by all odds the best the Village had to offer, but Potter decided not to stay there himself, not because of any worry that it might be too expensive, but rather out of some obscure, private-eye-story notion that he shouldn't be registered in the same hotel as Marilyn since no one was supposed to know he was down there to come to her aid. The only person who could possibly care was old Herb, who knew Potter by name but probably wouldn't recognize him from the New Year's Eve party, but the whole bizarre and clandestine nature of the business led Potter to decide he should get a room at the Earle Hotel, which was handily situated nearby on Waverly Place.

He had heard people long ago praise the Earle as a nice little Village Hotel, but he hadn't been in it for years, and it was obviously on the decline. The hallway smelled of urine, and when Potter began unpacking his bag in a paint-peeling room with a soiled print of a vase of flowers hanging tilted above the bed, he wished he had stayed at the Fifth Avenue. It was done, though, and to check out now would only create a greater hassle for himself. He splashed cold water on his face, brushed his teeth, straightened his tie, put on his overcoat, and went over to Marilyn's hotel.

Herb was due in an hour, and Marilyn had dressed for the crucial meeting with him.

"What do you think?" she asked.

Potter walked slowly around the room looking at Marilyn and her outfit, studying the effect. "No," he said thoughtfully, "I don't think so."

Marilyn looked down, disappointed, at the maroon velvet gown she was wearing. It showed her cleavage, and was split way up the side, revealing lots of leg. "I thought you told me it was sexy," she complained.

"I did. It is."

"So what's the matter?"

"Let me think a minute."

Potter loosened his tie, and sat down in an armchair. "Let me have a drink, will you?"

Marilyn sighed, and poured him a Scotch over ice. Potter stirred it with his finger, reflectively.

"If you wear that," he said, "it's like you're saying 'Here—take me. I'm all yours, whatever the conditions.' "

"But I'm *not* saying that. I don't *want* to say that."

"But the gown says it."

Marilyn crossed her arms over her chest, holding herself as if she were chilly.

Potter got up and walked around the room, rattling the ice in his glass. "You want to look sexy, but not obvious. You don't want to make it so he can just come in and throw you on the bed and then tell you later he's sorry but he can't leave his wife."

Marilyn nodded. "So what should I wear then?"

"The effect, I think, you want to create, is of a very beautiful, sexy woman on trial for murder who is dressing for the jury—dressing so they know she's beautiful but not loose—that she's cool, and in possession, and wouldn't do anything crazy."

"A pants suit?"

"No no. You don't want to hide yourself—but on the other hand you don't want to flaunt yourself."

Potter looked through the considerable wardrobe she had brought and settled on a plain, dark blue dress. Short, but still rather prim and severe. A simple strand of pearls.

"And no makeup," Potter said.

"Not even eye shadow?"

"That's OK. Yeah. Eye shadow. But try to look pale."

"Pale."

"Like you might faint."

"Actually, I might."

"No, no. You mustn't *really* faint. Just have the *aura* of fainting."

"I'll try."

"You can do it. And remember, above all, don't give in. If he's not splitting with his wife, this is it. You won't see him anymore. He's got to make the choice. And try not to cry. Let *him* do the crying."

"Oh, Phil."

"You can do it."

They hugged, and Potter left her to her preparations.

Potter went back to his room and had a Scotch. It was a little after four, and he had the evening before him. Till midnight, anyway. That was when Herb would have to leave Marilyn to go back home, and she would most be in need of Potter's company. To help her celebrate or keep her away from the window.

So he had Saturday night in New York ahead of him, alone. It was the first time he'd returned after moving to Boston, and he hadn't told anyone he was coming.

He wondered what Jessica was doing. She was sure to have a date on Saturday night. He wondered whatever happened about the guy who wanted to marry her, whether it was all off or she was still seeing him, still considering the proposal. He wondered where she was living, how things were going for her. But he didn't want to go through the scene that would be required to find out.

Maybe he should call up one of his old buddies. One of the guys from the office. But then he would have to explain. His life. His work. His plans. He would have to defend and justify.

He had another Scotch. It might be fun to see Al Kolonkis, a buddy from the old theatre days. But that would mean hearing about Al's life—the old frustrations, the fragile new hopes.

Maybe there was a party somewhere. He thought of Lorna Cassell, a sharp, striking blonde who had her own boutique on the East Side and always knew where the parties were. He called information, and they confirmed that an L. C. Cassell on East Sixty-first Street indeed had a telephone, but that the number was unlisted. Potter smiled. She was moving up.

He heaved the Manhattan phone directory onto his lap, and began to flip through it, hoping that suddenly a name would pop up from the page of someone he was dying to see. Looking through the H's, he thought of Agnes Hyer. She lived—or used to live—on Bank Street, with a lot of cats and plants. A fat, philosophical girl. He once got drunk and laid her and the next morning couldn't look her in the eyes, but they managed to stay friends and he never made that mistake again. During the day she was a commercial artist at one of the big agencies, and at night went home and put on her leotards and her string quartets and drank wine until she resembled the image of who it was she started out to be when she came to New York. Potter found her name—she still lived on Bank Street. He called the number, but after it rang once he hung up.

He really didn't want to plug into his old life, in any way. He wanted to remain anonymous, a tourist.

Around six he went out walking through the

Village. He was hungry, but he didn't want to
go into a good restaurant, alone, and sit at a table, alone, and have a good drink and dinner and
wine, alone. Nor did he want to go into one of
the floodlit greasy spoons and wolf down a hamburger and a Coke, mashed among junkies and
winos and speeded-up kids. Finally he chose La
Crêpe, where you could eat alone in relative
comfort, have a glass of wine, and perhaps be
sized up as a busy fellow who was just grabbing
a bite on his way to a big party or late date. He
had the sausage-and-egg crêpe, number thirty-
seven, and two glasses of chilled rosé.

Back out on the streets, he felt alien and un-
comfortable. It seemed to him that New York
was even more crowded and desperate than it
had been only six months ago, though he figured
that was probably because he was accustomed
now to the relatively slower, less strangled
streets of Boston. Whatever the reason, he felt as
if he were drowning in flesh and neon, the stench
of stale vomit and the squeal of sirens. He hurried, faster, back to his room, threw off his coat,
poured himself a Scotch, and flipped on the television. He was happy to choose what seemed the
lesser of a vast array of evils.

Saturday Night at the Movies.

Marilyn called a little after midnight, her
voice noncommittal, and he yanked on his coat
and rushed to her room.

She was focussing on the lighted tip of her cigarette with a concentration that suggested an attempt at self-hypnosis.

Potter already knew the answer so didn't ask. He poured himself a drink, sat down, and waited until she felt like talking.

"His shrink said no," Marilyn said.

"Just plain 'no' or No with a theory?"

"Compulsive patterns. Anal and oral fixations. Hasn't worked out his real feelings."

"He agrees? I mean about the 'no,' not about the symptoms."

"He has to think it over."

"How long?"

"I told him to let me know tomorrow, I had to go back."

Potter looked at the bed, which could have passed for the scene of a six-day orgy. "You know, of course, he'll come tomorrow, fuck you some more, and say he still needs time to think it over."

"I won't let him."

"Fuck you tomorrow?"

"Think it over anymore. After tomorrow."

"OK."

Potter suggested they take in the late-late show. After that they watched the late-late-late, and then, connoisseurs that they were, stayed glued to the late-late-late-late-late, which brought them into the early. One thing you could say in favor of New York, its TV stations knew what the citizens needed.

Continuous numbing.

The morning was cold and soot-speckled. Potter went out and got orange juice for them, put Marilyn to bed with a call for ten, and said he would meet her that afternoon at four. He went to his own cubicle across the street, took a shower, and passed out. He slept fitfully, woke around noon, and went out for the Sunday *Times* and something to eat. *The Times,* like the New York TV stations, filled its most important mission of providing enough material to blank out the customer's mind as long as needed. It kept Potter going till four.

The special sad sunlight of Sunday afternoon spread over Marilyn's room. Maid service had cleared the traces of whatever had happened with her and Herb, but there was no type of service to clear her face of what anyone who saw it could surmise had occurred.

Passion. Pleadings. Pledges. Post mortems. Protests. Promises. Parting. Packing.

She sat quiet and prim, like a political exile who has been ordered to leave the country on the next train.

Potter looked around the room and found the bottle of Scotch with a tiny bit left. He poured it into a bathroom water glass, sat down, and guzzled it. "You ready?" he asked.

"No hurry."

"No booze, either."

She shrugged. "Order some if you like."

"You join me?"

"If you like."

Potter dialed room service and ordered a double Scotch on the rocks and an extra dry martini straight up with a twist.

They finished those off without saying anything, and Potter ordered up two more rounds
of the same.

When they neared the end of those, Marilyn
said they might as well have some more, since
Herb was paying. She hadn't checked out yet,
and he would pick up the bill.

"Fuck it then," Potter said. "Let's celebrate."

"Celebrate what?" she asked.

"Don't ask what, ask how."

"All right. How?"

"We'll figure it out as we go along."

Because it was to be a celebration, they started with champagne and caviar. Since Herb was
paying.

The notion that Herb was paying served as an
incentive.

Since they had such a hard time deciding what
to have, Marilyn hit on the idea of simply ordering the most expensive item offered in each cate-
gory of the menu, from appetizer to dessert.

And more champagne.

After the feast, with a fine bottle of brandy,
they decided it was silly to go out into the night
and fight their way to a cab and on to the next
shuttle flight. Marilyn said in the past couple
months she had learned there was nothing so depressing as catching a Sunday night shuttle
flight back home. They decided to take an early
one next morning. What the hell. Potter had already checked out of his hotel, but Marilyn had
already stayed past check-out time and had told

the desk she wasn't sure when she was leaving, so the room in effect was paid for the night anyway. There was a double bed, with plenty of room for Potter.

But they didn't need the extra space. For the first time since they had stopped being lovers they fucked, in a kind of spontaneous frenzy of anger and lust, mean and low-down and totally abandoned, hurting and liking it, saying no words, only making sudden squeals or grunts or moans or shouts, tearing and clawing and pumping and thrashing. It was like a "grudge fuck" only the grudge was not against the partner involved but against Herb, against all betrayal and loss and frustration, against the whole damn rest of the world.

On the plane going back the next morning, they were silent, and exhausted. They never spoke again of what happened that night. They were friends.

2

The faint hint of spring in the air at the end of February was only a temporary tease, and the day after Potter and Marilyn returned from New York, Boston was hit by a full-scale blizzard. Potter woke to an arctic scene outside his window. The cars parked up and down the block bumper-to-bumper, including his Mustang, were one solid chain of frozen silver humps. He didn't even attempt to scrape and shovel his own car out, but literally bundled himself to the teeth, wrapping a woolen scarf around his mouth and nose, and set out in full winter regalia to go for supplies. He tromped back home from Mass Avenue with a half-gallon of Cutty Sark, a dozen eggs, a dozen knockwurst, a Sara Lee cheesecake, a jar of Maxim freeze-dried instant coffee, and a carton of Pall Malls. He felt secure and self-reliant, a plastic era pioneer.

Potter welcomed this early March regression to winter. It constituted a kind of postponement of a spring he was not looking forward to. It would bring, among other things, his thirty-fifth birthday. It would also bring decisions about his "future," the very thought of which depressed him. He no longer saw "the future" as he once had in his mind's eye as a vast road widening purposefully before him toward the horizon, but rather as a rocky, downhill path that dwindled darkly below, a not-very-smooth slide toward oblivion.

The blizzard allowed him to hibernate, which suited his mood. Classes were cancelled, traffic was stalled, and for several days Potter was able to burrow into his apartment, into himself, without feeling irresponsible, having the legitimate excuse of being a common victim of the elements just like his fellow citizens and neighbors. He read Shakespeare, took long hot baths, watched television, and felt himself recuperating from the ordeal he partly shared with Marilyn. If the whole thing had left him feeling beaten and bruised from what was mainly vicarious participation, he figured it must have laid Marilyn out flat, and he didn't think he should even call her until she too had time to recuperate.

On the first day of warm sunshine and melting slush. Potter slogged his way to the subway and in to school, and arranged to stop by Marilyn's for a drink when she got off work. Her own office had carried on with business much as usual during the storm, and Potter expected to find her bleary-eyed and distraught, depressed and down at the mouth.

Instead, he found her humming.

It surprised and even annoyed him a little. He

hadn't expected any sign of cheeriness and wondered if it wasn't even . . . improper, somehow, her recovering so quickly from what was supposed to have been a major crisis. After dragging Potter down to New York and her dire dilemma with Herb, did she now consider the whole thing had only been a lark?

Humming indeed.

"What's that?" he asked irritably.

"What's what?" she said, her eyes large and fresh and blinking.

"What you're humming."

"Oh, *that.*"

"Yes, *that.*"

"Probably something from the new Cat Stevens album."

"Cat *who?*"

"Cat *Stevens.*"

"Who the hell is that?"

"A singer. Singer-composer. You know—like your Judys and Jonis—except—"

She grinned gleefully, and said, "He's a guy instead of a girl."

"That's swell."

Potter got up to make himself a drink, since the usual pitcher of martinis was noticeably absent. "You want me to mix the martinis?" he asked.

"Oh, no. Not for me, anyway. I'm just fine."

Potter made himself a Scotch and sat down, eyeing Marilyn suspiciously. "What's up?" he asked.

"Hmmm? Why, nothing."

She was rummaging around in her purse.

"Looking for a cigarette?" Potter asked.

He reached in his pocket and held a pack of Pall Malls toward her.

Marilyn giggled. "Not *that* kind," she said.

Proudly, she pulled from her purse a rather bulkily-rolled joint.

"Oh, for godsake," Potter said.

"I know you don't think you like grass, but this is something special."

"Oh, Jesus. I suppose you're going to tell me it's Acapulco Gold."

"Not at all," she said smugly. "Vermont Green."

She lit the twisted end and it flared, almost singeing her eyelashes.

"For Christsake, be careful!" Potter shouted.

Marilyn coughed, patted herself on the chest, and opened her eyes, cautiously.

They were watering. She held out the joint to Potter.

Resigned, he took the damn thing and did his best to inhale. They passed it back and forth until it was too small for either of them to hold, and when Marilyn tried to stub it out she burned a finger and the roach dropped to the carpet, under the couch. Potter went after it, as if the goddam thing were a live animal, which in fact it might as well have been. When he mashed it out he sat back up and had a long sip of his Scotch. Marilyn was sitting back smiling, her eyes closed, looking like St. Teresa just prior to lift-off.

"You want a drink now?" Potter asked.

"I'm *fine*," she said. Not opening her eyes.

Potter freshened his Scotch.

"Try to go with it," Marilyn whispered, her eyes still closed, her voice unbearably mystic.

Potter lit a Pall Mall, deciding to wait out Marilyn's trance.

When she finally stood up, opened her eyes, and got herself a drink, Potter felt he could talk to her again. Rationally.

"Where'd you get that goddamn stuff" he asked.

"A friend," she said coyly.

"Come off it. What's going on?"

It turned out that Marilyn had seduced a cute hippie dropout boy who worked in the mailroom at her office, and he had given her the grass.

"What's he like?" Potter asked.

"Beautiful," Marilyn sighed, "and only nine-teen."

Potter felt a flush of anger rising, and then it just as suddenly subsided as he saw that she was doing what he had so often done. She had simply gotten herself a young pretty one of the opposite sex to forget things with, no doubt providing an instructional and enlightening experience for him, too, in the process; hopefully a matter of mutual profit.

"Hey," he said, "that sounds terrific. Your boy-friend."

"It is," she said. "Just what I need now. Mind-less fucking."

"Terrific. But now that you're all set, what

about me? Alone in the world."

He expected friendly mockery, but instead Marilyn smiled, and gazed mysteriously at her glass.

"I've been thinking about that," she said.

"You *have?* Tell me!"

Marilyn lit a cigarette, slowly, and took a long, dramatic drag, blowing a line of smoke at the ceiling. "What do you think of Southern girls?" she asked.

"As a rule, they smell good," Potter said. "Also as a rule, they are not very bright, or they go to great lengths to pre*tend* they're not very bright. But they make up for that by this delicious odor they have. Per capita, they probably bathe more often than your average Northern or Western girl. Why do you ask?"

"There's the Southernest girl you ever saw in my office. In accounting. She and her roommates are having a Sunday Brunch, and you know what they need for it, honeychile? The lacking ingredient?"

"Let's see—a sack of grits?"

"No. They have plenty of that."

"What do they need, then?"

Marilyn smiled. "Men."

"Aha."

"Do you volunteer?"

"It's the least I can do."

"OK, but try to behave. These are delicate flowers."

"Of course. I'll do anything you want."

Marilyn smiled. "Try not to let your nostrils flare," she said.

Potter had thought that Marilyn would take him to the Southern Girls' Sunday Brunch, but she said she preferred to stay home and smoke grass and fuck her new hippie dropout boyfriend, so Potter had a bracing Bloody Mary for breakfast and set out all by himself.

The Southern Girls' Sunday Brunch was at a large, sunny apartment on Mt. Vernon Street. The "good side" of Beacon Hill. It must have been expensive as hell. The place was beautifully furnished, and there were lots of plush pillows and cushions all over the place. The apartment had two bedrooms, and was shared by four girls.

Amelia, Lilly, Samantha, and Pru.

It sounded like a garden. Potter wondered which flower to pick.

The four roommates were all from Georgia. There were also girls at the party from Virginia, Alabama, and North Carolina. They seemed to have banded together in the cold, foreign clime of Boston according to their states of origin, rather like the Puerto Ricans who settled in New York with people who hailed from the same hometown on the island.

Only one man at the party was an identifiable Southerner, an insurance man from Savannah. None seemed to be native Bostonians. They were the usual male Singles crowd that is almost interchangeable in any large city, former fraternity types grown into accountants and bankers, realtors and lawyers, ad men and department store buyers, not really rooted anywhere, looking for the action, saving their money for orange Porsches and mirrored bedrooms, subscribers to *Playboy* who ski and scuba-dive according to season, have their own home wine-making kits and hang their college diplomas in the room they refer to as The John. Many of them belonged to churches, few had abandoned their faith in God, and most believed secretly that if they lived a reasonably honest and hard-working life they would go to Swinging London when they died.

The brunch featured marvelous homemade biscuits laden with hot butter and thick preserves. There was also scrambled eggs, ham, and fried apples. There were weak Bloody Marys and strong coffee. Potter snuck into the kitchen hoping to perk up his coffee with a secret shot of whiskey, but finding none, resorted to sousing it with cooking sherry.

One of the Georgia Peaches caught him. The tall one, with thick brown hair the color of molasses. Large chocolate-y eyes. Cherry red lips, moist and sweet-looking, as if they might be sugar-coated. She smelled of marmalade and honeysuckle.

"Mistah Potter!"

"Oh, I was just—"

"Heah," she said, extracting the coffee cup from his hand and pouring it down the sink.

Oh, God, he thought, I have sinned and been seen. I will be given a lecture and asked to leave. All of Boston's Southern society will scorn me. Magnolias will close when I pass. Honey will harden at my touch, and biscuits will burn in outrage.

But the sweet peach only smiled, her perfect teeth gleaming in friendly glory, and said, "That stuff'll curdle a man's stomach."

"Well, I just—"

"You just thought you wanted a good, stiff drink, and if that's what you want you should *have* one. Now heah."

She stretched to reach a high cabinet, and pulled down a bottle of Johnny Walker Black Label.

"You just pour some of this over a little ice, and enjoy yuh-seff."

She whispered it, conspiratorially, as if such pleasure and privilege were reserved for him alone.

"Hey, thanks. That's great. No kidding."

Her head tilted, her lips made a pout, and she said, gently cooing, "Honey, a man should have what he *wants*."

A tingling sensation swept over the surface of Potter's whole body.

That night, he dreamed of molasses.

"So you liked Amelia?" Marilyn asked.

That was the one who had caught him in the kitchen. Amelia.

She was the one he had picked, of the four roommates.

Pru was too much like her name; tight-lipped and careful.

Samantha seemed prone to eating too many biscuits; she wasn't quite yet an out-and-out fatty, but a couple of extra pralines would do the trick.

Lilly was quiet, fragile, and her eyes were sad.

He might well have gone for Lilly, though, or the dark, husky-voiced Alabama girl, or the bouncy little lollipop from North Carolina, but it was Amelia's act of mercy in the kitchen that he couldn't forget, and the way her big brown eyes fixed on him when she said, "Honey, a man should have what he *wants*."

A world of honeyed comfort seemed promised in the phrase.

Marilyn, pouring a second martini, asked that most unanswerable of questions. "What do you see in her?"

"Molasses," Potter said.

"Mo*lasses*?"

"Don't you think her hair is like that? Brown and rich and thick?"

"Oh, fuck," said Marilyn.

Amelia would never say that, Potter thought warmly. *She is a lady.*

He smiled. "You asked what I see in her," he said. "I guess I see—everything I'd like to imagine."

Marilyn sighed, shook her head, and took a drink.

"Do you understand what I mean?" Potter asked.

"Molasses," said Marilyn.

Potter splurged.

On his first date with Amelia, he took her to Locke Obers. Just because it was supposed to be the best, the most chic, expensive, grandest place in all of Boston. He knew that with many girls that might blow the whole thing, make them suspicious or contemptuous of his showing off, or coolly reserved in knowing they already had the upper hand because he was going all out.

But Amelia loved it, exclaimed over each choice on the menu, spoke of food and of Living Well. Her molasses hair was clean and shimmering.

When he took her home, she apologized for not being able to ask him in, and allowed him a swift, sweet kiss good night.

The next day he sent her yellow roses.

3

Potter sent Amelia more roses, which she absolutely *adored,* and took her to lunch at Joseph's, which she praised for its *elegance.* They held hands, and pressed their cheeks together in public. When Potter came to call, Amelia's roommates grew giggly and pink-faced, like sisters in some turn-of-the-century family who realized the new gentleman caller was a serious beau.

Potter's feeling of enchantment and generosity toward Amelia overflowed into other areas of his life, and he made a private declaration of amnesty to all those people he was or had been mad at. He called Marva Bertelsen, mentioning nothing of their past unpleasantness, and said he had a marvelous new girl friend he was anxious for her and Max to meet. He knew Marva wouldn't be able to resist a close-up look at the new woman in his life, and, as he expected, she invited them to dinner. Potter was pleased, for in addition to his altruistic feelings of forgiveness, he secretly suspected that Amelia would be most impressed with his fancy friends the Bertelsens and their classy townhouse on Louisburg Square.

He was right. Amelia thought the place a *palace*, raved about Marva's impeccable taste, went unerringly to the most precious antique pieces with knowledgeable appreciation, and praised Max's study as being as warm and charming as Max was himself. Potter sat back basking in her glow. He realized that one of the factors enabling him to resume friendly relations with the Bertelsens was having a new girlfriend he knew they would approve, and who made him feel safe in this or any other potentially ticklish social situation not only because she was gracious and diplomatic but because she gave Potter the sense that she was *with* him, would be on his side in any argument or attack, would support his own cause and protect his best interests. Potter found these qualities especially comforting since his old rival as the Bertelsens' most available bachelor, Hartley Stanhope, was also at the dinner, with a rather mousy and colorless lady who worked as a researcher in Stanhope's firm. Stanhope asked Potter about his teaching at "that little college of yours, I can never remember the name," and when Amelia spoke up brightly about how *fascinatin'* she thought Potter's courses sounded, Stanhope attempted to Southern-bait her with some heavy-handed questions about Nixon administration policy on school desegregation. Amelia parried politely by expressing pride in "how much has been done down home, even though so much more remains to be done—just as it does up heah, I understand. Though I understand your Mrs. Hicks feels things have gone too far already?"

"She's not *my* Mrs. Hicks," Stanhope grumbled.

"Nor is the recent governor of Georgia *her* Lester Maddox," Potter said firmly.

Though Stanhope seemed eager to carry this on, Max deftly moved the conversation to the subject of inflation, which everyone was against but no one seemed to know how to stop. Potter and Amelia exchanged a glance of loving camaraderie across the table, and Potter recalled approvingly a friend's definition of a successful marriage as "a conspiracy of two people against the outside world."

Marriage?

He was surprised, and a little bit scared, to have thought of it. But it was an exciting kind of fright.

When they left, Marva pulled him aside to say how wonderful Amelia was, and how "right" she seemed for Potter. He agreed.

Amelia didn't want to get home too late because she had to go to Church in the morning with her roommates. They all went to church together every Sunday. They were Methodists.

Potter didn't go so far as to offer to join Amelia and her roommates for Sunday services, but he did propose something that was almost as much out of character for him. He offered to take Amelia to a concert she had mentioned Sunday afternoon at the Gardner Museum. She said she'd adore it.

The concert was some kind of quartet playing works of a minor contemporary of Bach. Potter, in a warm sort of daze, let the sound slip through his head, like distant water running. Tootly-tweetly-toot-ta-tee-toot ...

My God, he thought, *what am I doing?*

But just then Amelia's hand closed softly over his own, and her fingers intertwined with his, making a slight pressure, a comforting hold, and Potter let doubt slide from his mind, let himself be lulled by the music.

Tootly-tweetly-toot-ta-tee-*teet* ...

Potter moved with cheery absent-mindedness through his class preparations, his classes, his office hours, his daily life, all of which seemed only interludes between the times with Amelia; pleasant enough interludes, but pale and one-dimensional compared to the bright, full feeling that came when he was in her company.

After one Communications class, Miss Linnett asked Potter if he was high on something.

He only laughed.

"*Wow,*" she said with envy. "I wish I had some."

"You will," he assured her with a wink, and waltzed away down the hall.

In much the same spirit that had made him want to make up with Marva and Max Bertelsen, he wanted to resume his friendship with Gafferty in the old, trusting way it had been before Potter started getting his fantasy hangups about what student the guy was fucking. There had been no open split between him and Gafferty, but it was obvious that Potter had cooled toward him, and Gafferty had not again asked for the use of his apartment. Potter didn't care now who the guy was fucking there. In the glow of his feeling for Amelia he didn't even mind if Gafferty was making it with Miss Korsky or Miss Linnett. He would still give them A's.

He found Gafferty in his office, reading papers, and invited himself in. He apologized for having forgotten about letting him use the apartment, but hoped he would do so again whenever he wanted to, most any afternoon that week would be all right. Gafferty, surprised, said that was asking a lot of a man, maybe he should never have done it, but Potter insisted it was fine, what were friends for, why didn't they go over to Jake Wirth's and have a couple beers. Gafferty said he just had to finish reading one paper, it would only take a few minutes, why didn't Potter just make himself at home.

"Terrific," Potter said. "Take your time."

He picked up a copy of the *Globe,* and read about an interview President Nixon had given on the Today show. The president had said that the "fundamental cause" of unrest among American youth was not due to war, poverty, or prejudice, but "a sense of insecurity that comes from the old values being torn away. . . ."

The old values. It reminded him of Amelia. Everything reminded him of her. Maybe the president was right. Maybe if there were more women like Amelia. . . .

His musings were interrupted by a hesitant tap at the door, and he looked up to see a shy, studious-looking girl whom he recognized as one of the students who worked part-time in the Administration office. She was one of those pleasant-seeming but unobtrusive people, neither fat nor thin, tall nor short, ugly nor beautiful, the sort of person of whom it is said that they blend into the woodwork.

Gafferty looked up, reddened, and said, "Ah— Miss Griffin. Do you know Mr. Potter? Miss Linda Griffin."

"Sure, I've seen you in the office," Potter said.

Miss Griffin said, "Oh, yes," looked nervously at Gafferty, and said, "I'm sorry Mr. Gafferty, I didn't mean to interrupt."

"Oh, no, not at all—"

"I can wait outside," Potter offered. "I was just waiting, anyway."

"Oh, no," Miss Griffin said.

"No, no, it's all right," Gafferty said, leaving Potter wondering what was all right for whom and what all the fidgety business was about.

"I'll stop by tomorrow," the girl said, and scurried away before anyone could say anything else.

"Sorry," said Gafferty.

"Huh? What for?"

"No, nothing. I'll just be a minute."

He turned back to his paper, coughed, riffled through it, and stood up, saying why didn't they go for the beer.

Over the second one he said, "Miss Griffin. That's the girl. The one I see."

Potter, at first astonished, then amused, not at Gafferty or the girl but his long needless torturous suspicions, started laughing, then tried to apologize, explain without explaining, tying himself in more complex knots, finally saying, "Brother, forgive me. I'm a little bit light-headed these days."

"Ah," said Gafferty, "anything serious?"

"Yes," Potter said with a huge smile, "I'm afraid it is."

Potter had neglected Marilyn since his courtship of Amelia had moved into high gear, and he felt guilty about it. Hoping to make amends, he invited her to meet him at Trader Vic's for dinner, but once there, it seemed all wrong. She had quickly become bored with the pot-smoking mailroom boy, and fallen into the depression over Herb that what she called her "hippie thing" had only briefly forestalled. Marilyn refused to join Potter in one of the exotic drinks that he thought might cheer her, explaining she was not in a festive mood. She wanted a serious drink, and ordered an extra dry martini straight up with a twist. Potter, still hoping to jolly her around, ordered some damn thing that came in a huge bowl with a flower and a purple parasol floating in it.

"Jesus," Marilyn said with disgust when the gaudy business was set in front of him, "that thing looks like a chorus girl's dream."

"Look," he said, "I know you're pissed off, and I'm really sorry I haven't called, but—well, I've been seeing Amelia all the time, and—you know, it's just been one of those things."

"I assumed," Marilyn said coolly, "that things were going well with you and Miss Molasses."

"Oh—hey, has she said anything? About me? At the office?"

"She doesn't have to."

"What? What do you mean? She doesn't even say anything about our dates?"

"Not directly."

"What do you mean *not directly?* Either she says something or she doesn't."

"It's not her style—to say anything." Marilyn made a mock smile and her voice raised an octave: "She just *oozes*—sweetness."

"But—about what? How do you know it's about me?"

"Oh, she says something like, 'Ah saw Phee-ul lass night.' Then she oozes."

"Does she?" Potter asked anxiously.

"Ooze?"

"No—mention me."

Marilyn sighed. "Yes, yes, of course. Jesus. This whole thing is getting sickening. Can't we talk about something else?"

Somehow Marilyn's obvious dislike of Amelia's manner excited Potter even more. "Really," he said, "she has something—different. I don't know how to explain it."

Marilyn lit a cigarette, and looked at Potter with a not very friendly grin. "I bet I can explain it," she said.

"You can? Really? What is it? How do you figure it?"

"How many times have you seen her now"

"Five. Five times. Tomorrow night will be our sixth date. Counting lunch and the concert yesterday. Why? Are you going to tell me I hardly know her, I haven't had time to know what she's really like?"

"No. I wasn't going to tell you that."

"Well? What *were* you going to tell me?"

"I wasn't going to tell you anything. I was going to ask you something."

"OK, what?"

Marilyn dragged on her cigarette, her mouth pursed and she blew a large, perfect smoke-ring at Potter. "How is she in bed?"

"In *bed?*"

Potter was shocked.

"You haven't fucked her yet, have you?"

"Why do you have to use that word?"

Marilyn began to giggle.

"What the hell's funny?" Potter demanded.

Marilyn's giggling got louder, more hysterical. She doubled over, coughing, wiped at her eyes, and sipped some water, then broke out laughing again while Potter, annoyed and impatient, waited for the fit to pass.

"Ohhhh," said Marilyn, partially recovering. "Ohhhhh—you poor sap."

4

It was not until after their seventh date that Potter took Amelia back to his own apartment. He had feared that the mere suggestion of it might have seemed . . . lewd. That she might be offended by the very idea. Going alone to a gentleman's private apartment!

The afternoon of their Saturday date, he had tried to straighten it up. He took out the trash, piled his ungraded papers into neat stacks, washed a two-week accumulation of grimy dishes, and even cleaned the grey ring out of the bathtub. He hid his dirty laundry in the closet, and—*just in case*—he put clean sheets on the bed. This was a real problem because the only "clean" sheets he had still bore stains on them from someone or other he had fucked during their menstrual period. Ordinarily, he would have just put them on, stains and all, but the idea of Amelia touching such sheets was a prospect too shameful to even consider. He jumped in his Mustang, sped to the Sears on Mass Avenue, and bought a set of lime green sheets and pillowcases.

It crossed his mind that buying the new sheets might be bad luck, might make Fate or God think he was counting on getting Amelia to bed, and so jinx the whole thing. But on the other hand, if he didn't put on clean sheets, and it turned out she wanted to go to bed, he would be too embarrassed to take her there. And she certainly wasn't the sort of girl you fucked on the couch or the kitchen floor.

After dinner at Stella's, which was noisy and crowded, Potter suggested they go to his place to have a brandy.

He had bought a bottle of Remy Martin. And he had two fine snifters that were part of his share of the spoils from the wedding presents of his marriage.

At the suggestion Amelia lowered her eyelids, smiled sweetly, and said, "Aw right, Phil."

Amelia declared what a charmin' apartment Potter had, and he said, "That's very kind of you, but I know it isn't nearly what it could be. It's the kind of place everyone says what a lot could be done with it, but I don't know how to do it."

"But *ah* do," Amelia said with a quiet smile.

"Well, of course, I'm sure you do, but I can't ask you—I mean it's my own place and I ought to be—uh. You know. It's my responsibility."

"But darlin', if you don't have the touch—you can't help it."

"Well, I certainly lack the touch, all right."

"Of course, everyone has different taste. You might not like what I'd do at all—"

"Oh no, I'm sure I would—"

"You mean you'd *let* me?"

"You mean you'd *do* it?"

"Darlin', ah'd adore to do it. I just love fixin' things up, and organizin' things."

"Jesus. That's what I can't do at all. I'm the most disorganized person in the world."

"Well then," she smiled, "ah guess a person like you needs a person like me."

"God," he said, "you're wonderful."

He clutched her, held on to her, buried his face in the sweet richness of her honeysuckle-smelling hair, while she rubbed her hands softly over his shoulders, down his back, cooing "Darlin' darlin'" as if comforting a homeless child. He felt safe, sheltered. And the comfort Amelia gave him was not only soothing, but stimulating. He drew back, staring at her face, gently running the tips of his fingers over it like a blind man trying to memorize it, as she smiled and closed her eyes, offering herself like a cat to be stroked, and making a sound that was the closest human equivalent of a purr.

"Mmmmmmmmmmmmmmmmmmm . . ."

When he kissed her then, long and hard, her mouth for the first time opened to him and she pressed her body against him.

It was not until, prone, on the couch, when Potter reached back for the zipper at the neck of her dress that Amelia stiffened, drew away, sat up. Cigarette time; but Amelia didn't smoke. Potter did. Neither of them said anything. It was obvious that negotiations were necessary before further intimacy was achieved.

Amelia took his hand. "Phil, darlin'."

"Yes?"

"Ah guess I'm real old-fashioned."

"Yes?"

"Ah just don't—go around—doin' these things."

"Of course not. I know you don't."

"Matter a fact, ah guess you could say—ah'm practically a virgin."

"Practically?"

"Well, there was only this one man. And we were engaged. We were plannin' to get married acourse, but it didn't work out. Ya see, I know it's not popular now, but I was raised to b'lieve that a woman should—save herself—for the one man, she would marry. And give him—everything."

Potter swallowed hard, the *everything* reverberating in his imagination. His mind tried then to absorb the fact of an attractive, twenty-six-year-old woman being "practically a virgin." The phrase itself was an old joke, and he wondered if she was putting him on. Then, looking into the wide and misty sincerity of her eyes, he was ashamed of himself for doubting her.

"All I know," he said helplessly, "is I love you."

"I know, darlin'," she said sympathetically. "And I love you, too; that's what makes it so difficult. Ah love you, and ah'd love to be able to—give myself to you."

"Oh, God," he said.

"There, there," she soothed, stroking his forehead.

Later, they necked some more.

Later still, back home alone in bed, Potter mas-
turbated, imagining "everything."

That Saturday morning Amelia came over in
bluejeans and a man's white shirt tied at the
waist, and began the redecoration of Potter's
apartment. Part of the redecoration included
cleaning up the accumulated debris, the dirt and
grime that he had allowed to grow, like some
kind of experimental bacteria, throughout his
living quarters. After taking a moldy piece of
cheesecake out of the refrigerator and tossing it
into a trash can, Amelia sighed, kissed Potter on
the tip of the nose, and said, "You know, darlin',
you met me just in time."

By five in the afternoon they were able to sit
down for a drink in the sunny, glistening living
room with bright yellow curtains fluttering at
the windows, books neatly arranged in orange-
crate shelves that Amelia planned to paint bright
green the next weekend.

Amelia had brought supplies for dinner, and
while Potter sipped a second drink she prepared
a feast of boneless chicken breasts, brown rice,
asparagus with hollandaise, a chilled Pouilly
Fouissé and ambrosia for dessert. Ambrosia, food
of the gods. Amelia made everything seem am-
brosial, and Potter indeed felt like a god.

As well as bringing groceries, Amelia had
brought two of the lush cushions from her own

apartment so that she and Potter could dine at the living room coffee table in a simulation of oriental comfort. She had also brought a change of clothes, so that she wouldn't have to sit down to dinner in the bluejeans and shirt she had worn for working around the house all day. For dinner she wore a long gingham dress with lace at the cuffs and collar, and an old-fashioned brooch. She looked like one of those wonderful young ladies in Degas, the kind who were taken for rides in canoes, holding a parasol and letting one hand gently drape itself into the water.

"You look wonderful," Potter said.

"It must be because I feel wonderful."

Potter, on hands and knees, crept from his pillow over to hers, and put his arms around her. "You *are* wonderful," he said.

"Oh, Phil. Darlin'."

They rocked into one another, clutched, kissed, stroked, licked, bit, nibbled, rubbed, gasped, gurgled, grew hard, and groaned hot declarations of love, until Potter, dizzy and breathless, broke away, sat up straight, slightly shaking, holding one of Amelia's hands with both of his. "Listen," he said, "will you marry me?"

Her eyes, large and moist and intent, searched his face. "Oh, Phil. Darlin'. Are you sure?"

"Yes. I think I am. But I want to be even more sure. I don't want to make a mistake again. I want us to wait a while. To take our time."

"Of course, darlin'."

"Think of everything. Plan."

"Oh, yes."

"And Amelia. I don't want to tell anyone yet, I mean like having a formal announcement or any of that. Not till we've decided everything, have everything worked out."

"Of course, darlin'. It'll be our secret."

"You don't mind?"

"Mind? Oh, darlin'. I think it's wonderful. It's exciting—a secret engagement!"

Potter hadn't wanted to use that word. "Engagement." It sounded too—certain. Irrevocable. But if Amelia wanted to think of it that way, he didn't want to object. What the hell. It was only a word.

It turned out to be a magic word. The engagement, even though secret, was enough to satisfy Amelia's scruples about further intimacy, and she allowed an escalation that led to removal of all her garments except for panties, a final barrier that couldn't fall until Amelia was able to arrange for what she called "precautions."

Amelia thought it would be nice if she and Phil could go away somewhere for the weekend after she obtained her precautions; instead of making love for the first time in Potter's apartment, she felt it would be so much more romantic to have it happen in a new and lovely setting. The ocean, perhaps, or the mountains. Somewhere in the country, maybe.

Potter immediately agreed, but was privately apprehensive. He knew how disastrous "roman-

tic weekends" could turn out to be. Like his
weekend with Marilyn in Vermont. He felt su-
perstitiously it might be bad luck to go to a
Country Inn again, after the fiasco in Middlebury. He was also concerned about Amelia's
sense of protocol and propriety, fearing a motel
room might seem shabby or illicit to her, might
make her anxious or embarrassed and turn her
off. She wasn't experienced at this sort of thing,
and Potter grew even more worried when he realized that in Amelia's case "this sort of thing"
not only included staying with a guy in a rented
room somewhere but also the very act of making
love. That is, if he believed her story about being "practically a virgin."

He had known her for less than a month, knew
nothing about her past except what she had chosen to tell him, and for all he knew she perhaps
had moved to Boston not out of her proclaimed
love of its historical and cultural attributes, but
because she had such a wild reputation in
Georgia no Southern gentleman would deign
to marry her; perhaps those weekends she spoke
of so dreamily at the Sigma Chi house at Chap-
el Hill had been drug-crazed orgies, perhaps she
had been a football groupie and had laid every
starting quarterback in the Southeastern Confer-
ence . . . *Shit.* Potter stopped himself, condemned
himself, and felt ashamed and ridiculous for
doubting Amelia's account of her practically
virginal past, a noble and remarkable record of
purity stained but once, and even then only be-

cause she thought she was going to marry the guy. Though the fellow had scored with her, it was not, in retrospect, according to the rules, so the score was not really a legitimate score but more like a touchdown that is called back because of a penalty; it didn't really count. On the other hand, when Potter thought about it, Amelia never said that she had only done it once with that guy but that she had only done it with that one guy, which left open the possibility that he had fucked her hundreds or thousands of times, that his fantastic love-making had turned her into a sensual beast, a creature of passion, and she hadn't done it with anyone else because she knew it would never be so good again. . . .

Good*damn*it, there his mind went *again,* irrationally, tormentingly, foolishly. He shamed himself *again,* not only for his doubting Amelia, but for falling into such an old-fashioned hang-up about a woman's relative virginity for christsake, when he had never in fact been turned on by the notion of making it with virgins, when he knew things would be a lot easier all around if Amelia had had some experience with her former fiancé. But he couldn't help hoping that the experience hadn't been all that great. A woman friend once told Potter that if she were a man she would not ideally look for a virgin, but would prefer to find a girl who had already been fucked a few times, but badly. The logic of that seemed indisputable, and he secretly hoped it was the case with Amelia.

Finally making his mind focus back on the real problem of where the hell to go for the romantic weekend, Potter hit upon what he considered the brilliant notion of the Bertelsens' farm in New Hampshire. They had bought the place about a year ago, and it was just a little less than two hours from Boston. It would provide seclusion and privacy, a quiet pastoral atmosphere, and eliminate all the hassles of room registration, motel illicitness, and Country Inn bad luck.

Marva said she and Max had been up the weekend before and Potter would actually be doing them a favor to go up the coming weekend and use the place, see that the furnace was working all right, make sure everything was in order.

"Are you taking that marvelous Southern girl?" Marva asked.

"Yes, Marva."

"It sounds like things are getting serious."

"Yes, I guess you could say that."

"Oh, Phil, this is so exciting. *How* serious?"

Potter held his breath for a moment in an effort to hold his temper.

"Medium serious," Marva persisted, "or very serious?"

"More serious," Potter said, "than I expected."

"Oh, Phil, this is marvelous. Will you tell me all about how the weekend was when you get back to town?"

"Sure," he said, not meaning he'd really tell everything, but enough to repay Marva for the use of the place. That would be the fee for the weekend, instead of a regular motel bill.

The day they drove up was wet and blowy, perfumed with spring. A perfect day for sitting inside, by a fire. A perfect day for coziness.

On the way they stopped at a shopping center grocery store and bought supplies—much more than they needed. Shopping with someone else, with someone you loved, was altogether different from shopping alone. It had a design, a purpose; it brought two people together, as in a conspiracy. Potter kept popping things into the cart, whatever caught his eye, much more than was needed. Amelia was going to make an old-fashioned beef stew for dinner, but besides the ingredients for that, Potter grabbed the biggest porterhouse steak he could find.

"What's that for, Phil?"

"Well, you never know. Maybe we'll have it for breakfast."

"But we got bacon and eggs."

"You never know. We might wake up and wish we had steak. Besides, having a steak around gives me a sense of security."

"Mah heavens, we have enough to live for a week!"

"Well, we might get snowed in. Or rained in. If we're lucky."

She smiled, moistly, her eyes wide and adoring. "Oh darlin', you're such a fool. Such a sweet fool."

The farmhouse was old and small, with floors

tilting, foundation sinking. It was furnished with plain, rickety, unmatched chairs and couches and tables, not antique, just aged and tattered and teetering, yet it seemed like a magic place, a palace in disguise. It was on a winding road off the main highways and interstates, and from its windows you could see no other houses or buildings or stores or lights. It came with twenty acres, once cultivated, now dormant, and a leaning, unusable barn that looked as if one good wind could knock it down. The Bertelsens had paid a pretty penny for it, but they knew its value could only go up, land was one sure thing of real worth. Prices for places like this had sky-rocketed all over New England, not only because of the obvious investment value, but also because such former farms were now the new vacation and weekend havens of the well-off middle class. Only the relatively wealthy could afford now the luxury of keeping warm by wood fires and planting their own vegetables, of hoeing their own gardens. The price of simplicity and privacy was high. Owning such a place was like having your own time machine, in which you could be transported back on weekends and vacations to the fantasy of living fifty years ago, the pretended peace of the pre-atomic age.

Potter indeed felt happily farther than two hours away from the world in which a jury had just voted the gas chamber for Charles Manson and a military tribunal had found Lt. Calley guilty, a world of senseless massacres at home and abroad, of a war that kept "winding down" but wouldn't stop, of brand new Pinto automobiles being recalled by the Ford company because even though they looked colorful and cute they were also defective and unsafe; a world of bright imagery and crummy insides, of plastic and smog and tear gas and lies. All that seemed years instead of hours away.

They ate in the kitchen, by the warmth of a big pot-bellied stove. Potter had chopped wood, and built fires in the living room fireplace as well as the kitchen stove, feeding them fondly, tending them with ritual care, while Amelia concocted the fragrant stew.

The intimacy of the farmhouse fed the intimacy between Potter and Amelia, and helped them feel relaxed. At dinner they talked and laughed a lot, not from nervousness but a sense of rapport and pleasure. After a couple of brandies they went to bed, and Potter's apprehensions proved pleasantly ungrounded. It started out tender and sweet and slow, grew into passion, and finally ended in fulfillment for both of them.

They lay there for a while, hands touching, and then they got up and went down to sit in front of the fireplace. The living-room lights were off and the flames threw shadows, mysterious but friendly; the oldest light show of all.

This is what there is, Potter thought.

Man, woman, house, fire.

Nothing else seemed necessary, or even important.

"Amelia," he said, "let's not wait a long time."

"For what, darlin'?"

"Getting married."

She nestled against him. "Whatever you say, darlin'."

"Spring vacation's coming up. I'll have a week, and we can take a nice honeymoon."

"When does spring vacation start?"

"A week from Wednesday."

"*A week from Wednesday!* Darlin', wha—ah hardly—there's so much to do, so many things, arrangements, plans—"

"I don't want a big lavish ceremony, I couldn't do that anyway."

"Ah know, darlin', but even so—"

"Even so, I want to marry you a week from Wednesday. All the rest can be worked out. All you have to say is yes."

She looked at him for quite a while, her face intent and serious, her eyes looking straight at him and into him, as she balanced all the factors, the pros and cons, the rightness of the moment, the pitch that might not be reached again, and finally, calmly and quietly, she spoke.

"Yes," she said.

They had the porterhouse steak for breakfast.

"You're kidding," said Marilyn.

"Is that your idea of congratulations?"

"OK. Congratulations."

"Wow. This is really something. I rush over here to tell you so you'll be the first one to know and you act like—like I've told you I lost my job."

"Well, it's awfully—sudden, isn't it?"

"What's sudden about it? I've known her over a month."

"Over a month."

"What do you advise? A two-year engagement?"

"I don't advise anything. You're the one who said you didn't want to get married again. Unless you were absolutely sure."

"But I am."

"OK, fine. Congratulations."

"Fuck you."

Marilyn made a new batch of martinis. They drank for some time in silence.

"I'm sorry," she said finally. "I just hope it isn't a mistake. I mean that really."

"Yeah, I know."

"But if you're sure—"

"Hell, Marilyn, who's sure about anything ever? If you waited till you were sure you wouldn't do anything."

"OK."

"A month isn't long, but it's enough to really know how you feel. About someone."

"You thought you loved *me* for almost a month."

"Well—uh—that was—"

"That was different, I suppose."

"Yes, it was different."

"How?"

"We never talked about getting married."

"That was my fault," Marilyn said.

"It wasn't anyone's fault. It just didn't come up."

"I didn't *bring* it up. But from now on, brother—the next time I get into it with an available man, I'm going to play it just like little Miss Molasses."

"Shit, Marilyn, you didn't want to marry me. That would have been—awful."

"Maybe, but here I am again, goddamned alone, and that sugary little Peach is getting married."

"Come on, Marilyn. We're buddies."

"Yeah. Well—do I get to be Best Man at the wedding?"

"Jesus, you ought to be. You're sure as hell my best friend."

"I'll buy a tux and top hat."

"God, wouldn't it be great? If we could pull it off?"

They got to giggling, and started on a third batch of martinis. Marilyn became a little more mellow about the whole thing.

"I do hope it works," she said. "I honestly hope it's not a mistake."

"Well, who knows. It may turn out to be. But at least she's different than Jessica. I mean, at least if this doesn't work it'll be a *different* kind of mistake."

Marilyn nodded. "Yeah," she said. "I guess that's progress."

The Tuesday evening after the fateful farm weekend Amelia came over to Potter's and fixed a fantastic meal that featured a cherry pie she had baked the night before. In the living room after dinner she made him close his eyes, and stuck a fine Corona in his mouth. She lit it for him, poured him a brandy, and nestled beside him on the couch. "Darlin', have you decided yet whether you plan to go on teachin'?"

"Why?" he asked. "What's wrong with teaching?"

"Wha nothing, Phil, it's one of the noblest professions a man can have."

"Well?"

"Well," she said, playing her fingers along his lapel, "you've said you weren't sure about it, about goin' back to get another degree and all—and, well, a girl wants to know what her future husband wants to do, so she can *help* him."

It was, in essence, the old "what are your plans?" routine, but stated so sweetly, and in such conditions of comfort and well-being, that Potter hardly experienced a shudder. A man who has a great meal in his stomach, a fine cigar in his mouth, a glass of brandy in his hand, and an adoring woman on his shoulder is likely to look on the future with a certain cool confidence. Plans? Fine. Why not have plans?

"Well, if I decide not to go on with teaching, there's this guy Charlie Bray I told you about, the big PR man here who as much as told me I could write my own ticket if I wanted to come with his firm."

"That's mah-velous."

"On the other hand," Potter said, grandly flicking an ash from his cigar, "I might well go in some other direction."

"Of course, darlin', ah know you could do just *anything*."

"Well, not *anything*," Potter said modestly.

Nor was it just "anything" that Amelia had in mind. Amelia had a plan. A very specific one. All she wanted Potter to do was have lunch with this marvelous man she knew, Dick Dalton, who was high up in one of the best Boston advertising firms, but was restless and wanted to strike out on his own. When she first came to Boston she had worked for six months in the accounting office of Dalton's firm, became friends with him and his wife and two children, and still kept in

touch with them. She had lunched with Dick only yesterday—a happy coincidence!—and told him
all about Potter, whose background seemed to interest him a whole lot. Amelia only asked that
Potter meet him; she was sure they would hit it
off.

Much to Potter's surprise, they did.

Dick Dalton was a sharp, wiry little guy, with
quick thoughts and movements, full of restless
energy. Potter was relieved that he spoke without jargon, and soon sized him up as a no-bull-
shit kind of guy. Dalton said he had faith in himself as a copy writer, he had a good friend who
was tops in layout and graphic design, and they
needed a man with something like Potter's background to start a nice little operation—a man
who could deal with the press, make presenta-
tions to clients, stage the right sort of publicity
parties. Dalton explained that he was almost
forty and he figured if he was going to strike out
on his own, it was now or never.

"You know," Dalton said with intense sincerity, "I'd like to be on my own now, I'd like to
—well, have *fun* at what I do."

He paused. "Fun," he said reflectively; then
he smiled, and waved toward the window, the
street, the world beyond: "I know it's out there.
Somewhere. It *must* be!"

Potter and Dalton both laughed, together,
feeling an immediate trust and kinship. They
would work something out, they would work together, and, in the pursuit of mutual profit they

would try along the way to find that elusive, al-
luring promise that some men are said to discov-
er in their work: fun.

They shook on it.

As Amelia had seemed to produce Dick Dalton, genie-like, she also quickly and efficiently
came up with marriage plans, arrangements, details, schedules, participants, principals. It turned
out she had a cousin who owned a lovely home on
Cape Cod, in Wellfleet, right on the ocean, and
the cousin was delighted to offer the house for the
wedding. This took care of Potter's qualms about
a Church wedding for a man who was on his second time around and had never been religiously
committed anyway. Through her Methodist minister in Boston she was able to drum up a local
Cape Cod Methodist to perform the service, an
ocean-side, unorthodox kind of ceremony keyed
to God's natural wonders. Her cousin arranged
for a caterer, and her mother handled flight plans
for a small delegation of Southern relatives.

The plans moved swiftly and inexorably forward, like a powerful freight train that has gathered steam and now possesses a force and direction
of its own beyond the control of any individual
to change its course or slow its momentum. As
he watched this Marriage Express hurtle onward,
Potter's mood varied from joyous giddiness to
sudden, stark terror. But when the doubts and
fears assailed him, like a stone-throwing mob, he
would make the chamber music come into his
mind, the music he had heard when he took Ame-

lia to the Gardner concert. He told her how much
the music meant to him, and she bought him a
record of the principal piece that was performed.
He played it countless times, at home on his stereo,
and away from home, in his head, letting it fill his
mind, dispelling all the dark questions and doubts,
soothing him into a wordless rhythm, a suspended
state of calm.

"*Tootly-tweetly-too-ta-tee-toot . . .*"

Potter's first lie to Amelia was about his Bachelor Dinner. It wasn't exactly a lie, it was more
of an omission. He told her that Gafferty and Ed
Shell were going to take him to Stella's for the
ritual celebration, and that was true. But he
didn't mention that Marilyn was coming too.
Women weren't supposed to come to a bachelor
dinner, a rule that would no doubt apply even
more strongly if the woman was a former girlfriend.

It seemed only right though that since Marilyn
was his best buddy but couldn't be "Best Man"
she at least should be allowed to attend the Bachelor Dinner. There wasn't any hanky-panky intended, but Potter just thought that Amelia
might not understand. There was no sense in
causing unnecessary trouble right before the
wedding.

The group agreed to meet for the dinner at
Stella's, which Potter had now firmly established
in his mind as his favorite Boston restaurant.
Potter picked up Marilyn, nervously looking

over his shoulder as they walked out of her apartment building, feeling guilty already about being seen alone with another woman. He was glad that Gafferty was already there when they arrived at the restaurant, so in case he saw any friends of Amelia it wouldn't look like he had a date on the eve of his wedding. Gafferty said Shell would be a little late, something about a business call.

"Oh, God," Potter said. "The poor bastard. It's probably another one of those hot movie deals that will fall through in a couple of days."

They had a round of drinks, deciding to wait till Shell came before ordering the celebratory champagne. When Shell finally arrived he was breathless, beaming, and carrying a suitcase. *The* suitcase. The one he kept packed for the fantasy trip to The Coast. Potter wondered if the poor guy had finally flipped and was going to The Coast whether anyone asked him or not.

"Sorry I'm late," he said. "And Phil, I'm sorry I won't be able to come to your wedding. It's a damn shame I have to go to The Coast the same time you pick to get married. But, I guess that's the breaks."

"When are you leaving?" Potter asked.

"Tonight. The red-eye special."

"The what?"

"Oh, I'm sorry. That's kind of a show business name for the late night flight to The Coast."

Potter winced. "The term 'red-eye special,'" he said, "is used in reference to night flights from the West Coast that arrive on the East Coast in the morning—going from East to West is not a red-eye."

Shell merely shrugged.

"Lad, this is marvelous!" Gafferty said with obvious enthusiasm. "Now we have two celebrations to drink about!"

"Congratulations," Marilyn said. "I'm really impressed."

"Yeah," said Potter, oddly unable to sound enthusiastic. "Tell us about it."

Shell said he sold a script to a major studio. They wanted him to come out and work on it with the director. As the actual details unfolded —names, figures, terms, dates—the realization came over Potter that this was indeed a real deal, that Ed Shell's dream was actually materializing. Shamefully, he found himself having to fight back his own resentment and jealousy, having to force himself to pretend to be happy over Shell's success. It was like having to listen to a man tell about winning a woman you had loved yourself and lost, and even though you liked the guy and were glad about his good fortune, it hurt because it hadn't been yours.

Potter's Bachelor Dinner turned into a farewell celebration party for Shell, but after a while Potter didn't care. It took his mind off the wedding. After dinner Potter said he'd better get going if he was going to get up early enough to be on time for his own wedding, and he mustered as much heartiness as he could to give a final shake of congratulation to Shell.

Marilyn invited him in to have one final drink, a kind of farewell drink, and Potter said well, just one.

Marilyn offered a toast to Potter's happiness, and after they each took a sip of brandy she said, "Phil, I've been wanting to talk to you. About what I think I'm going to do."

It seemed to Potter that the celebration marking the end of his bachelor days (for the second time in his life) was for some reason the perfect occasion for everyone else to talk about their plans while Potter served as an interested audience. Well, what the hell. Maybe he'd get some attention tomorrow. Though Amelia would probably steal *that* show. Resigned, he attempted to focus his full attention on Marilyn's plans.

"So what have you decided?" he said.

"I want to leave Boston."

"How come?"

"Well, a lot of things. I feel like it's kind of the end of an era here. Also, I haven't told you, but I've started seeing Herb again."

"Really?"

"Yeah. I know. It's crazy. But this time I don't have any illusions. And besides, we still have good sex and good times, so why shouldn't I enjoy it?"

"Sure. Why not?"

"But I don't want to make it a way of life."

"No."

"And if I stay in Boston, so close, I'm afraid it'll just drag on and on."

"So what are you going to do?"

"I think I'm going to The Southwest."

"The Southwest?"

"Yeah. You know. Arizona, New Mexico."

"Why The Southwest?"

"There's lots of space, and clean air—and," she grinned, "millionaires."

"The Southwest," Potter said.

He pictured expanses of desert, and mountains with mansions on top, and lots of millionaires riding around in shiny new limousines, just waiting for Marilyn.

It struck him as odd at first, the notion of someone deciding to go live in The Southwest, as an answer to what they should do. But it was really quite common, like the people he had known in college and the service who, when asked what they were going to "do," answered that they were going to live in San Francisco. And perhaps it was no more unreasonable than what he was about to do tomorrow. Get married. That was another "answer" people had when confronted with what to do with themselves.

I'm going to get married.

I'm going to The Southwest.

It probably wasn't much different.

Potter stood up, and said he really had to go home. Marilyn walked him to the door. They wished each other good luck, and then kissed. First it was light and gentle, and then they embraced, harder, and Potter could feel his prick getting stiff. Marilyn was rubbing her legs up against him; his hands moved down her back and shaped themselves over her ass, squeezing.

With all the will he could muster, his determination strengthened by guilt, Potter finally pulled away, shaky and perspiring. "No," he said. "Listen. I've got to go. *Now*."

Marilyn breathed in deeply, and folded her arms over her chest. "OK," she said. "See you at the wedding."

"Yeah, right."

Potter hurried out into the street, walking in an awkward crouch, trying to hide his shameful hard-on.

The day of the wedding was bright, but terribly chilly. A cold wet wind gusted in off the ocean, and Potter wished he had a brandy in his hand. It seemed to him that would be a civilized addition to the ceremony, sipping brandy while the minister read his piece: in this case, an informal string of pleasantries highlighted by some passages from Robert Frost. Frost had been a compromise. Amelia had wanted something from Rod McKuen, and Potter had blown his stack. He said if there was going to be any poetry in the ceremony it was going to be the best and the best was William Butler Yeats. Amelia said she had to read Yeats in college once and hadn't the faintest idea of what he was trying to get at. Potter said he was trying to get at The Truth, and Amelia countered that if that was the case he shouldn't have made it sound so complicated. The whole wedding plan—the marriage itself—

nearly foundered on the poetry issue till Potter
came up with the compromise of Frost.

Amelia was squeezing his hand, and Potter
stared out at the ocean, past the minister, his
mind wandering from the words. There was a
young slim girl with long blonde hair walking
along the shoreline, hopping back as the water
licked her feet. She stopped and tossed some
stones out, then pranced toward the waves; carefree, frolicking. She had on a baggy sweatshirt
and tight dungarees cut off at hot-pants length.
Her firm little ass twitched and teased. Potter
felt a tug at his arm and realized the time had
come; everyone was waiting for him to make the
big vow.

"I do," he whispered.

Another tug, and he turned to see Amelia's
face lifting toward him, presented like an offering; eyes closed, lips parted. He pressed his
mouth down against hers, enclosed her with his
arms, and they clutched, tight, as the seawind
swept over them. From the corner of his eye,
Potter watched the receding ass of the blonde,
twitching away down the beach, reminding him
of freedom, soon to be out of sight.

There was rice in the salt spray air, and people
were clapping Potter on the back and laughing
and he tried to smile, tried to focus on who and
where he was now, as hearty voices offered congratulations. Max Bertelsen squeezed his shoulder, red-faced Gafferty whooped and gave him a
manly poke on the chest, and all hands hurried

him toward the warmth of the house, where champagne and caviar waited and a woodfire crackled.

At the doorway Potter took one last glance over his shoulder at the now tiny figure of the disappearing girl. Then he was hustled on in to receive, with Amelia, the toasts to the new bride and groom as they began their new life, man and wife, till death or divorce did them part. The voices ran together, cheery and buoyant.

"Congratulations . . . You're a lucky man . . . Ah, and isn't that the truth . . . This is your lucky day, Phil . . . Congratulations . . . Lucky man . . ."

Potter was lucky; everyone told him so.

Dell Bestsellers